THE TRIO

D1354193

THE TRIO

Johanna Hedman

Translated by Kira Josefsson

HAMISH HAMILTON
an imprint of
PENGUIN BOOKS

HAMISH HAMILTON

UK | USA | Canada | Ireland | Australia
India | New Zealand | South Africa

Hamish Hamilton is part of the Penguin Random House group of companies
whose addresses can be found at global.penguinrandomhouse.com.

Penguin
Random House
UK

First published 2022
001

Copyright © Johanna Hedman, 2022
Translation copyright © Kira Josefsson

The moral right of the copyright holders has been asserted

Excerpt on p. 9 from 'Invisible Dark Matter' from *Poems 1959–2009* by Frederic K. Seidel.
Copyright © 2009 by Frederic K. Seidel. Reprinted by permission of Farrar, Straus and Giroux.
All Rights Reserved.

Set in 12.25/15pt Fournier MT Std
Typeset by Jouve (UK), Milton Keynes
Printed and bound in Great Britain by Clays Ltd, Elcograf S.p.A.

The authorized representative in the EEA is Penguin Random House Ireland,
Morrison Chambers, 32 Nassau Street, Dublin D02 YH68

A CIP catalogue record for this book is available from the British Library

ISBN: 978–0–241–55166–0

www.greenpenguin.co.uk

MIX
Paper from
responsible sources
FSC® C018179

Penguin Random House is committed to a
sustainable future for our business, our readers
and our planet. This book is made from Forest
Stewardship Council® certified paper.

CONTENTS

PART ONE

Frances calls one day in late April and asks if she can come by next week. That's how she puts it – *come by* – as though it's a question of stopping in for an afternoon coffee, as though they don't live on opposite sides of the Atlantic. Her voice over the phone is breathless and he can almost picture her: red cheeks, hair tousled by the wind, probably dressed in a jean jacket that's too light for the season. She explains that she's found cheap tickets to New York and emphasizes that it's a direct trip, as though he should congratulate her on the find. It's been a long time since they last saw each other. He tells her that of course he'd love to see her, and asks if she wants to stay at his place, but she says she's made arrangements with some friends already. Then there's silence, and he understands she didn't call just to schedule a coffee.

'There's something I'd like to talk to you about,' she says.

'Sure, what do you want to talk about?' he says.

'Mom.'

'Frances,' he says, but stops short of finishing the sentence; he assumes she'll understand what he's getting at by the way he says her name.

'I know, I know,' she says. 'That's why I didn't want to have this conversation over the phone.'

He can tell from her tone that she's holding her hand a small distance from her body, palm facing up, like she's waiting for him to hand her something. This gesture – he's always wondered if it's something she picked up as a child at private school in France. It seems too flamboyant to be associated with the dispassionate Stockholm temperament.

'Is she on her deathbed?' he asks, sarcastic.

'No.'

'Sick?'

'No—'

'Okay then,' he says. 'I'd love for you to come by when you're here, but I don't want to talk about Thora.'

'I'm worried about her.'

'She probably wouldn't want you to talk to me about her either.'

'How can you be so sure of that?'

He shakes his head even though Frances can't see it. His laptop is open on the desk but the screen has gone to sleep, and when he brings his finger to the touchpad a blank document appears. He looks at it for a few seconds and then shuts the computer.

'You know her,' Frances says.

'I *knew* her.'

He hears Frances breathe, the sounds of traffic in the background. He tries to imagine her somewhere in central Stockholm, but he's no longer sure if the places he pictures actually exist or if they're just an amalgam of memories invoking a city suffused by a strange blue light, like on an old postcard.

'That's not why you're coming, is it?' he asks.

'No,' she replies.

'Are you mad at me now?'

'I'm not crossing the Atlantic just to discuss my mom with you.'

'Okay. Good.'

'Do you still want to see me?'

'Yes, of course.'

'You never know.'

He doesn't like the way she says it, but he doesn't protest.

'Get in touch when you arrive,' he says before they hang up.

It's been several years since the first time Frances rang his doorbell. Since he opened the door and Frances said:

'Hi.'

And then:

'I think you knew my dad.'

He didn't ask who her dad was. He didn't need to. He let her in.

Frances was an exchange student that year. She'd initially been staying with one of Thora's cousins, before moving into a dorm on the Upper West Side. She told him she didn't know anyone in New York. She was lonely.

He soon got accustomed to having Frances in his life. In the afternoons she'd hop on the subway downtown and camp out in his living room or kitchen, studying until the evening. She said it was easier to focus at his place than at the dorm. He gave her keys to his apartment. It was nice to come home from work and find her on the couch or at the kitchen table, surrounded by textbooks, notebooks and highlighters. In the evenings he'd get her a cab home. He'd take her out for dinner on Sundays, and on those occasions she'd eat as though she hadn't had a proper meal all week. She'd ask questions about her father which he tried his best to answer, but at that point he hadn't talked about August in many years and his answers probably weren't as exhaustive as Frances was hoping they'd be. He didn't have the nerve to ask about Thora. From throwaway comments, he was able to glean that she was married to a Frenchman with whom she had two sons. She still lived in Stockholm.

He introduced Frances to his friends and invited her whenever he hosted dinner parties. In response to their questions about her, he responded, truthfully, that she was the daughter of old college friends of his, but he didn't elaborate and they seemed content to leave it at that. His friends were all from elsewhere, many of them from other countries, and they weren't in the habit of prying into each other's past lives. During this time he lived in a small apartment with a dining table so rickety it made every meal a balancing act, but his friends liked to get together at his place since it was conveniently situated between everyone's subway lines. Towards the end of the evening they'd crowd onto the fire escape and smoke weed while they spun loose dreams of moving somewhere else, where the buildings were less like cardboard houses threatening to collapse. He prohibited them from offering Frances weed or cigarettes. She liked to sit at the short end of his long table and listen to his friends gossip about their colleagues and bosses. Sometimes he looked at her across the table and was overwhelmed by a sucking feeling; it was like turning a kaleidoscope of memories until the patterns clicked, a tunnel through time to a place he thought he'd never see again.

When Frances's academic year ended, he helped her move out of the dorm. He drove her to the airport, trunk full of suitcases, and she went back home to Europe. He thought then that everything would go back to normal, and in some ways it did, even though she left the apartment in a new kind of silence.

Nowadays she works as a journalist. They rarely see each other but she calls him regularly to tell him about articles she's about to write, articles she wants to write and articles she can't get anyone to publish. When she writes something in Swedish she likes to read him sections before asking: Is that correct? Is that how you say it in Swedish? It makes him smile – this trilingual kid who moves between languages with casual swiftness, like she's trying on various garments and doesn't notice that her sweater is inside out before she's already out the door. He tends to respond that he's not the right person to ask, that she's one of the few people with whom he still speaks Swedish. If she keeps insisting, he'll silently try the sentence for any irregularities, though he can no longer instinctively sense details like erroneous prepositions or dangling modifiers. Answering Frances's questions feels like trying to get his mobility back in a hand that's fallen asleep. He never lets on how uncomfortable it makes him.

Once, on his way to work, he saw Thora. Or at least he thought it was her standing on the opposite subway platform: red coat, loose hair, eyes on her phone and one hand resting on a shoulder bag. Fat rats were scurrying across the tracks, and out of the corner of his eye he could see their small grey bodies scampering about as he tried to get a better look between the beams that separated the platforms. Was it her? He broke into a cold sweat and his heart hammered in his chest while the rest of his body tensed up. He'd forgotten this feeling – or rather, how powerful a feeling could be.

It wasn't her.

It *was* her.

He waited for her to look up; all he needed was a glimpse of her face to know for sure. Then the train came shrieking into the station – and by the time it left, the woman in the red coat was gone. Over the days that followed he kept looking for her in the rush-hour crowds, raising his gaze over the masses of heads in search of a scrap of something red, something to make his heart lurch. But he didn't see her again.

Now and then he'll walk past someone on the street and catch a snippet of a conversation held in Swedish. For a few seconds he has time to wonder what language they're speaking before realizing that it's *his* language. Sometimes he'll sit at a bar or in a restaurant next to people speaking to each other in Swedish, and eavesdrop with an unassuming look. Nobody ever imagines he's anything but American, and in any case, he's never lived up to the cliché of a Scandinavian, he thinks. It happens that Americans, upon learning where he's from, scrunch up their noses as though some distinctly Nordic quality might appear if they squint. Whenever this occurs he adds that his paternal grandmother was American, and for some reason that information tends to produce an *Ah!*, as if the US heritage explains some kind of lack in him.

Frances texts him when she arrives in New York, and they decide to meet up that weekend. It's the end of the spring semester and classes are over, but students sometimes email or show up outside his office with questions about finals and grading. On Friday night there's the traditional end-of-term celebration where the department and the students gather in a red-brick building near Washington Square Park. Officially there's only tea and coffee on the menu, but almost everyone shows up at the start of the evening already high or tipsy. He's sitting on the stairs by the entrance, surrounded by friends and colleagues. Someone touches his arm; it's not clear who, and he doesn't care. He has the sense that if he put his hands out, his palms would touch some invisible material that separates him from other people.

In the dead of night he is startled from sleep by a muscle pain that keeps him up for several hours. It's a familiar agony that always follows the same trajectory: starting as a shooting sensation in the right shoulder, then intensifying as it spreads to the left shoulder, radiates up through his neck and jaw, burrows deeper. Finally he gets out of bed and walks into the kitchen, where he lies down on the floor and stares at the ceiling while water comes to a boil so he can make himself a cup of tea. Then he abandons the tea, pours himself a glass of whisky and takes a shower instead. With the stream of hot water directed at the centre of the pain in his right shoulder, he opens his mouth in a silent moan. Afterwards he lies down on his bed, naked and still wet, and he doesn't know if he ultimately faints or just falls asleep from sheer exhaustion. When he wakes up in the morning all is back to normal again, his body a battlefield that's already been cleaned up.

There was a night when Thora mumbled a few lines from a Frederick Seidel poem in his ear. She'd complained about not being able to

8

sleep and he'd told her to recite something, anything. He didn't think she'd take him up on the challenge, and she lay silent for a long moment, so long that he thought she'd finally drifted off. But then she rolled over to face him, and the words came, warm and humid against his skin . . . He'd heard her repeat these lines several times before, like a song she hadn't been able to get out of her head ever since she bought the poetry collection in a Paris bookstore: *I read my way across / The awe I wrote / That you are reading now. / I can't believe that you are there / Except you are.*

How strange that English could sound so beautiful. In the mouth of an upper-class girl from Stockholm.

Frances rings his doorbell on Sunday morning. It's warm outside and her face is shiny with sweat as she enters the air-conditioned apartment.

'It gets so hot here,' she says while taking off her shoes. 'Do you really stay in town over summer?'

'Not if I can help it.'

'My friends say it's awful here in the warm months.'

'It *is* awful.'

They look at each other. She's taller than her mother and doesn't need to get on her tiptoes to hug him. They move into the kitchen which connects to the living room, making an L-shape around the long, narrow hall. Frances tells him there was a leak in the roof of the subway station in Greenpoint. He gives her a glass of water with ice. While he starts up the coffee maker, she steps into the living room and asks if he lives here alone.

'Most of the time,' he replies.

'Isn't it too big?'

'Probably. I rent it from the university.'

'You must be paid really well to be able to live like this,' Frances says when she comes back into the kitchen.

'Do you need money?'

'What? No.'

'I thought recent graduates were always short of cash.'

'I don't need your money.' Frances sits down at the kitchen table, folds her hands and rests them on the table. 'I know you think I'm spoiled.'

'You're fine,' he says, and adds with a smile: 'Things could have gone really badly with you.'

When he thinks of Thora and Frances, he pictures them moving above a fine mesh safety net that cushions each fall. It's always maddened him, but he still wants them to remain safely buoyed by the freedom only money can buy.

Frances tells him about her flight – long and uncomfortable; about the apartment in Greenpoint where her friends live – run-down but pleasant; about how her younger brothers are doing – one of them in Paris, in school and in love, the other in Stockholm, where he works as a stage actor. She doesn't bring up her mother and he keeps expecting her to do it, thinking, annoyed, that they might as well get it over with. He's convinced she will at some point start talking about Thora, as if his previous refusal were invalid since it was communicated over the phone, and maybe she can convince him now that they're speaking face-to-face. He *knows* this is how she reasons. But Frances doesn't mention her mother. Instead she talks about her move to Copenhagen, what it's like compared to Stockholm; she lists, with deliberation, the Danish words she's learned, as if lining up a collection of small treasures found on an excursion.

Then she looks at him over the rim of her coffee cup with a serious expression, and asks: 'Are you never coming back to Stockholm again?'

'I don't think so.'

'But it's your home.'

'Not anymore.'

'So you're going to stay here?'

He smiles at her concerned face. He could tell her he's never loved Stockholm the way Thora and August did, but he knows that Frances, like them, is deeply attached to her native city. She is likely to take his ambivalent relationship to Stockholm as an insult, so he just shrugs in response, as though it's not a topic that interests him.

'You've fallen for the Big Apple,' she says. 'I thought you were above such clichés.'

'No, you are the one who's above them,' he says. 'Did you tell Thora that you were going to see me here?'

'Yes.'

'Does she ever talk about me?'

'Not really.'

'But?'

'There's no *but* – she doesn't . . .'

He stops himself from asking if Thora still thinks about him. How would Frances know.

The last time he ever saw Thora in Stockholm was at a café near Vasaparken; the trees in the park had just bloomed. He's replayed their conversation in his head so many times that it's like he has the scene folded up in his pocket, available to revisit whenever, though he never knows what he's looking for.

They were sitting across from each other at a small, unsteady table; he was drinking a coffee and she was eating a salad. Later, he thought about how this was probably a strategic choice on her part; it allowed her to focus on the food as she painstakingly cut the lettuce and vegetables into small pieces, chewed slowly, wiped the corners of her mouth with her napkin. The few times she did look up, her gaze slipped over his face as it had done so many times before, as though there was nothing there to hold her attention. And yet he'd been there, trying in vain to catch it. He observed her eyelashes lowered against freckled skin, her earlobes adorned with a pair of small gold earrings, her perfectly straight middle parting. He rested his palms on the table. Everything around them seemed to be falling, collapsing. Like the landscape frames of a train window, the café seemed to flicker past him, but vertically, from ceiling to floor.

'Tell me what you want me to say,' he said finally.

'I can't. That's not how it works.'

In English, he reinvented himself. He dismantled the self that had been manhandled by forces outside of his control, and built a new one which the impersonal English language couldn't penetrate. His experience of the world is less immediate in English. There's no direct link between feelings and the words that label them. It's all detour.

During Frances's year in New York he hadn't yet started working at the university. He was still employed by the large international organization, and spent his workdays in a grey cubicle in an office whose low ceilings were only partially compensated for by the skyscraper vista. He told Frances about the hours-long negotiations over singular words, the budget discussions and austerity, but she never listened, or maybe she just wasn't interested. She wasn't receptive to accounts of reality that portrayed adulthood as a matter of repetition and routine, shaped by an odd mix of stress and boredom instead of excitement and adventure. He suspected she never missed a chance to inform her roommates that she knew someone who worked at the headquarters. He explained to her that he couldn't get her an internship, and repeated the same thing when she asked if he could at least invite her for a tour.

'Everyone is welcome,' he said. 'You just need to reserve a time.'

'It's different when you know someone,' she said and gave him a knowing look.

He felt she was too young for such crass awareness of the differences in access. Then he remembered the members' clubs where Frances's maternal grandfather would take her on his visits to New

York, her manner of talking about European cities as if the world was one verdant neighbourhood. So he didn't protest. She was right; it *was* different.

One morning he joined Frances in the line, along with the various groups of tourists and schoolchildren that waited each day by the tall fence and the flagpoles. He showed the guards his ID and access card and then he waited for Frances to pass through security. In his recollection it was a sunny fall day; bad timing for pulling the plug on Frances's optimism. She beamed at him as they walked through the revolving doors, her hands around the straps of her backpack like she was a taller version of the kids in school uniform. He showed her the conference rooms, his favourites among the paintings and sculptures in the collection, the small café on the windowless ground floor where diplomats held hushed conversations, the ostentatious reception rooms decorated by wealthy oil nations, and the terrace bar on the second floor where pass-holders gathered on Friday nights to drink wine. Frances was no stranger to this world, and she didn't move like someone expecting to be ejected at each turn. He realized, when he watched her joke with the elevator operators and play hopscotch on the chequered floor in an empty corridor, that Frances belonged to Thora's world, not August's, even if her scruffy shoes, backpack and jeans gave a different impression. She looked like August but talked and moved like Thora. It was confusing.

They go for a walk. Everyone on the street moves slowly, as if the heat has transformed the air into an object they have to push out of the way in order to advance. The humidity bears down on the skin, creating a shiny layer that brings to mind the transparent plastic sheets that cover the screens of new electronics. He rubs his hand over his arm like he wants to find the tab that will let him peel it off. People in their weekend best stream out of the churches that line the avenues, blinking, as if newly woken, when they step into the strong

13

sunlight that batters the city. The tables outside the restaurants abut cars and buses.

Frances asks if he'd like to go to a museum. He has grading to do but he already knows he won't be able to focus, so he says yes. They take the subway from Union Square and walk a few blocks to the museum. The stairs to the entrance are crowded with posing tourists. He's rolled up his shirtsleeves and hung his blazer over his arm. Once inside, Frances picks up a map and studies it carefully while they wait in line to pay the admission fee. The woman at the register asks if they want to buy tickets to the memorial exhibit about the pandemic. She smiles and gestures towards boxes of face masks on the counter. 'It's immersive. You have to put one of these on.'

She looks about the same age as Frances; probably too young to remember it herself. He declines, returning her smile.

As they walk up the stairs, Frances holds the map in front of her, looking like she's guiding them through a foreign city.

She takes them straight to the American wing. They pass through several hallways and rooms until she comes to a halt in front of a few portraits by Sargent. He watches her stand there in silence with her arms crossed, hands cupped around her elbows, as if the portraits are engaged in a conversation she's not sure she's welcome to join.

'Mom says Dad loved these paintings,' she says. 'Look.'

And he looks, but he doesn't say anything. He can sense the spring warmth outside, a snarling animal banging its head against the building.

Frances glances at him. 'Do you like them?'

He recognizes the portrait of the pale woman in a black dress. August had a poster of it hanging in his student apartment. A drop of sweat trickles down his neck. He wishes he could get rid of the blazer – why did he bring it?

'A bit too traditional,' he says.

'*Traditional?*'

He gives her a smile and moves on to the next room. When he

turns and looks at her through the doorway, she's back to examining the portraits.

After the museum they go for a walk in the park. The greenery is effervescent and the skyscrapers rise up behind the trees like an artificial mountain range, glass summits reflecting the sunlight. In the round pond close to Fifth Avenue, children play with model sailing boats.

They walk in silence for a while, until Frances asks: 'Would you say you're happy?'

'Frances. Come on.'

'What?'

He shakes his head. 'It's not a question you just ask like that.'

'Why not?'

'Are *you* happy?'

Frances lifts her hand to block the sun and looks at him. 'Sometimes I am.'

When he got his first office job, he got dressed each morning with a certain ironic remove. It was a game that everyone had to play to make a living. To be an adult is to sell out, but as long as there's someone to recognize the irony you bring to this game it's easier to maintain a sense of self-respect. These days there's nobody in his life who would understand that irony, and he suspects that he's transmitting his signal on a wavelength only he can hear. He knows that the outside observer will think of him as at one with his blazer and button-down shirt; there's no crack for the irony to push through and unhitch the image of an indifferent, middle-aged man. When the students look at him, what do they see? A hypocrite? Thora and August would have laughed about it.

He didn't like New York at first. Not that he disliked it either, but he'd never understood the people who came back to Europe looking like they'd been born again. It was just a city. Tall buildings and wide streets and a decrepit subway system. Then he started taking long walks in the evenings. It was pleasant to meander aimlessly, winding his way in and out of neighbourhoods until he at some point realized that he had no idea where he was. He'd have dinner at a small restaurant he knew he wouldn't return to since he had no memory of how he'd got there. He didn't consult a map; at the end of the night he'd simply hail a cab. Reading the street names, he knew it would take hours to walk back home. Feet sore, he'd sink into the back seat of the taxi while commercials played on the TV screen mounted on the seat in front of him. He would lean his head against the window, looking out at people and shops; restaurants and cafés and construction sites; parks and bus stops. In these moments he would experience a rare sense of peace, a kind of exhaustion and repletion of impressions that made him feel dissolved, as if the boundaries between him and the city had temporarily softened. He was nobody and everyone at once. On such nights he always slept well.

They walk to a café on Amsterdam Avenue, close to the park. He gets in line for coffee and something sweet while Frances rushes to get the one free table in the back. She waves at him once he's paid.

'I used to come here all the time when I was a student,' she says.

'I know,' he says, and reminds her that she would bring pastries in a small box when she came over to study for exams; flaky Danishes that fell apart at the slightest touch and scattered buttery crumbs all over the floor, where they would lodge between the planks and attract mice at night.

The coffee is so hot it burns his mouth. He drinks it slowly, while Frances eats in silence. As soon as her plate is empty she moves it aside, clasps her hands on the table and looks seriously at him, as though this entire day has consisted of things they just had to get out of the way.

'I'm worried about Mom,' she says.

'Yeah?'

'She's started getting rid of things. She's planning to sell the big apartment in Lärkstaden.'

'Where is she moving to?'

'I don't know. She won't tell me anything about her plans. I happened to come across the sales listing, otherwise I wouldn't even have known that she's selling. Mom *loves* that apartment.'

'Maybe she thinks it's too big.'

'But isn't it weird? That she's suddenly decided to sell her childhood home?'

'I don't know.' He thinks about what it was like to stand in the corridor that ran the length of the apartment and look at the rectangles made by the flooding sunlight on the floor, stripes of darkness and light on the fishbone parquet. 'Maybe.'

'She says that she wants to be *free*.' Frances pronounces that last word as though the idea of an old person's freedom is laughable – preposterous in a way that a young person's desire for freedom is not.

'If you think I can stop her from selling—'

'No. That's not what I think. I just think you should know.' She looks at him in a demanding way, as though she's nevertheless expecting forceful action on his part. He looks back with a mild expression and wonders why she feels that he should be concerned with Thora's real estate dealings, but he doesn't ask. The person they're discussing seems like a mythological creature – a being which might have existed in the real world at some point in the distant past. He can no longer imagine Thora's everyday – what she eats for breakfast, how she dresses, what she thinks about before she falls asleep. In rare moments, he has a flash of what she'd have thought of someone or something, but it usually happens in banal contexts. He might be in a meeting with a colleague and all he can think is that Thora would have noted the bad fit of those trousers, that the shirt is too long and the shoes too casual for the office.

'She says we don't need her anymore, that we're adults now, with our own lives. Sometimes I'm scared that she'll disappear,' Frances continues. 'That she's going to take off.'

'Like I did,' he says, because he can hear the thing she leaves unsaid.

'Yes,' she says. 'Like you did.'

He brushes the table with his hand, collecting a neat pile of crumbs. He avoids looking into her eyes.

'I wish I could have known Dad,' she says.

'Of course you do,' he says, and tries to sound gentle, but the sentence comes out unintentionally harsh in Swedish, more nonchalant than the reply had sounded in English in his head.

Frances shifts in her chair and straightens her back, as if to adapt to the altered shape and direction of the conversation.

'You can be hard to talk to, do you know that?' she says.

'No.'

'You're good at small talk, just like everyone here, but sometimes there's this closed-off thing about you. Like when I try to talk to you about things that mean something.'

'Closed-off?'

'Yeah, like, you become distant.'

'Just because you want to talk about something doesn't mean that I want to talk about it,' he says.

Frances looks at him across the table and it's like she's watching him from afar, and he doesn't know if it's because she's moved away from him or because he's moved away from her.

'I'm just a faint copy of them, aren't I?' she says.

'You remind me of them.'

'When you look at me you see them.'

'I see you too, Frances.'

'Do you love her?'

It strikes him that these days Frances is the only person who would think to ask him such a question. Nobody else would have the impulse to discuss love with him as anything other than a theoretical concept. *Love is a social construct*, one of his students said once during a seminar, and for a short moment he considers recycling that answer.

'I love them both,' he says instead, unsure what tense to use.

Frances looks surprised. Maybe she didn't expect an answer. Her posture softens and it makes him feel strangely pleased. They're silent for a moment, him eating his croissant, Frances rummaging through her bag. She finds a notebook and pen, tears out a piece of paper and scribbles with the book on her lap, pen cap between her lips. Then she returns both pad and pen to the bag and looks at him again.

'It's never too late,' she says and slides the scrap of paper in his direction, a challenge. He looks at the numbers, recognizing the Swedish country code. It might be the most childish thing he's ever heard her say, but he accepts the piece of paper without protest.

'Shall we?' Frances says.

He nods.

They walk a couple of blocks together before they part ways at an intersection. He wants to keep walking; she's meeting some friends in another neighbourhood. He watches her cross the street through a cloud of steam from a manhole and then disappear down the subway entrance. The piece of paper she gave him burns in his pocket.

When he gets home and unlocks the door to his apartment, he momentarily expects to find Frances on the living room floor, hunched over her textbooks and notes. Time is the fourth dimension. But Frances is not in the living room, just as Thora is not in the office working on an essay, just as August is not at the kitchen table drinking coffee. Time breaks its neck. His apartment is empty, dark. He walks from room to room and turns on the lights. Then he gets the scrap with Thora's number on it and puts it on the kitchen table. The chairs he and Frances were sitting on earlier are still pushed out, as though it was just a moment ago that they stood up. He turns the piece of paper and reads Thora's number again. He reaches for the computer and sits down to write, maybe to her, he's not sure. By the time he's done, dawn is breaking behind the water towers on the rooftops. It's going to be a hot day.

PART TWO

Hugo

The first time I saw Thora and August together was at a dinner party hosted by Thora's parents. I had heard August's name mentioned in passing before, but I'd never met him, and my conversations with Thora had been limited to short exchanges. Whenever I was in the same room as her she would either ignore me or look at me as though she was trying to expel me with her gaze, and every time she looked at me that way I lingered for longer than I had to. Over the course of that dinner I noticed the way Thora and August's hands kept finding each other. I don't know why those discreet gestures made such an impression on me; maybe it was the contrast between the ease with which they chatted to the others around the table and the vulnerability with which they touched the backs of each other's hands. At one point I glanced across the table and locked eyes with August, and it felt as violent as if I'd flung my arm across the table and toppled over the wine bottles. August smiled. As he looked away he disentangled himself from our eye contact without effort. I was left watching him with tender eyes, as if I'd stared at the sun too long.

After that first dinner I started seeing Thora and August in various places around Stockholm: on the lawn outside the National Library, at the outdoor tables of Södermalm restaurants, in line for the nightclub under the Skanstull bridge. They were always far enough away that I didn't feel obligated to say hi. I wasn't sure if Thora would acknowledge me and I didn't want to risk embarrassing myself in front of them. A week after the dinner August sent me a friend request, which both surprised me and made me feel uneasy. I wondered if I'd slipped and liked one of their pictures, and I scrolled through my activity log to make sure I hadn't left such clumsy tracks. Thora on the other hand never sent me a friend request but I studied her page too. They both had carefully chosen profile pictures and cover photos, but neither of them posted regular updates. I accepted August's friend request and then sat there staring at the screen, waiting for something to happen that might restructure my life. Nothing happened. I saw that I had several friends in common with August and I wondered if he was the kind of person who indiscriminately added everyone he met. For some reason that thought depressed me.

One day I saw them at the corner of Sveavägen and Odengatan. My bus was waiting for the light to turn green, and looking out the window I noticed Thora and August outside a fast-food place. Thora was searching in the pocket of her jacket while August talked and gesticulated as if he was trying to convince her of something. Finally Thora fished out a pair of sunglasses but she didn't put them on; she just held them in her hand and looked at August with an amused expression. August stopped talking, seemingly in the middle of a sentence, leaned forward and kissed her forehead before he took off his hat and put it on her head. There was a gust of wind and she used her hand to hold the hat in place. When the lights changed she looked at the street, laughing with one hand still on her head and the other around the hair that blew across her face, and for a moment she looked straight at me through the bus window. I wasn't sure if she recognized me, but in the midst of her laughter there was a small crease between her eyebrows. I resisted the impulse to duck. A few seconds later the bus moved on and I was tense in my seat with the unpleasant sense of having been caught snooping on a private moment.

I had been renting a room from Thora's parents, Aron and Laura, for a few weeks when a book about the Stiller conglomerate sparked a debate in all the big newspapers. The attention was so upsetting to the family members that they got together for multiple days of meetings to discuss the articles and the critics now blacklisted. It was high summer and to me it seemed like nothing mattered. Laura's mother and siblings came filing through the apartment, and I could hardly tell them apart. They'd enter the hall in the morning without ringing the doorbell, then kick off their shoes and head straight to the living room – the site of the deliberations. I didn't understand why they had selected Aron and Laura's home for these meetings, since the hosts seemed the least perturbed by the book's publication. In contrast to their relatives they were mostly quiet, and they never read out loud from screenshotted paragraphs. Sometimes I noticed them looking at each other as if they were exchanging secret packages, the contents of which were for their eyes only.

I was in the habit of taking my morning coffee on the living room balcony, and Aron and Laura insisted that I continue to do so during their meetings. I wondered if they used my presence to indicate an ironic remove from all the hubbub, but it wasn't clear to me for whose sake they would be doing this – mine or their relatives'?

During these days, the coffee maker rumbled incessantly in the kitchen and the towers of stacked cups grew taller while milk soured in little pitchers nobody bothered to put in the fridge. The news-papers lay scattered over the tables, and as the morning turned into afternoon they were folded up and turned into temporary fans or conversational baseball bats. Jacob Stiller, the oldest of the siblings, was particularly fond of smacking the living room table with a rolled-up magazine to emphasize a point, a consciously clumsy ges-ture that made his siblings roll their eyes. In the mornings, while I was having my coffee, Aron would often sit next to me with his arm on the balcony railing and his fingers in the air, like he was trying to grasp something in the wind. The trees extended their green can-opies over the Lärkstaden streets. We could have leaned over the railing and touched the leaves with our fingertips.

Aron explained to me that Laura's two oldest siblings, Jacob and Charlotte, had board positions in the companies and foundations that were part of the conglomerate, while neither Laura nor Philip, the youngest of the four, had any formal role in the family business. Laura was an art history professor; Philip the editor-in-chief of a magazine.

'Bridges to the cultural world,' Aron said.

I asked if Laura and Philip owned any stock in the conglomerate and Aron gave me an ironic smile, as if I'd just made a joke.

Laura's siblings said hi in passing while Karla, Laura's mother, took the time to shake my hand. She inquired, briefly, about my name, age, occupation. Then she asked if I spoke German – I had just moved from Berlin to Stockholm to study at the university – and when I said yes she nodded again, in approval.

The siblings always took the same positions in the living room, and the view reminded me of a mise-en-scène for some kind of strange portrait. Jacob and Charlotte faced each other from different couches, Philip stood leaning against the bookshelves, and Laura sat in the armchair next to Aron, her legs folded in front of her. Karla was the only one without a dedicated place; she'd stand by the fire-place, pace back and forth around the couches, sit down for a moment, only to get up again shortly thereafter. Every now and then the siblings would look at Karla as if to anchor the conversation to her, but she rarely acknowledged these glances.

I realized that the Stiller family actually enjoyed this artificial state of emergency, which stirred up the lazy July atmosphere that dulled the warm Stockholm streets.

'What we need to do now is focus on damage control.'

'Jacob, you've taken far too many management classes,' Charlotte said.

'We can't appear weak.'

'There's basically nothing new in it. It's just a compilation, a strategic repackaging of facts that have been available for decades.'

'The big question is whether we should offer ourselves for interviews.'

'No. We're not a public family.'

'Now we are though, right? When we're in the media like this?'

'They can talk *about* us. But we don't talk *with* them.'

'So we're just going to sit here and do nothing?' Philip asked.

'If we don't respond somehow, we run the risk of being seen as detached elitists,' Jacob replied.

'Isn't that what we are?' Philip said.

'If that is what we are, the Swedish people don't need to know it,' Charlotte said.

'It's becoming increasingly obvious that the entire witch hunt has been built on speculations that have been combined to create this' – Jacob made a sweeping gesture with his hands – 'this exaggerated, entirely fabricated scandal. Which, in any case, is old news.'

'Old news?' Philip said with a laugh. 'It's not more than three years since you were courting those dictators.'

The word made Jacob and Charlotte flinch. They looked at their younger brother with detached sympathy, like he'd evidenced a stupidity he couldn't be blamed for. Philip looked at Aron and Laura, as if to seek support.

'It's not a long time ago,' Laura said.

Jacob cleared his throat. 'News is slow this season. The media decided to make a thing out of it right now because they don't know what else to publish in the dead of summer.' He was quiet for a few seconds, during which he allotted a smile to each person in the room. 'Journalists feed off of other people's tragedies. I think we can all agree on that.'

'I don't think we need to go as far as portraying the fourth estate as our enemy,' Karla said, but she smiled back at Jacob.

On my way out I would sometimes pause in the doorway and look at them, and at one point Aron caught my gaze through the hum of voices. He had dark, deep-set eyes, and glasses that followed the shape of his eyebrows. His smile brought out the wrinkles around his eyes, a small network of lines, and his brows hiked up over the frames, emphasizing the smile. It was like he was inviting me to laugh at all the fuss. I didn't laugh, but I nodded at him before turning around and heading out into the stairwell. From the courtyard-facing window, light poured in over the marble steps.

When Thora's cousins came over later they greeted Karla first, followed by Aron and their aunts and uncles, after which they gathered in the kitchen, where they crowded around the table and snacked on fruit and biscuits they dipped in their coffees. It was a smaller-scale mirror image of the scene in the living room, and their loud voices carried, just like their parents', into the apartment's hallway, which meant I could hear snippets of their conversation.

'I think they're overreacting.'

'*I* agree with Grandma, personally.'

'You always agree with Grandma.'

'It's our name being dragged in the dirt.'

'What do Aron and Laura think, anyway? I've hardly heard them say a word.'

'Who knows,' Thora said. 'My guess is as good as yours.'

The group of cousins fell silent when they noticed me. Thora had her legs pulled up to her chest and was resting her chin on her knees while she spun her phone between her fingers. Sun from the tall windows bounced off the black screen and sent the light trembling over her impassive face.

'One of Mom and Dad's guests,' Thora explained, her voice bored, to the cousins, and they picked the conversation back up while I put my coffee mug in the dishwasher.

Nobody said anything when I left.

Aron and Laura had been renting out rooms in their apartment for several years. Their lodgers were usually students or young scholars who had a hard time finding an apartment in Stockholm, or who had been put in touch with Aron and Laura through their friends, colleagues or acquaintances. Aron and my parents knew each other from university in Lund; that's how I had been offered the room. My mom had given me Aron's phone number when I told her about my plans to move to Stockholm for school.

The room next to mine was occupied by a young doctoral student named Tigran, who informed me the first time we met that he basically hated all abstract art. He was trying to get a read on my thoughts about the Berlin art scene, and when I told him I had none he seemed to relax, and he launched into a description of his thesis, which dealt with symbolism in figurative art. He spent his weekdays working on it at the National Library, but on Sundays the library was closed and he took long walks by the water around Riddarfjärden and Årsta Bay. Sometimes I joined him. In the evenings he'd often play Sidney Bechet or Janis Joplin, and whenever I heard 'Summertime' or 'Me and Bobby McGee' through the wall between our rooms, I was filled with an unusual sense of calm. I never told Tigran how much I liked the music he played.

My bedroom was by the kitchen, with an inconspicuous private entrance that had been used by servants in the past. Tigran and I shared a small bathroom near the hall. We were at a bit of a remove from the rest of the apartment, which made it easy to come and go without attracting attention. My room was simple: a bed, a closet, a desk, and a sink with a mirror over it. It didn't take long to settle in by putting my small book collection on the desk. I bought sheets and towels and a few storage boxes, which I pushed under the bed, where my black suitcase lay like a large, punctured lung. I liked not having to get any furniture because I didn't want any more belongings than were necessary, and I liked knowing that everything I owned could be easily packed into one suitcase.

Tigran's thoughts on abstract art fuelled frequent arguments with the third guest in the apartment: Vera, an artist. Vera painted 'abstract art', something she told me the first time we met. This introduction was accompanied by air quotes as she looked at Tigran, who shook his head and gazed skywards. Unlike Tigran and me, Vera didn't live in Aron and Laura's apartment; she just went there to paint, in an attic room that had been remodelled as a studio. It was only if she missed the last subway home that she would sleep on a couch by the studio door.

Vera and Tigran had both studied under Laura at some point. Tigran was a PhD candidate in Laura's department and Vera had Laura as her adviser for her dissertation a few years earlier. Despite their divergent opinions on what constituted good and bad art, Vera and Tigran often exchanged looks or made references to lectures that earned a nod of recognition from the other. They told me that Laura would come up whenever they talked to anyone who had studied art history in Stockholm. When I asked what made Laura so popular, Tigran looked at me as if he wanted to make sure we were talking about the same person. But he just replied, concisely: 'She's good.'

Laura confirmed my assumptions about the way wealthy people in Stockholm looked. She was always impeccably styled in smart trousers and white blouses or simple shirt dresses, embodying that thing my Berlin friends loved to hate: the North European bourgeoisie and its subtle expressions of excess. Nevertheless, there was a kind of quiet intensity in Laura's eyes, which in combination with her low, slightly gravelly voice gave me some indication of how magnetic she must be as a lecturer. She was friendly but not prone to unnecessary small talk, and there was something reserved in the way she looked at me that made me feel like the object of a study intended to categorize my weaknesses. I found this unpleasant, since I for my part had no idea how to get a sense of who she was. Still, I couldn't help but wonder what she thought of me.

I came to understand that Laura rarely smiled just to make others comfortable. She didn't use smiles to fill the silence, or try to put whoever she was talking to at ease. I realized this the first time I saw her face break into a sincere smile followed by laughter. That smile, that laughter: you wanted to be near it, but most of all you wanted to be the reason for it, and I imagined that's what Vera and Tigran hoped for when they spent time with her.

Thora was Aron and Laura's only child. She had spent a little over a year in Paris, and was now returning to Stockholm, the week after I moved into the apartment in Lärkstaden. Aron told me she was starting law school. Tigran had never met Thora, but even so there was something dreamy in his eyes when her return to Stockholm came up; maybe he thought he was about to encounter an amalgamation of the best of Aron and the best of Laura.

Thora did not match his expectations. She came from the airport early in the morning one day at the beginning of July, and Tigran and I woke up to a hall strewn with bags and the small family reunited in the living room. When she turned to look at us, her face made it clear that she saw us as interlopers. She got up and introduced herself, apologized for the luggage in the hall and asked if she had woken us up, but I got the impression she would have ignored us had her parents not been present. Her eyes scanned my face without looking.

Soon thereafter Tigran noted: 'She's not like Laura.' Nevertheless, he made a few more attempts to befriend her, knocking on her bedroom door to invite her to eat with us, but she always said no, without explanation. This annoyed him, and he would return to the kitchen in frustration, complaining that she didn't even have the courtesy to lie and say she wasn't hungry. So he stopped trying to get to know her.

I didn't interact much with her either. Sometimes we'd pass each other in the narrow hallway that ran through the apartment. She neither smiled nor glared; we could have been strangers on a crowded commuter train. We rarely spoke.

Now and then, Vera would invite Tigran and me up to her studio. We joined her there one night after Thora had been back in Stockholm for a few weeks. Vera had met both Thora and August before in various contexts. She liked August but found Thora difficult.

'It's weird, right? That someone with parents like Aron and Laura should end up like that.'

'So what's she like, then?' I asked.

'You can't tell by now? She's spoiled. A brat.'

'I guess Aron and Laura would be the reason for that,' I said.

'I'm sure it's a family trait,' Tigran said. 'Families from Östermalm, that's just the way they are.'

Vera laughed. 'Families from Östermalm?'

Tigran made an impatient hand movement. 'The *upper* class.'

The attic room was draughty, and we were all wrapped in blankets even though it was summer. We were seated on rag rugs on the floor, forming a circle around a collection of glasses, coffee mugs, a French press, a wine bottle, an ashtray. Vera's oil paints emanated a strong smell that made me feel a bit dizzy. Through the skylights you could see the sunset, shades of pink that brought out the purplish colours of the rugs. I moved my fingers over the lumpy texture, the stripes that called to mind ocean waves. Once we'd finished the coffee and wine, we went out. Some friends of Vera's were doing a reading at the used bookstore on Birger Jarlsgatan, and we walked over, passing the last couple of Tigran's cigarettes between us. Sitting on wobbly folding chairs, we listened to students reading work they'd produced in a writing programme. Everyone seemed to have gone for lyrical prose pieces with themselves at the centre. Lukewarm wine flowed into plastic cups. After the reading we stepped outside to smoke. A couple of people ran across the street to get snuff and hot dogs at the 7-Eleven. Tigran and Vera's friends discussed the housing situation in Stockholm, compared their sublets and aired plans to move to Malmö; things were cheaper there. And, everyone added in chorus: 'It's so close to Copenhagen and Europe.' It didn't seem, however, like anyone had any serious plans to move.

I liked being in settings where nobody knew me very well. For as long as I could remember I'd avoided bringing people together who had only me in common, and this had created a zigzag pattern across the different areas of my life, one I alone could chart. As a child, I'd realized with sudden clarity that I was multiple persons in one; that the person I was with my mother was different from the person I was with my father, and that this person was different from the person I was with my friends, and that that person was different even with different friends. Small, crucial shifts in the shades of my personality – there was a certain comfort in it. No person existed who could give an account of my life in its totality, and this to me was evidence of freedom. At the same time, there were deep fissures between the different parts, and sometimes I was struck by anxiety at the thought that someone might discover them, and thus be able to stick their fingers inside the cracks, explore the contradictions and tear down the entire construction.

Week by week, fewer and fewer articles came out about the Stiller conglomerate as the onrush of opinion slowed to a trickle. The end of the articles also marked the end of the appearances by Laura's mother, siblings, nieces and nephews in the apartment, and the rhythm of the home changed. I never heard Thora state her opinion; I wasn't even sure if she had one. At breakfast she barely glanced at the articles with her surname in the headline before she turned the page.

I had got a bit of work at a restaurant near Humlegården; they called whenever there was a shift for me. I spent the days when they didn't wandering through Stockholm. I figured out how the islands and the neighbourhoods were connected. I learned where to stand on the platform to get on the train at the right end for my exit. I drank beer or coffee while people-watching from sidewalk cafés and bars. I got a library card and borrowed old movies that I watched on the bright nights I couldn't sleep. After work I went to the bookstore on Stureplan. Passing the section for new non-fiction, I noticed a table with a stack of books titled *The Iron Triangle: The Stiller Empire Hits Back*. I picked up a copy but, seeing the price tag on the back, returned it to the table. In any case, I didn't feel that the Stiller family had anything to do with me. Instead I headed to the fiction shelves and bought a paperback which I brought with me to the stairs at the entrance of the National Library, where I sat down against the wall of the building, face tilted to meet the afternoon sun.

One day I took the subway to the university to scope out the area before the semester started. The campus was empty; the buildings looked like banged-up pieces of Lego flung out on a green field by the highway. The desolation and the contrast between the bright blue sky and the pale blue buildings was depressing, so I returned to the city after a short stop at the main building. I met up with Tigran at a dive bar on Hornsgatan, and listened to him expound on the ways in which he was stuck on his thesis while I tried my best to ignore the familiar feeling of emptiness. It was hard for me to understand why anyone would spend several years of their life on an academic work that only a handful of people would read. Obviously it would be tactless to say what I was actually thinking, so I just advised Tigran to take a break from writing for a few days and to try to think of something else for a while. Meanwhile, I was attempting to catch the eyes of a group of girls a few tables away, all of them dressed in black with tote bags hanging from the backs of their chairs, but none of them looked our way and I didn't feel like getting up and walking over.

On the bus home, Tigran pulled up pictures of Eugène Jansson's paintings. Scrolling down the grid of images, he declared that Jansson was the artist to most successfully capture Stockholm's blue palette. I looked out the window, comparing the blue of the paintings with the great blue outside the bus, and I thought I saw August strolling down the quay, but I might have imagined it.

Aron and Laura left the house early in the mornings and returned late at night. They'd bring home takeout for dinner, which they ate in the living room or the kitchen in front of a computer or book. I'd pass through and spot them sitting next to one another, each with a laptop, faces lit by the white light of the screens and with the dusky sky as their backdrop outside the windows.

On weekends they hosted dinner parties that seemed to go on forever. I sometimes joined them in the dining room, where they made space for me and offered a plate with a hodgepodge of what was left from dinner and dessert. Aron and Laura's friends always introduced themselves with their first names and profession, as if their work was their surname. Karolina the art critic, Samir the professor, Maggie the journalist, Joel the lawyer.

Those dinners represented my most substantial interactions with Thora. When she was present she was usually absorbed in conversation with Aron and Samir, who seemed to be her favourite among her parents' friends. She rarely spoke with Maggie. On one evening I saw her look at Laura, who was seated at the end of the table with Karolina and Maggie on either side. Maggie rested one arm on Laura's shoulder as the two of them listened intently to Karolina. They didn't sense that Thora was studying them with a look I couldn't define – jealousy? irritation? – and in her black roll-neck sweater, with the darkness of the hallway behind her, her face appeared in pale relief, as if she belonged more to the shadows than to this gathering of people seated in the light of the lanterns on the table.

When August was there, Thora was more at ease. She'd immediately slip into the same kind of jargon her parents' friends used with each other. Joel spoke of her future legal career and said that once she graduated he would expect nothing less than greatness from her. I couldn't tell if he was joking. Thora looked at him, and said calmly: 'I look forward to disappointing you.'

I didn't find it particularly funny but everyone laughed. August put his arm on the backrest of Thora's chair and looked at her with a quizzical expression. She didn't seem to notice. She added that she was still waiting to hear about Joel's great deeds, and he responded that she would be *the first to know*. He used the English expression, paired with a jolly glance at Maggie, who was from the US and therefore the intended target of every English word and phrase tossed into the conversation. Maggie received these volleys with great poise.

August and Vera had gone to the same high school, Vera one year above him, and at their end of the table they were discussing friends and acquaintances they had in common. Thora chimed in with more details, and I noticed Vera observing her with reluctant curiosity. Neither Tigran nor I had grown up in Stockholm, but unlike me, Tigran was fascinated by the friendships that formed within and between the prestigious city-centre schools, networks that lasted long past graduation. Tigran asked what distinguished each school, what characterized their students, and the others provided comprehensive answers, as if they were accounting for complex cultures with deep historical roots. I was seated next to Tigran and didn't say much. I had an instinctive aversion to the world they discussed, an aversion I wished I could explain in any way other than as a result of having learned to look down on anything typically Stockholm.

Later that evening we headed up to Vera's studio. August came with us but Thora stayed behind in the dining room. I watched her as we put on our shoes in the hall, my gaze tracing the contours of her head, neck and shoulders, her hair gleaming in the candlelight. Then I looked away, as I felt Vera looking curiously at me. August steadied himself on me when he put his shoes on; I didn't move.

'Thanks,' he said when he straightened up.

In the studio, Vera opened the skylights to air out the paint smell and then she pulled out a few paintings to show August. She told us about her art projects, what her classmates were doing, and Tigran complained that video installations were boring. I had nothing to add, so I was silent. Smoking gave me something to do, but August looked at me as though he saw through me. He smiled.

'My brother loves this type of stuff,' he told Vera. 'You could probably sell him a few.'

'Tigran is sceptical,' Vera said in an amused voice and looked at Tigran, who had sat down on the couch.

'It's not my cup of tea exactly,' he said.

'Still better than a video installation,' Vera said.

It was raining, and it was only when I felt the cool raindrops coming in through the open window that I realized how warm I'd been.

I put out my cigarette and stepped up on a stool to gaze out. A landscape of dark rooftops, shiny with rain, extended before me. I closed my eyes. I could still distantly hear the others' voices. My face was all wet by the time I stepped down, and Vera tossed me a towel but it was covered in oil paint so I declined to use it.

'You'll catch a cold,' Tigran said when I plopped down next to him on the couch.

I wiped my face with the sleeve of my sweater.

'It's warm out,' I said.

I felt soft in my body, and content for the first time since I came to Stockholm. As if I was precisely where I was meant to be.

Vera sat down cross-legged on the floor. August accepted a cigarette from Tigran.

'No offence to your brother,' Vera said, 'but I can't quite picture my stuff hanging in a fancy apartment in London.'

'It's money, Vera,' Tigran said. 'Who cares.'

'*I* care,' Vera said.

'I never let my brother buy art from me,' August said. 'But that's just because he would do it out of pity. With your stuff, he'd buy it because he thinks it's good.'

'Are you that bad?' I asked.

'I might be,' August said with something insouciant in his voice.

'No, you're not,' Vera said. 'There's nobody in Stockholm who paints the way you do.'

August gave a wry smile. 'I'm not sure that's a good proxy for anything.'

'August.'

We turned around. Thora was at the door. Even though we were all looking at her, her eyes were on August alone, as if willpower could make the rest of us go away. Out of the corner of my eye I noticed Vera and Tigran shift where they sat. It was quiet for a few seconds, then August nodded at Thora. He stood up and gave Tigran the cigarette, then thanked Vera for showing him her work. He paused, looking at me. It seemed like he was trying to think of some way to acknowledge me the way he'd acknowledged Tigran and Vera. During this short silence I began to worry he'd forgotten my name. He placed a hand on my shoulder – the touch was heavy, palpable – and said: 'I'm sure we'll see each other again, Hugo.'

He left before I could meet his gaze. We all looked after him, smiling.

Thora was already on the landing.

Later, when Vera shared what she knew about Thora and August, I made an effort not to seem overly interested. I let Tigran ask the questions and pretended to focus on tapping the ash from my cigarette into the tray. Vera explained that the two of them were childhood friends who had known each other more or less their whole lives.

'So they're like siblings?' Tigran said.

'No,' Vera said. 'They used to be a couple. A long time ago. In high school.'

I tried not to picture them having sex.

Tigran hummed.

'But Thora is a snob,' Vera said.

'Or just shy,' Tigran said.

Vera pursed her lips.

'You never know,' he hastily added.

'I think Vera is right,' I said and squashed the cigarette on the ashtray, brushing off my hands. 'Thora is a snob.'

Vera winked at Tigran, as if my support had settled it.

The last day of August, I went to campus to confirm my registration. I'd applied without any clear sense of purpose, and when the admissions offers came in I enrolled in both a full-time course and an evening course, surprised at having been accepted at all. I took a walk and pondered whether I'd chosen an easy out by moving back to Sweden. I wasn't sure what this move was an escape from, but I thought about how effortless it would be to fall back into a false

sense of contentment, to act as if the world was graspable and struc-
tured, with orderly lines at the post office, efficient bureaucracy,
recycling. That's how my Scandinavian friends in Berlin conceptu-
alized going home – that you'd chosen to return to a type of comfort
you might reject on the level of aesthetics and politics, but which
nevertheless couldn't be completely disavowed. It was difficult to
convey this contradictory attitude towards our home countries to
other Europeans, and even more so to non-European immigrants.
There was a kind of communal shame in being both attracted to and
repelled by the orderly middle-class life of Scandinavian cities. And
here I was, surrounded by people at cafés with their baby strollers
and laptops, enjoying brunch and drinking freshly ground coffee,
unwitting representatives of that life of comfort. I assumed I'd
become one of them in due time. The rows of brand-new sneakers
under the tables and the outfits in black, white and dark blue brought
to mind the United States suburbs of the 1950s, with their well-
manicured lawns and shining cars in the driveways.

I took the subway from Slussen. Every time the train stopped I
considered getting off, not registering for the class. I could return to
Berlin. I could fly as soon as the next day if I wanted to. The train
rattled through the darkness, one of the old models that are so noisy
they make it hard to speak at a regular volume. A few seats away
from me, two women were yelling to make themselves heard. I got
off at the university stop. The platform was crowded with students
lining up for the two escalators to the ground level.

The intro to my class took place in a windowless auditorium.
Afterwards I went to the university bookstore and bought used copies of a few of the titles for the poli-sci course. And just like that, I
began the unstructured existence of a student.

(Later, I would return in my mind to this short subway ride to the
university. The doors opening, closing behind me, the lamps in the
tunnels. And every time I went back to that memory, I wondered
who I would have become if I'd got off the train at T-Centralen and

flown to Berlin instead. Then, at some point, I stopped having these thoughts because it became too difficult to imagine that person, that hypothetical version of myself.)

When I came home that evening I encountered Thora in the hall. She was sitting on the floor putting on a pair of shoes, and looked up when I stepped through the door.

'Dad wanted me to tell you there's food in the fridge if you and Tigran want some,' she said. 'Mom and Dad are out.'

'I already ate,' I said and hung up my jacket. 'Where are you going?'

Thora got up, put on a light trench coat and tied the belt around her waist. She didn't seem to have heard my question. She fixed the hair that had got caught in the collar. I watched her from behind as she checked her own reflection, and she met my gaze. She smiled.

'Do you think I should put on lipstick?'

'Sorry?'

She pulled a finger across her lips. 'Red lipstick?'

I heard Tigran in the kitchen and wondered if he could hear this conversation over the din of cooking.

'Sure,' I said and looked away from her reflection. 'Red.'

I felt stupid, as if she had outwitted me in a game I hadn't even understood the rules of. I turned and walked off without waiting for a reply. When I heard the door close I couldn't help but wonder if she'd worn the lipstick.

Thora

I knew from the moment we first met that I disliked Hugo. I never liked any of my parents' charges. August said this was due to an unfortunate combination of being an only child and jealous by nature. I'd just come back to Stockholm and I wanted everything to be mine. I could tell that August took an instant liking to him, but August always liked new people, so I didn't bother to point out what a cliché he was with those worn sneakers, jean jacket smelling of cigarettes, and the faded t-shirts with silly prints he must have picked up at some cheap second-hand store in east Berlin.

That summer, August and I would bike to Djurgården in the mornings, and pick a tree close to the water where we'd park our bikes and lay out our towels and then spend the day swimming, sunning and reading. I'd bring a thermos of coffee and August would come with tuna sandwiches wrapped in tinfoil. The empty wrapping glittered in the sun after we'd eaten. I would lie on my stomach and watch the silvery light through half-closed eyelids. August always made sure to dispose of the garbage in a trash can, and if there was none nearby he'd put it back in the plastic bag we'd brought the stuff in, something that both amused and annoyed me.

It was a hot summer. The sun had bleached the green trees, scraped off their most intense colours. Stockholm was overlaid by a haze that softened the contours and made the building facades seem like they were dissolving in the heat. Viewed from bridges and hills, the city increasingly looked like a mirage.

For me, the season had always been synonymous with the archipelago. Leaving Stockholm on the boat marked the beginning of summer break – a small eternity. I spent the first summers of my life on an island where we stayed in a red house with a glass veranda that Aron and Laura had bought as newlyweds. When I was a bit older, I joined Laura on her travels in Europe, while Aron, who loathed cities in the summer, stayed behind on the island. From these travels I came to understand that most people thought of Stockholm as a remote town in the Nordic backwoods, and ever since I've carried with me an image of a city perched high atop a snow-covered mountain. Aron smiled when I told him this. He'd grown up near the northern border and informed me that I knew nothing about mountains or snow. In Vienna, Laura took me to the opera and to old cafés where I always ordered Sachertorte with whipped cream. In London, Laura's British friends all tried to talk to me even though I hadn't yet mastered English and could only look at them with an indulgent expression that made them laugh. In Paris, I tried to keep up with Laura on the boulevards; I learned to greet people with cheek-kisses. And in Aron's care, far from the European metropolises, I biked down gravel roads, swam in cold water, scraped my knees on stones, dozed on smooth rocks, scratched up bug bites, and stopped brushing my hair as the freckles exploded over my face. When Laura joined us at the summer house she brought a scent, a subtle waft of the Continent, that made me dizzy with a nostalgic joy I'd have described if I only knew what words to use.

When July turned to August, the atmosphere in Stockholm changed with a kind of quiver in the air. Small shops and cafés opened back up. Cars and cyclists grew in number. The nights became marine blue, a premonition of the darkness that would descend on us in a few months. Everyone returned from their summer homes and vacations abroad, their tans varying degrees of even. I met up with friends at bars we picked because of their supply of cava, and we discussed our plans for the fall and the future with a sense of fateful anticipation.

I tried not to look as bored as I felt.

I checked off the list of friends I hadn't seen in a long time, and realized, with growing discomfort, that I felt distant even from people I'd previously enjoyed spending time with. I couldn't tell if the problem was with me or the others. I heard myself nonchalantly describe my year in Paris. The small, round wine glasses at the bars, the Americans who still came to the city to find themselves, the men in suits who tenderly took hold of each other's arms and kissed each other hello; the empty wings of the Louvre, the conversations had over café tables and the mumblings of nameless men (who might, in fact, have said their names; I always forgot). When I finished my account I always felt sad and a bit sticky. I didn't know how to explain the freedom I'd felt there, a freedom maybe best described by the simple fact that I'd been able to commit mistake upon mistake and none of them meant anything, none of them weighed me down. There wasn't the same space for missteps in Stockholm. Here, everything I did seemed to encircle me like the growth rings of a tree, triumphs and let-downs etched into the pavement. The city was witness to all my failures.

It was a feeling I'd often had as a child, and even as an adult I'd frequently wake up in the morning with a kind of surprise. Why had I been born into this body, this life, with these people? I'd speak my name slowly, then quickly, stressing different parts each time, until the word transformed into an inscrutable term in a foreign language.

At the end of the summer, August moved into a new apartment with some friends. I'd lost count of how many times he'd moved long before. He didn't consider it necessary to officially change his address each time, so he was still registered at his grandmother's apartment on Folkungagatan. On weekends he'd go there to pick up his mail, and she would usually make him dinner. Sometimes I joined him. Dessert was Eton mess served with coffee, and Alma insisted that we drink it from a saucer. She laughed when we inevitably spilled the coffee on our clothes.

I liked these dinners at Alma's, sitting around the table in her tiny kitchen, looking out the window where the street lamps swayed in the wind and talking about simple things. Next to the potatoes on the stove and discarded pea pods on the cutting board, I felt ensconced in a warm tower of light, protected from the cold and the darkness outside. I liked who I was with August and I liked who I was with Alma, and the two of them together made me feel safe, part of a little group that didn't need anything from me. I was often preoccupied with trying to assess what kind of person I would be if I liked something or didn't like something, if I was silent on some topic, if I argued for or against something, but in the company of Alma and August that all evaporated. Alma made me feel trivial in a salutary way, and with August there was no point in trying to shape his image of me – it was too late for that.

The apartment August moved into was located at Mariatorget. My excitement about the move was greater than his; I liked to be able to stay within the city limits. For a year he'd had a sublet further out, in Högdalen – a run-down apartment, with yellowed wallpaper that smelled of cigarettes and a mint-green stairwell with a constant stench of the same. During the day this neighbourhood was ordinary and pale, as if the colours had seeped from the facades over the decades, but I liked it when it got dark and the lights came on in the windows of the tall apartment buildings. From August's kitchen you could just about make out the people waiting on the train platform, and I'd raise a hand in the direction of his window whenever I got off the subway. The apartment belonged to an older man who lived in Spain, but now his grandchildren were moving to Stockholm and so August had spent all spring looking for a new place. The one he found at Mariatorget had belonged to a recently deceased relative of his pal Christian, and Christian and his friends had been given permission to stay there while the family quarrelled over how to divvy up the estate. Delighted, Christian had explained to August that this dispute could take months to resolve.

I helped August and his friends with the move since I, as opposed to the rest of them, was in possession of a driver's licence. We loaded the small elevator with moving boxes and went up and down between the street and the apartment. The roommates drew lots for the bedrooms, and the one that fell to August was small but had a view over the verdant square. I stepped over his boxes and looked out the window, at the children running around the fountain where Thor raised his hammer at the Midgard Serpent. The tree crowns were softly rounded and seemed to be floating over the ground, liberated from both trunk and roots. I sat down on the windowsill and watched August arranging his things. When I suggested different ways of furnishing the room, he looked up at me and smiled.

'We won't be in this apartment for long,' he said. 'I can't make myself too at home.'

I shrugged and traced my finger over the white windowsill. His friends entered the room and I wiped off the dirt I had picked up.

'We've hauled up the last of it,' Christian said. 'We can return the trailer tomorrow.'

'Crazy that this is where we live now,' Elif exclaimed.

'Just for a few months though,' Brita reminded him.

'But like . . . I'll be able to *walk* to work from here,' Elif said. 'I won't have to get up at 5.30 anymore.'

'I'm sure the ticket controllers will miss you,' August said. 'You have far too much respect for the law.'

'Thora won't travel with me if I jump the turnstiles.'

'You're so smooth you can talk your way out of a ticket,' Elif said.

'You guys are ridiculous,' I said from my spot at the window. 'You complain about people who don't pay their taxes but you won't even buy your own bus tickets.'

'You're missing the point completely,' Christian said and shook his head.

That afternoon we went to a bar on Bellmansgatan. August and his friends toasted to having become temporary residents of Söder-malm. They had been in the same class at high school, and Brita noted how funny it was to be back in that same neighbourhood, in the midst of the cafés where they had spent their breaks. I'd never liked August's classmates and I knew the feeling was mutual. Ultimately it seemed like they had agreed to view me as a piquant feature of August's life. *A typical childhood friend*, I once heard Elif tell Brita.

Since high school, we'd found and refined a way of talking that dictated the rhythm of our conversations. We often got into political territory where I'd willingly take the role of the Old Right while the others represented the Left. These exchanges entertained me not because I had strong political convictions in any direction, but because in August's friends I saw the political opponents my uncles and some of my cousins were referring to whenever they mentioned 'the leftist press'. August called us the *bourgeoisie* (with intentionally bad French pronunciation), whereupon someone would retort that it's a privilege to be able to be apolitical. In this way, the debate repeated itself; the details were different but the framework was always the same. The predictability of it was oddly satisfying – a way of fixing the world, strapping it down like some rowdy animal you wanted to be able to better observe and deal with.

Afternoon turned into evening but there was no darkness, just a deeper, bluish light, as if the sky had been turned inside out to be aired out for a few hours. August and I walked to Ivar Lo's Park while the others returned to the apartment. We sat down on the sloped lawn. All around us, people were spread out in pairs on blankets and jackets, watching the sunset over the Västerbron bridge. August lay down on his back, his hands on his stomach. I looked at him. He tapped his fingers on his belt.

'Samuel called me yesterday,' he said.

'What did he say?'

'He asked what I'm doing this fall.'

'The seasonal update, huh?'

August sighed. He jabbed my hip with a finger. I removed his hand.

'Quit it,' I said. 'You can't get all grumpy just because your brother gets in touch.'

'I don't call him to ask what *he's* doing in the fall.'

'You're such a child.'

'That's what Samuel says too.'

I pulled my legs up to my chest and put my arms around my knees. 'And what did you tell him you're doing in the fall?'

'I told him the truth. That I'm going to advertising school. He liked the sound of that. Better than art school. Honestly, I think he was googling the name of the programme while we talked. He told me that if I work as an *art director*, at least I'll make money.' August sounded derisive when he said 'art director', the way he and his friends always pronounced English words.

'What a horrible idea. Making money. And from advertising, on top of that. What will your activist friends say?'

August sent a foot kicking in my direction. I ran my hand through his hair.

'You can always justify your chosen profession by promising you'll fight for greater diversity in the advertising world,' I said. 'Even if you'll be a cog in the capitalist system.'

August grabbed my wrists. He pulled me closer.

'You're so . . .' he mumbled.

'So what?'

'*Frustrating.*'

On our way back to the apartment we stopped at a grocery store on Hornsgatan and August bought milk, yoghurt, coffee, bread and peanut butter. I added a bouquet of asters to the shopping basket. We spent the rest of the evening in his room, surrounded by moving boxes and bags. August plugged in a round paper lantern and placed it on the floor. Its yellow pool of light only just reached the mattress. The room was cold. I pressed myself against August, and his body welcomed me.

'Your feet are cold,' he said.

'You'll have to buy a space heater,' I said. 'Before winter comes.'

'Mm.'

He moved his hand over my arm, invisible strokes of warmth.

I woke early the next morning and couldn't fall back to sleep, so I lay watching the crack of light that pushed through the window blinds. I thought about the Midgard Serpent in its permanently frozen pose in the fountain down in the park. Then I put my clothes on and kissed August's forehead before I walked into the hall and slipped into my shoes. August's friends were all still asleep. On the street the morning sun was so bright. The city was quiet, save for a few early-bird tourists photographing buildings in the Old Town. I took a shower when I got home, and underneath the harsh light of the bathroom I traced the silver-white lines on my hip, absent-mindedly remembering being a teenager and crying myself to sleep over the stretch marks as August tried to convince me they didn't matter. I had spent a few summers looking for the same ruptures on Laura's body, but I was never able to spot any.

After the shower I pulled the curtains in my room closed and got into bed still wrapped in my towel, wet hair loose over the pillow. I could hear the others making breakfast in the kitchen. I slept until late afternoon.

For a short while in Paris I'd dated a philosophy student who jumped at every chance he got to talk about Rancière. I couldn't follow his reasoning and finally I bought a few used copies of some of Rancière's writings in one of the bookstores on boulevard Saint-Michel. I started going to Jardin du Luxembourg after my afternoon classes, struggling through page after page in French. I wanted to pry Rancière out of the hands of the philosophy student. When I felt I'd discovered an error in the argumentation of his capstone project, I saw it as a childish victory – as if I'd won several rounds of Ludo. The student took my findings more seriously; he removed me from his social media, and after that I didn't get in touch with him again. I told August about it, acting out the events like a farce. He asked if I was upset, and I said I was absolutely not. Later I told him – and this became something I liked to repeat – that it was thanks to the French philosophy student that I had discovered the joys of meeting another mind on the page. It was thrilling to engage in that kind of mental arm-wrestling. These books contained the thoughts of another person, thoughts that were every bit as winding as my own. I tried to communicate this insight but failed – it fell flat from my mouth. I began to wonder if the only way to meaningfully communicate with others was through writing. Even with August I felt like I could capture my thoughts better in email or text message than when we were face-to-face. And it was when I read August's messages to me that I sometimes experienced vertigo before his thoughts, as if I was standing at the chasm where I ended, looking out across the borderlands to the unmarked point where someone else's mind took over.

I spent many afternoons during that spring in Paris visiting the bookstore on boulevard Saint-Michel. I bought the English and French editions of the same book to make sure I understood. I underlined and translated passages in *Mémoires d'une jeune fille rangée*, *Le plaisir du texte* and *L'Homme révolté*. I mumbled the French phrases to myself until I no longer stumbled over the syllables, until they became a chant that put me in a state of total concentration. Darkness fell in the park around me, and the sound of retirees playing pétanque faded. In the end it was the guards blowing their whistles that yanked me back to reality. I'd pack up my things and leave, feeling wide awake as I walked through the gates, over the street and on across Place Saint-Sulpice, where the smells and the sounds and the people seemed to be in higher definition.

When the admissions period opened at Stockholm University, I applied to a course in literature. I added it alongside my application to law school, like a footnote. I didn't tell anyone about it, and had more or less forgotten all about it when I received an email from the department with the date and time for the first session of the semester in September.

When the day arrived, I took a seat in the front row of the auditorium. The lecturer called the names on the list with his orator's voice and paused briefly to leave space for each hand to shoot up. I was scrolling my feeds, but when the name Hugo was called I looked up. The phone was suddenly heavy in my palm. I turned around to get a better look at my classmates, but nobody had raised their hand. Hugo wasn't there. I wasn't sure about his surname, and of course it's not an unusual first name. I'd been classmates with several, and these days I'd run into them in the neighbourhood around the Stockholm School of Economics, where they hung out dressed in beige chinos and quilted vests. But it was unlike a Hugo of that sort to enrol in an evening class in literature. Humanists tend not to wear quilted vests.

As I left the auditorium, I confirmed that my parents' lodger was nowhere to be seen. When I saw August later, I didn't ask if he knew Hugo's surname.

These evening sessions took place twice a week. Attendance was voluntary for the lectures, but mandatory for the seminars. Two weeks after the start of the semester, at the first seminar, Hugo showed up. He looked at me apprehensively when we caught sight of each other, as if he was trying to figure out how I wanted him to act. I smiled at the classroom in a general way. I was surprised to discover that he was well prepared. He'd done the readings, and whenever he spoke he paged through the books until he found the section he was referring to. The classroom was much smaller than the auditorium, and the tables were arranged in an angular U-shape, with the teacher's table at the whiteboard. I was in a corner, leaving Hugo just outside my field of vision unless I turned his way. When he spoke, I tried to find things to attack in his argument – thoughts and ideas I could tear apart privately until they collapsed – but there was nothing.

When I got home that evening I considered emailing the administrator to ask if I could switch seminar groups. I sat at my bedroom desk, dressed in my pyjamas, with my hands resting on the keyboard, fingers spread, wiggling the Q and P keys, both of which were loose. The oak tree in the backyard was still green, lit by the moon. Then I shut my laptop and went to bed.

Whenever the students got together after class for a beer or coffee, I made sure to pick a seat far from Hugo. I felt silly, and I could picture August laughing at me; this imagined hilarity became more real since I had the sense that Hugo and August sometimes bumped into each other around town, just as you always did with people who ran in the same circles.

Before long, Hugo started to appear at the lectures too. I heard him tell Ella, a girl in our seminar group, that he'd been able to swap a work shift that conflicted with the lectures. They were sitting a few rows behind me so I made sure to look straight at the whiteboard, pretending I couldn't hear them. I knew that Ella had a septum piercing she touched whenever she was trying to think of what to say. She spoke a southern Swedish and I couldn't help but wonder if she emphasized her drawl to make a point of her difference from the rest of us.

The evenings were still temperate and people took the chance to go outside during the break, gathering around the stairs to the entrance. Some headed to the convenience store by the subway station for coffee or bananas.

One of these evenings I was standing at the top of the stairs, talking to some people about the amount of reading we had for the next section of the course. Someone had counted the number of pages and a murmur rose from the group. Hugo was standing at the bottom of the staircase, turned towards a different conversation. I noticed him glancing my way when I said something, as if he was trying to hear better. I caught his eye, at which he came up a few steps and leaned against the wall of the building. He smiled, cautious, like he was planning to toss me something fragile and wanted to measure the distance first to make sure I'd catch it.

He held out his hand. 'Hugo.'

I raised my eyebrows but left the cigarette in the corner of my mouth for a few seconds while I shook his hand.

'You really want people to like you,' I said as I exhaled the smoke.

'Everyone wants people to like them, no?' he said.

'Sure. And yet almost no one wants to be known for who they actually are.'

He gave me an odd look. I couldn't interpret it. He looked at the ground and moved his foot lightly, as if he was putting out an invisible cigarette with his shoe.

'I thought you were going to become a lawyer,' he said when he looked up again.

He was still standing a few steps down, which put him closer to my eye level than normal.

'I am going to become a lawyer.'

'But you felt they don't make you work hard enough over there?'

'Does it bother you that I'm here?'

I was surprised by the edge in my voice. August sometimes told me I was too reserved. Once he sent me an article with the headline 'Do You Make Things Hard by Being Defensive?' It was meant as a joke; I hadn't replied.

'No,' Hugo said.

I looked down at him and tried to think of something to say that could soften my sharpness after the fact and set up a more casual dynamic between us, but the break was over and everyone was heading back inside. Hugo fell back with the group he'd been talking to. Ella said something and he leaned down to hear. He didn't look at me.

Taking my seat, I sensed a small yet noticeable shift in the power balance between us, and I did not like it.

I discovered that I took easily to legalese. I liked the way the real world crackled when filtered through the legal method. It was satisfying, like finding the logic behind a secret code, even though the writing was dry and I rarely cared about the cases themselves. In school I'd always resisted doing things that didn't interest me, and I had spent much of my time teasing classmates and questioning teachers, who in response would sometimes send me to something called a 'group room', where they left me alone to solve problems that seemed too easy to me. I once had a teacher crouch in front of me and explain that I would have a difficult life if I was going to be this combative. I looked him in the eyes and felt sure I was better than him.

Similar scenes played out in other contexts – featuring ballet teachers, piano instructors, after-school programme tutors – and I was steadfast in my resolve not to cry, since this was exactly what the teachers wanted. They wanted me to break into tears and plead for forgiveness, a restoration of balance through my submission. The only people I respected and acquiesced to were my parents and a few of their closest friends. My parents took advantage of this by telling me off during dinner parties, and I'd sit there at the table, face burning with shame. When I got older I realized it was better to be liked than disliked by authority figures. Still, my combativeness seemed to appeal to many of my law professors, and I enjoyed having my legal arguments tried by someone who knew better than me. Moreover, I enjoyed the validation I got from others whenever I mentioned I was in law school. These comments were small nudges towards the future, steady hands placed delicately on my back to shepherd me in the direction of something (I always tried to find a word other than *safe* here) promising.

Laura was the exception. There were no validating nods from my mother. One day we met for lunch at a campus restaurant and I observed the way she grew distant during my account of the first weeks of school: she arranged her face in a cool smile, nodded slowly and avoided any comments that might have functioned to deepen and broaden the story. I'd seen her use this subtle power move many times before, and it annoyed me since I knew it set you up for accusations of overreacting if you protested. Because Laura did listen. But she didn't care about what was said, and it was hard to demand proof of an interest that didn't exist. I knew that she had no real complaints about what I was studying, it was just that she had no interest in law and would, had I confronted her, characterize it as a boring choice.

Saying goodbye after our lunch, she caressed my cheek and placed a few strands of hair behind my ear.

'To think that I've nursed a lover of fine print at my bosom,' she said with a smile.

I watched as she crossed the campus lawn. The wind tugged at her beige coat like a restless child. Leaves tumbled over her from the trees, yellow and bright in the sun.

That evening, one of Laura's colleagues came over for dinner. Aron cooked. I hopped up on the counter and watched as he sautéed vegetables in a frying pan. I told him that the first question asked during the Q&A in the auditorium that day was what kind of salary a lawyer might expect.

'What did you ask?'

'How many of us had in fact chosen Stockholm School of Economics as their first choice.'

Aron stirred the pan. Olive oil splashed onto the stove. I dangled my legs over the floor.

'Thora,' Aron said. 'You don't have to set out to make enemies of everyone.'

Aron, like August, tended to use my name only when he wanted to indicate displeasure. Hard emphasis on the T. I pictured the horizontal line being pushed down on the vertical line, which bounced back in defiance, like a coil.

I'd enjoyed these dinner parties as a child. Nowadays I tended to sit through them with a strained tolerance. The glamour that used to surround them had faded once I realized how much Aron and Laura enjoyed the attention. Gradually, the combination of a studied choreography, recycled conversation topics and my parents' tendency to adjust their opinions according to whoever was the guest of the hour, had worn away my admiration for their skill at making everyone feel at home.

August was the first to make this observation. After the guests had left and it was just the two of us, he said that Aron and Laura had no political convictions of their own. I protested; he was exaggerating, it was just that they didn't share his viewpoint. But once I'd seen it, I could never unsee their perpetually shifting positions. One evening they'd condemn the EU's efforts to keep migrants out and criticize the US president's usage of armoured drones. A few days later they'd praise the EU's strengthened borders while they defended the US president's Nobel Peace Prize. It was no coincidence that my mom's most radical artist friends never came over on the same night as my dad's most conservative diplomat colleagues. Had they shared the table, they would certainly have been confused by their hosts' ability to both support and criticize something at once. At some point I brought it up with Samir and he nodded in agreement with a serenity that irritated me.

'You can't just change what you think like that,' I said. 'You have to choose.'

'It's good you're not planning a career in the foreign service,' Samir said, adding that there was a difference between changing your point of view and changing your opinion.

I didn't find this to be a satisfactory answer. When I told August what Samir had said, he nodded with a smirk. It made sense in a cynical way, he said, shrugging. I was aware that August didn't like my parents, and I knew they didn't like him either. They'd never said it out loud, and they never would. It wasn't a strong aversion, just a disaffection, like standing in a cold draught nobody cared to admit to or fix.

That evening's guest was a colleague writing a book about Soviet art. He wore thick glasses and had a ring in one ear. My parents regaled him with anecdotes about their trips to St Petersburg. I got the sense that this colleague had a crush on Laura, from the way he laughed at the things she said that weren't funny. Tigran talked about Russian Orthodox iconography. Hugo didn't say much. Maybe he had no knowledge of Soviet art or Russian Orthodox iconography. I wondered what he thought about Aron and Laura. He didn't seem enamoured like Tigran, but beyond that I couldn't discern his attitude towards them. Now and then I'd perceive a shadow of scepticism crossing his face, as if he was trying hard not to roll his eyes. Maybe he'd heard August call my parents bourgeois bohemians and agreed with this characterization.

'Do you think Russia will move on Gotland?' I asked out loud during the dessert.

The others stopped talking. Our small silver spoons gleamed in the light from candles and oil lanterns. Hugo looked at me, but he must not have expected eye contact since he immediately turned his attention to his plate. Nobody answered my question. Instead they turned to a discussion of the writing dreams of civil servants at the Ministry for Foreign Affairs, and a newly published novel my parents adored and wanted everyone to read. The colleague promised he would. Hugo and Tigran nodded.

I didn't say anything.

Out of principle, I was critical of the authors and artists Aron and Laura loved. As a child I could never relax at the concerts and plays they took me to. I'd been so focused on interpreting their body language – the way they breathed, how they held their hands, if they were leaning back or forward – to figure out their opinion. I'd wait for their assessment before I shared what I thought. By the time I was a teenager, I'd grown so tired of this that I decided that everything they liked was bad, and everything they disliked was good. Accordingly, I could stubbornly defend the quality of a play Aron hated just to spite him, and he'd let me have at it for a while, before laughing and calling me his little contrarian. Then we'd make peace, at least officially, though in secret I felt resentful that the only acceptable measurement of the world was theirs. In unguarded moments this anger would seep out, and it made Aron and Laura look at me like I was a stranger in their daughter's body.

Hugo

I came home one evening and found Thora and August in the kitchen. It was unusually warm for September, and I'd walked home, jacket flung over my arm, past parks full of people lounging on blankets and eating dinner and toasting with plastic cups under vaults of leaves that had not yet shifted colour. The air was sweet with flowers and greenness.

Thora and August were drinking wine at the kitchen table. There was a laptop on a stool by the windowsill, and from its speakers came a playlist Thora had put on several times before. She had pulled her legs up to her chest, her toes peeking over the edge of the chair. She was bare-legged but had on a knit sweater over her summer dress. August sat with his back to the door, and smoke from his cigarette rose slowly to the tall ceiling and coiled through the open window into the night. I paused in the doorway. When Thora saw me she straightened her back, as if my presence called for a less relaxed pose. Apparently August noticed her changed posture since he turned around.

He smiled at me.

'Hey,' I said, and added, because I didn't know what else to say: 'Where's Tigran?'

'I don't know,' Thora said in a tone that made it clear she thought it was a stupid question.

'Did you just come from work?' August asked, and made a gesture as if to invite me into the kitchen.

'Yes.'

I took a pot from the cupboard, filled it halfway with water and put it on the stove.

'How was it?'

'It was fine,' I said.

I dumped spaghetti in the water and took a jar of supermarket pesto from the fridge. I could feel the weight of Thora's and August's eyes on my back. I turned to face them only when I had no more tasks to busy me.

'How long are you planning to stay in this apartment?' Thora asked.

'I'm not sure,' I said, pretending not to understand the subtext of her question. 'I hope I'll get a room in the student residences soon.'

'You won't.'

'Sorry?'

'You won't,' Thora repeated. 'This is your first semester in Stockholm, right? You don't have enough days on the clock.'

'I guess I'll have to think of something else in that case.'

'Stockholm's housing market is pure hell,' August said. 'Aron and Laura will let you stay for as long as you want. They'll just bring someone new in as soon as you move out anyway.'

Thora glared at him.

August continued with a smile: 'You could always take Thora's room when she moves out.'

'Are you moving?'

'Yes,' she replied curtly, as if I should have known. She turned to August. 'We should head out.'

He looked up at me. 'Do you want to come?'

I waited a few moments to answer since I thought Thora might protest, but she didn't say anything. She just ran her finger around the rim of the wine glass, and rolled her upper lip over her lower lip as if to make sure her lipstick was evenly distributed.

'Where are you going?' I asked.

'We're going to . . .' August said slowly, and looked at Thora.

'To a party,' she said. 'In Djurgården.'

'We were planning to bike there,' August added.

'He doesn't have a bike,' Thora said.

'You don't have a bike?' August asked.

'No,' I confirmed, and refrained from asking how Thora could know this.

'That's fine,' August said. 'We can double on mine.'

They got their stuff and I turned off the stove. Thora went to get something from her room while August and I put our shoes on in the hall. When Thora came back with her bag on her shoulder she was no longer wearing the sweater, and she beamed at August as if it was the first time she'd seen him all day. He gave her his arm to steady herself on while she put on her sandals and adjusted the straps around her heels. We crowded into the elevator and August closed the gate. Thora and I pressed ourselves against the mirrored wall to make room for him.

'Did you go to the liquor store?' Thora asked as the elevator rattled its way down. Her breath left a fog on the glass.

August picked up his backpack and shook it lightly. It clinked.

'You only keep me around so you can use me,' he said.

'Yes,' she said, calmly. 'You're nothing but a remainder from when I was too young to buy alcohol.'

August bent down and kissed Thora's shoulder. She turned away from him and in the mirror I saw that she smiled. The kiss left a slow-fading red mark on her shoulder. I resisted the impulse to touch it.

'You can share our drinks,' August told me.

I said thanks, and for some reason that made Thora laugh. I could smell the subtle scent of her perfume when she moved her head. Stepping into the street, August looked at me as if I was the reason for the joyful mood. While the two of them unlocked their bikes they debated which route to take, Thora impatiently asserting that

Karlavägen was prettier than Valhallavägen, as if that settled it, and ultimately it did. August's bike was old and rusty; he'd forgotten to put it in storage during the winter, he explained, and he instructed me to hold on to him.

The evening sky was deep blue. It was still light out. I would remember this bike ride – this I realized as soon as August started pedalling. I'd forget the work shift, the nearly done pasta, maybe even the red mark on Thora's shoulder, but the rest I wouldn't forget: August's soft cotton shirt between my fingers, the scent of laundry detergent and cigarette smoke, the evening sun braiding itself through Thora's loose hair, the light in the trees that lined the allées, and four statues on the bridge to Djurgården, rising like pledges to something – something as elusive as the shimmering foam in the wake of the boats.

The party was in a large house situated on the easternmost edge of Djurgården. Darkness fell over the course of our bike ride, and our lights shone yellow paths on the asphalt. The trees stood black and silent, lining the road, and nothing moved in the forest groves as we passed. We encountered no other people. I had never been this far out on Djurgården before, and if Thora and August were for some reason to drop me off at the side of the road, I might not have been able to find my way back to the bridge.

We heard the party before we saw it. The neighbouring houses lay in darkness, the streets empty. Then, on a hill, squares of light came into view between the trees and the bushes, and Thora pointed at a gravel road where we turned off. It looked more like a mansion than a house, and I suddenly became aware that I was still dressed in the same t-shirt and jeans I had worn all day at work. The windows and doors opened onto the garden. Thora didn't knock or ring the doorbell, she just walked right in, and August and I followed her.

People with wine glasses and beer cans in their hands were

stumbling back and forth between the rooms. Music was booming from a set of speakers in the living room, and a small group of people were playing knock-out ping-pong on an oblong dining table. Now and then the white ball would bounce into the chandelier, and whenever that happened everyone in the dining room froze and regarded the small, quivering crystals with a mix of fear and delight. August explained to me that we were in the home of the parents of an old classmate of Thora's. These parents were rarely at home. Thora said she hadn't seen her old school friends in forever. She was turned to August when she said this, not me.

'When we get bored we can go swimming,' August said.

'*If* we get bored,' Thora said.

She was quickly swept up by a group of people who loudly declared that they wanted to hear *everything* about her year in Paris. August and I watched as she let herself be whisked off.

The two of us walked through the rooms on the ground floor and August nodded at the people we passed; every now and then he ducked behind me to avoid talking to someone. I wondered how well he knew the other guests. As if he could sense what I was thinking, he started pointing at the various partygoers and described them to me in a hushed voice.

'The son of a government minister,' he said about one guy who passed us. 'And over there are the daughters of some of the country's wealthiest men.'

'How do you know this?' I asked.

'I don't know, I just do. Knowledge by osmosis,' August said, a hint of fatigue in his voice.

'So they're not your friends?' I asked.

'No,' August said, taking a small step closer to me. 'Honestly, I don't know if they're Thora's friends either.'

'So why are you here if you don't like them?' I asked.

'Thora likes them.'

'She does?'

'At least, she tries to like them. More importantly, I think she wants *them* to like *her*.'

I took a sip of lukewarm beer. 'I don't think Thora likes me,' I said.

'Do you want her to like you?' August asked with a sincerity that surprised me.

'No. I don't know.'

'Thora doesn't like anyone at first. It's nothing personal.'

'Are you together? You and Thora?'

'Why? Are you interested?'

We had paused in the dining room doorway. August leaned his head against the door frame and I pressed my fingers into the embossed logo on my beer bottle as I met his gaze, not sure how to interpret the question, or which of them he was referring to.

'No,' I said.

'We were together when we were teenagers,' August said. 'We're better as friends.'

'You behave like a couple.'

'Are we that boring?'

I smiled wryly, but I could tell from the way August looked at me that he wanted me to respond. I didn't like the thought that he might tell Thora about our conversation. I looked out across the dining room, at the ping-pong ball bouncing back and forth on the dark table.

'You're fine,' I said.

August smiled at me, as if he was holding back a laugh. I looked at my fingers. The logo had left marks on my skin.

We played a round of ping-pong. August seemed to aim for the chandelier and I had the sense that he would have enjoyed seeing it crash into the table; he smiled every time the room hushed. I wondered if everyone else in here was the child of parliamentary politicians or celebrities or C-suite executives. August and I headed to the kitchen for more beer and found a guy in a bow tie in front of the fridge, explaining how liquor bottles should be organized to take up the least amount of space. When he laid eyes on August he dropped his soliloquy. He extended the vowels of his 'hello' so much that it sounded like he was about to break into song. August introduced him to me as Carl, an old classmate of Thora's and, August added sarcastically, *our host*. Carl looked at me and then August as though August were in the midst of demonstrating a complex math problem, and it was only when August mentioned that I was staying at Aron and Laura's that a flicker of approval crossed Carl's face and he began to nod, eagerly.

'You know, we always said Laura looked straight out of a Hitchcock movie,' he said, without explaining who was included in his 'we'. 'And Thora is starting to shape up. Do you know the problem with freckled people?'

'They have a higher risk of skin cancer,' I said.

'They *collapse* when they get older.' Carl gestured with his hand over his face.

'I'll make sure to let Thora know,' August said in a crisp voice.

Carl looked at him, face vacant. 'Come,' he said. 'I'll give you the tour.'

Neither I nor August told him that we'd already looked around. Carl launched into an avalanche of questions: he wanted to know where I was from, why I had moved to Stockholm, what my parents did for work, how I knew Aron and Laura. August walked behind us. When I looked at him, uncertain of how thoroughly I should answer Carl, he gave me a smile, but I had the sense that it vanished as soon as I looked away.

We paused at the double doors to the veranda, where Carl introduced us to his girlfriend in the same tone he'd used when pointing out the paintings on the walls, the books in the bookcases, the objects in the vitrines.

'What's up,' Carl asked.

'I'm sick,' Jill said.

73

'Yeah, me too,' the guy next to her said.

'*You're* sick?' Carl said to him.

'Yes. No,' he said.

August and I glanced at each other. I had to look away in order not to laugh. I sensed an unspoken understanding between the two of us that I couldn't remember sharing with anyone in a very long time.

'Take a painkiller,' Carl told Jill.

'You're not supposed to do that with alcohol,' she replied with annoyance, and demonstratively raised her wine glass.

Carl turned to August and me as though he'd just had an idea.

'Where *is* Thora anyway?'

Jill straightened her back. 'Thora's here? I didn't know she was back in Stockholm.'

'I don't know where she is,' August said.

'You don't keep an eye on her?' the guy who was not sick asked, and offered me his hand. 'I haven't seen you before. Name's Casper.'

I gave him mine.

'Nice, nice.'

There was a short pause. Their cloudy eyes made me think of broken cameras, incapable of finding the right focus.

Two girls were seated on a chaise longue with their legs crossed. One of them said, loudly: 'Like, my first name goes with every surname. It'll be easy for me to get married. That's pretty nice to know.'

'That's good for you I guess,' the other girl said.

'Try to find a name it doesn't go with.'

I saw August tilt his face towards the ceiling and close his eyes. Without knowing why, I rested my hand against his back for a few seconds. The cloth of his shirt felt more real than Carl and Casper, who had moved on to discussing the value of different stocks, or Jill, who inserted a comment now and then in between humming along with the music and bouncing her head back and forth. August neither said nor did anything that indicated he had noticed my brief touch.

74

'August!' Casper said and clapped his hand over his forehead. 'Shit, I forgot. I ran into your brother in London the other week – looks like he's doing *good*. He wanted me to say hi to you.'

'You're not planning on following in the footsteps of your bro?' Carl asked.

'No,' August said. 'I don't think I have what it takes.'

'If you only knew the way my dad goes on about Samuel,' Casper said. 'And my dad is basically never impressed by anyone.'

'If you only knew the way *my* dad goes on about Samuel,' August said. From my angle I could see the tension in his jawline.

The girls on the chaise longue had stopped talking. I made eye contact with one of them and she smiled at me. The blonde fuzz on her thighs was lit up by the lights on the veranda.

A while later, we came across Thora out in the garden. She was sitting cross-legged in a wicker chair, glass of wine in one hand and cigarette in the other. She spoke slowly, with carefully orchestrated silences. I wondered if she didn't notice or didn't care that none of her listeners seemed to keep up with the story she was telling. Their eyes were glassy as they followed her hand movements.

August perched himself on the armrest of Thora's chair. He pinched the cigarette from her hand and took a drag.

After a moment of silence, as if they needed time to process what Thora had told them, one girl said, tentatively: 'So, like, things were good in Paris?'

'Yes, Selma,' Thora said. 'Things were *good* in Paris.'

'Do you speak fluent French now?'

'No,' Thora said, and jutted her chin out while August looked at her with an amused expression. 'But I'm much better.'

I sat down on one of the Persian rugs that had been pulled out into the garden. Several people lay on their backs and pointed out constellations even though no stars could be seen. Selma offered me a half-smoked joint and I accepted, watching Thora and August through the smoke. Thora had abandoned her audience and was now talking to August in a low voice. They were sitting so close together that their foreheads almost touched. Next to me on the rug I heard a guy on his back tell the girl he was talking to: 'Like, I get the concept of postmodernism, the *theory* behind it, but when I see a stick against a wall I'm just wondering – what's the point?'

The hours went by. I lost track of Thora and August. I wandered between the garden and the rooms on the ground floor. Carl and Jill were dancing in the living room. I heard some people discuss heading down to the water for a swim. I felt pleasantly distanced from everything going on around me. Thora's old classmates meant nothing to me. Normally I'd imagine the buzzing glances of everyone else at parties, in clubs and bars, as if I was moving through a soft mass of opinions shaped by how successfully I gave the impression of not caring. I was always worried about losing control of the image I projected to others, and this required constant vigilance, even if some slip-ups could be blamed on drugs and alcohol. *I was so high, I was so drunk* – excuses made to diminish the significance of something I'd said, even though I hadn't in fact been particularly high or drunk. The couple of times I'd gone out alone in Berlin – driven by restlessness, boredom, angst – the clubs and concert spaces had afforded me a rare sense of freedom. The anonymity represented a sanctuary from *myself*. And at this party I felt like a spectator rather than a participant. I didn't belong, that much was clear to anyone watching. I didn't look like them, didn't dress like them, and when I spoke it was obvious I wasn't from Stockholm.

In line for one of the bathrooms upstairs, I ran into the girl whose first name went with every surname. She smiled as though she recognized me too, and then she held out a hand and pulled me close – I assumed she'd got this gesture from some American movie or TV show – and kissed me until it was her turn to use the bathroom. She was gone before I could ask what her name actually was. My head felt heavy and precarious, an object I needed to steady with my hands. I wondered how I would get home. I went down to the living room and let myself be swept up by the bodies on the dance floor. After some time had passed I felt a hand on my wrist, and when I looked up August was there. Water was dripping down his face from his hair, and his t-shirt was dark with wetness. Thora was in the doorway, also with wet hair.

'Did you go swimming?' I asked, leaning closer to make sure he could hear me over the music.

'Yeah. It was freezing.' August's grip tightened, as if he was worried I'd drift away. 'Come, we're going home.'

I followed him.

Sitting on the back of August's bike, I intermittently rested my forehead on his back and closed my eyes. I didn't understand why my eyes were throbbing the way they were; I wondered if I was about to cry. August's wet shirt was cool, and it made me feel less dizzy. I felt his muscles drive the bike forward and tried to mimic the rhythm of his breathing.

A thin autumnal mist lay over the canal. The streets were newly awake, with the light of dawn grazing the asphalt, signalling that the morning rush was about to begin. The allée through Karlavägen was empty, and Thora and August biked side by side. When they stopped at a traffic light she turned to him and then, as if her eyes had just slipped back, to me. It was the first time I'd seen her look at me without a baseline of scepticism, but I couldn't tell if she'd meant for me to see that inscrutable gaze – there was something vulnerable in it, like a naked foot hanging off the edge of a bed.

After that party, August and I started hanging out on the regular. Tentatively at first, but it soon felt so natural to spend time together that I could hardly imagine Stockholm without him. Talking to August I discovered I had opinions and thoughts that I hadn't ever bothered to articulate to myself. Sometimes I worried that he saw me as a diversion, and I kept looking for signs that he was growing tired of my company. When I couldn't find any such indications I was relieved – at least for a while – but I couldn't quite shake the feeling that I had tricked August into thinking I was someone I wasn't, and that sooner or later he would find out.

August rented a desk in a studio near St John's Church, and I began to stop by in the early evenings, after my daytime class was finished, when the libraries and coffee shops had closed for the day. August would be working on projects for ad school, but as soon as I stepped through the door he pushed away his notebook and computer with a look like I'd come to liberate him. He didn't spend much time on his homework, said advertising was soul-sucking and amoral. Whenever he made this point it would be followed by a few seconds of silence, as if he was trying to figure out what bothered him about what he'd just said. Then he'd shrug and add that it was at least a way to make money. I realized after a while that he thought a lot about money, about how he was going to *make a living* – that's the expression he used. He was preoccupied with finding a profession that would allow him to support himself without being draining. Sometimes he'd mention, tartly, that this was stuff Thora didn't get, that she never wanted to talk about money or making a living.

'Then again, she's never had to worry about that kind of stuff,' he added.

On my way to his studio I'd buy something ready-made from the freezers in one of the grocery stores on Sveavägen. We'd micro-wave the food and eat it straight from the packaging. When we left the studio August liked to stop in at the church for a moment before heading to the subway station. I followed him even though I initially felt dubious about his enthusiasm for these church visits. I wondered if his family was religious, and when I asked he just laughed.

'But are you a believer?' I persisted.

'I don't know. Maybe. Sometimes I try,' August said. 'I guess I'm not doing it right. If this was a synagogue or a mosque I'd still come in.'

The church was situated on a hill and we climbed, rather than walked, up the stairs to the entrance. At the top I turned around, panting, and looked out at the rooftops and the cemetery below us. The scene was peaceful, even though the area was bracketed by heavily trafficked roads, tall office buildings and shopping streets.

Thanks to August I discovered parts of Stockholm I had never known before. He took me on walks, showed me parks, cafés and backstreet bars. On weeknights we'd often end up at a small jazz bar on Brunnsgatan, where black-and-white photographs covered the walls and the windows fogged up while the band was playing. August had manned the bar at one point and the owner let us stay after closing, when he put ashtrays on the tables as if to signal the transition from public bar to private living room. August took me home to his grandmother, who vividly described to me the old Klara neighbourhood, which she'd known well before it was demolished. August often spoke about Stockholm with a strange mixture of tenderness and condescension, not unlike the way someone might talk about an annoying younger sibling. Still, it seemed he wanted me to like it there, and I did, especially when I was with him.

The first time I met August's roommates, we ended up discussing Thora and the Stiller family. It seemed like there was a constant need among August's friends to talk about them. We were in the kitchen of the Mariatorget apartment, seated beneath a lamp someone had thrown a red shawl over, and the light brought out the shadows in everyone's faces, making us all look a little rough-hewn. Brita looked at me and asked if I was *friends* with Thora. I noted the emphasis and looked at August to gauge his reaction. He pretended not to have heard and passed me a can of beer from the fridge. I said that I didn't think Thora would call me her friend, which made August's roommates laugh.

'Brita doesn't like Thora,' August said in an even tone. 'It's mutual.'

'She would never admit it,' Brita said.

'Not *to* you.'

'Why do you not like each other?' I asked.

Christian laughed. 'Cultural differences.'

'City centre versus suburb,' August said.

'That's a simplification,' Elif said. 'Some suburbs are just as fancy as the city centre.'

'Call them the outskirts, then.'

'Right.'

'Thora is a city kid,' August explained to me.

'She's probably never taken the blue subway line in her life,' Elif said.

'Now that you mention it, I'm not even sure she's ever been on public transit,' August said.

'August, stop playing dumb,' Elif retorted.

'You have an inferiority complex because you're an art student,'

Christian told Brita. 'You have this feeling of needing to prove yourself.'

'Though we're part of the elite now. We belong to the cultural elite,' Elif said.

'Man, I hate that concept. Thora and her family – they have real power. *Economic* power. Who cares about my ceramics?'

'She didn't choose her family,' August said.

'Soon you'll tell me class isn't real,' Brita said and looked at the guy seated across from her, the only person yet to speak. 'Martin, why so quiet? You're our northern proletarian. You represent the perspective of the rural class here.' Brita looked at me and explained: 'Martin is Elif's boyfriend.'

'There's a stranger in our midst. Can't be too careful what you say,' Martin said.

'True. You never know who August is going to bring over,' Elif said, and she looked at August with tenderness.

'Right. He does fraternize with society's top dogs, after all.'

'You should have seen August when he was an usher at the Royal Dramatic Theatre,' Elif told me. 'The lady patrons of culture adored him.'

'The blue, the green and the red lady patrons of culture.'

'How do you tell them apart?' I asked.

'The bourgeois ladies have pearl necklaces and big hairdos. The environmentalist ladies wear loose-fitting clothes. The social democrats' – August paused and thought for a moment – 'those ladies have no particular look in common, but it's rare to see them dressed up.'

'Soon they'll discover August's potential,' Christian said. 'They'll be able to use you as a Scandinavian charmer on their export trips.'

'A gigolo for the dictators,' Brita said.

'It really is disgusting,' Elif said.

'Did you read the most recent stuff?' Martin asked.

'About the state visit? Yes.'

'With the royal family.'

'And a Stiller. Of course.'

'You make out like you're so *superior*,' August said.

'Aren't we though? Morally, I mean.'

'Economically we're inferior anyway.'

Everyone fell silent. August's friends looked at each other, as if they were deciding what direction to take the conversation.

'But it's true that Laura is a good teacher,' Brita said, finally.

Everyone except for August concurred. When I tried to catch his gaze, he seemed to sense my looking at him and gave me a small smile. Silence, again. Later I would think back to how that silence felt like a pulsing tumour that could only be punctured by a change of topic. And afterwards, everybody ignored the bad smell that came from the deflated lump. I came to know that stench well – it would return in many other situations, and in contexts that were drastically different.

I'd never thought of politics as relevant to me. When my mom took me to community meetings in various basement spaces all over Malmö and Lund during my childhood I had listened to the discussions with interest, but I hadn't linked them to anything bigger than the timespan it took to finish the coffee, cordial and cinnamon buns served at every meeting. I realized, sitting at the table with August and his friends under the red lamplight, that this, in practice, meant I had adopted my dad's attitude: that politics, fundamentally, were the result of the larger collective's vulgarizations and therefore not interesting. This insight made me uncomfortable, as though I'd seen my own reflection from a new angle. I wished I could discuss my new realization with August, but I didn't know how to bring it up and I was worried that he'd just dismiss me.

Thora

When August and I had sex I liked to lie spreadeagled, legs and arms extended across the bed while he kissed me wherever he liked. I never did this with anyone else, would never let myself be so vulnerable, but with him there was something exhilarating about closing my eyes, sinking into the bedding and feeling his mouth move over my body. It felt like I gave myself over not just to August but to something larger than the two of us. I could never guess in which order or how long he would kiss my feet, my thighs, my stomach, my breasts. I'd close my eyes and listen as his breath grew heavier, and when he entered me he'd do it with such sudden force that I'd grab hold of the mattress with my hands. Then I'd open my eyes.

There were long periods when we didn't sleep together. We never discussed it. Usually it was because one or both of us was dating someone else, or simply because there was no desire. But during that fall, August wanted to have sex with me a lot. He'd text me in the evenings and invite me over, and I'd bike through the city feeling like I was on the brink of something new and unknown. I'd missed August's touch when I lived in Paris and I didn't mind a replay of the frenzy from our teens. We discovered new kisses, new caresses, new favourite positions. It was like we were tracing and cataloguing our respective lovers, laughing as we asked who had taught the other to do this thing or that thing. I didn't comment on the fact that this new period – brief but intense – was concurrent with August's budding friendship with Hugo, even though I had the thought more than once.

Hugo had become hard to avoid. August introduced him to his friends, and they seemed to take to him. At parties and bars Hugo was seated among them, suddenly a natural part of August's social world. Now and then Hugo looked at me across the tables and rooms as though he was trying to return to a question I'd left unanswered. I didn't like the way it punctured the conversations with unspoken openings that seemed to insinuate there was something between us, floating on top of all the small talk. Sometimes I had the sense that the two of us were on the outside of the rest of the group, while August was at the centre, surrounded by his friends. There was a candour in Hugo's eyes I felt compelled to dodge.

Whether they discussed me when it was just the two of them, I didn't know. I didn't ask August.

One evening in mid-October, we found ourselves at another party, in an apartment on Kungsholmen where an acquaintance of mine and August's lived. Hugo and August showed up late. With them came Ella from our literature class who, August whispered in my ear, Hugo was now dating. It annoyed me that he felt moved to inform me of this, and I answered brusquely that she looked like Hugo's type – I made a circular gesture at my nose, where Ella had her septum piercing – whereby August raised his glass in a toast.

I turned my back on them, went into another room and struck up a conversation with a guy I knew was in the third year of law school. I'd recognized him immediately; we'd run into each other in the university library. His name was Simon, and while he demonstrated how to open a beer bottle using a jar of snuff he listed the classes and teachers he'd had over the course of his studies, an inventory of a past I was to inherit from him. I didn't tell him that I already knew how to use snuff jars to open bottles. The door to the little balcony was open and the people crowding out there were smoking, cigarettes glowing in the dark. The courtyard down below, split into rectangular sections by hedges and fences, was empty and quiet, covered with fallen leaves. It was warm in the apartment. Someone was frying eggs in the kitchen and called out the seasonings of each batch as though at an auction. The smell made me nauseous.

Simon asked what kind of practice I wanted to go into after finishing law school and I told him I didn't know. In that moment Hugo and Ella came out of the kitchen, each carrying a plate of omelettes, and I moved closer to Simon, trying to pay attention to his description of the firm he was hoping to join. I trained my gaze on his mouth and soon he leaned in and kissed me, tentatively at first. Then I moved in even closer. His mouth tasted of crispbread. After a short while he pulled away, maybe he thought I was moving too fast, and for some reason it almost made me laugh. I wiped my lips with my hand, but stopped myself from asking if he was into crispbread. Then my eyes got mixed up in Hugo's. He was leaning against the door frame. Ella was crouching by the couch, talking to someone I didn't know. It took a few seconds before I noticed that there was something like an open accusation on Hugo's face. Simon took my hand in an attempt to take me to the balcony for a smoke, but I pulled back and slipped out of his grasp. I paused by the wall-hung String bookshelf, stacked with colour-coordinated paperbacks, feeling at once curious and exposed. Hugo walked up to me and I crossed my arms.

'August and I are not a couple,' I said after he greeted me.

'I know. He told me.'

'So you've asked?'

Hugo smiled at me.

'It has nothing to do with you,' I said.

'No. I know.' He raised his free hand and rubbed his palm over his neck.

I glanced over his shoulder at Ella and then back at Hugo, unsure of what my gaze was communicating.

'You don't like her?' he said.

'Does it matter what I think?'

'No. I guess it doesn't.'

I found a space for my wine glass on the bookshelf and told Hugo to send Ella my regards. He raised his eyebrows, as if hoping to prolong the slippery exchange, but I turned around and walked into the hall.

I left the party without saying bye to anyone. Outside, the dark sky vaulted itself over the roofs, and the street lamps swayed in the wind. I felt strangely tender, as if my arms and legs were covered in invisible bruises.

The next day I called August. We talked about the party. He didn't ask why I left so early and I didn't mention my interaction with Hugo. Instead I tried to affect a playfully whiny tone, as if their friendship was an annoying fly in my field of vision that August was responsible for getting rid of.

'I *do not* like him.'

'Thora, you don't know him,' August said, patiently. 'I actually think he'd like to get to know you—'

'You always want me to like everyone you like.'

'You're too quick to judge.'

'And you don't judge often enough.'

I could hear August smiling on the other end of the line. I sighed. 'Whatever. Forget it.'

'Do you want to come over? Everyone else is out. We can watch a movie.'

I took the bus to August's and curled up on the couch under a blanket. He made tea, sliced up two oranges and brought it all on a tray into the living room. We watched two movies on his computer while I rested my head in his lap and he played with my hair.

'Are you going to fall in love with him?' I asked when the credits rolled.

His fingers in my hair were still for a few seconds.

'What if I'm already in love,' he said.

I turned around, put my head on the armrest instead. We looked at each other. I smiled. He stood up and got undressed, waiting for me to do the same before he got on top of me, lowering his full weight onto me. When he was deep inside me he put his lips to my ear and said: 'I think you'll be the one to fall in love with him.'

The kitchen cabinets at Karla's had no handles. To open them you had to press your hand against the smooth surface and wait for a small crack to appear, then you could slide your fingers in and pry the door open. The building was old, but her apartment was decorated in a modern style. At the centre of the living room a chaise longue in black leather sat like a lonely, bold exclamation mark. A large floor lamp reached over it, with a head that brought to mind an old-fashioned hairdryer.

Somehow Karla had learned that I was taking out a student loan, and she found this questionable. She found most things family members did without consulting with her first questionable. August had dubbed her the Matriarch at Humlegården and predicted a future where I would meddle in the lives of my children and grandchildren just like Karla did.

'I want to have my own money,' I told her.

'It's not your money, it's the government's money, which you have borrowed.'

My back did not touch the back of the chair. I folded my hands on the table. 'I'll pay it off after I graduate.'

'If you truly want to have your own money, you should get a job on the side.'

I nodded, despite having no intention of getting a part-time job. If I did, I would have basically no time for my literature class, though

Karla had no way of knowing that. I knew she would never understand that the class was like a room I could enter to make all the noise go away.

The autumn sun came flooding through the kitchen windows. I'd bought croissants from the bakery down the street, and the pastry flakes floated onto the white table like brown confetti. Karla sat facing the sun and she tilted her head back and closed her eyes for a short moment. She was dressed in a white silk shirt and a pair of loose beige trousers, an outfit that brought out her even tan from a summer spent mostly in southern France. I'd always found Karla beautiful. She was stately, with a chiselled face and large eyes that could stop anyone in their tracks. She usually styled her hair in a bun that showed off her neck. With her eyes closed like this, she seemed unusually vulnerable. But I could see them moving even now, the eyelids trembling like slumbering beasts of prey. A fly was buzzing in the window. I drank the last dregs of my coffee. Karla opened her eyes.

'Agnes received funding for her entire degree,' she said. Agnes was Charlotte's daughter and Karla's favourite of the grandkids.

'I know,' I said. 'But her university is in the United States.'

Karla brushed the table with her hand, making a small pile of croissant flakes. The rings on her fingers sparkled.

'Do those people still rent from Aron and Laura?' she asked.

'Hugo and Tigran? Yes, they're still there.'

'They have some ideas, Aron and Laura, they really do,' Karla said, more to herself than to me. 'And when you move out they might take in yet another person?'

'I don't know,' I said. 'I don't think so.'

I disliked the idea that a stranger would take over my old room.

'You never know,' Karla said.

I turned away from the window to avoid being blinded by the sun. The kitchen was separated from the living room by two open glass doors. In the far corner of the living room was a deep-red armchair with a softly rounded back. Shortly after graduating from high school, I had gone to visit Karla with a few of my cousins, and Karla had sat on that chair as if perched on a throne, lecturing us about how much more dangerous the world was for girls. The subject had come up because Harriet, who was my age, was going to travel around Asia that summer.

'There's a difference,' Karla had said, matter-of-fact, 'between girls and boys. It's not the same for you. You have to be *cautious*.'

This counsel had made me bristle. I'd thought about how the sons in the family were encouraged to explore and conquer the world, while the daughters could hardly dip their toes in before someone hastened to caution that the world would harm us. Later I recounted Karla's words to August. He was quiet for a short while before he said, hesitant: 'But it's true, isn't it? Even if you don't want it to be.'

Karla gave me the keys to the apartment on Styrmansgatan. Philip's daughters, Harriet and Iris, and I were all going to move in. It was Karla's apartment, and it had functioned as a transitional home for many a family member during their studies. There were three bedrooms, a bathroom, a living room and a kitchen. The bedrooms were long and narrow, but the tall ceilings made them feel larger. I got the middle room since the sisters didn't want to share a wall.

I was in law school, Harriet in med school and Iris was studying to become a teacher. We jokingly christened ourselves the three pillars of society.

'We should have a plaque on our mailbox,' I said. '*Here live three pillars of society.*'

'*Future* pillars of society,' Harriet said.

The night we moved in, we ate dinner on the living room floor. We cooked spaghetti and added sliced cherry tomatoes, olives and mozzarella, and on the side we dipped bread in a small bowl with olive oil and sea salt. To drink, red wine and water with ice. Harriet said she wished we had whisky for dessert. Iris, the most romantically inclined of us, had stuck tapered candles into a bunch of empty wine bottles.

We threw a housewarming party that weekend. August entertained himself by trying to guess which different guests were studying to become lawyers, doctors or teachers. He whispered his calls into my ear, and then he joined the party, introduced himself and chit-chatted with the guests, before he returned to me with his results. His rate of accuracy was surprisingly high.

'It's my artistic eye,' he said.

'So I look like a future lawyer?' I asked.

'No. You only look like you,' he said. 'You're in a category of your own.'

Hugo and Tigran came to the party too. August had invited them but they arrived late, at which point I'd begun to think they weren't coming. Tigran handed me a bouquet of red tulips.

'It was Hugo's idea,' he said, as if he wanted to distribute the blame in advance. 'But he didn't have time to go to the shop before work.'

'Thanks,' I said. 'That's so nice of you.'

The tulips were wrapped in plastic that crackled in my hands. I didn't know what to say. When August appeared with two glasses of wine for the new arrivals, I left them and went to the kitchen under the auspices of getting a vase for the tulips. I let the cold water from the tap run over my wrists before I filled a round vase halfway, unwrapped the plastic and placed the tulips, one by one, into it. Their green leaves unfurled as if they were sighing in relief. When I was done, I paused to take in my work. The bouquet was small and already drooping, the kind of tulips you could get from grocery stores all over the city.

'Tigran wanted to get lilies instead but I thought you might be bothered by the smell.'

I spun around. Hugo was in the doorway, observing me. I wondered how long he'd been standing there for.

93

'I was just coming to get a glass of water,' he said.

'Okay,' I said and stepped away from the counter, vase in my hands.

'Nice place,' Hugo said while he filled a glass with water.

'Yes. A little small.'

Hugo leaned against the counter. 'That probably depends on what you're used to,' he said.

'I guess so,' I said and placed the vase on the kitchen table. 'I think this is going to go here.'

I slid the vase to the centre of the table. Hugo nodded as if to show he had no objections to this placement. I had to stop myself from letting out a laugh.

'It's true, by the way,' I said as I left the kitchen. 'I don't like the way lilies smell. Too intense.'

The living room was dark. The only light came from a floor lamp and a string of fairy lights, as well as Iris's candles in wine bottles on the windowsill. Several phone screens glowed in the dark; small isolated rectangles of light. A couple of people were crowding around Harriet's computer to queue up their songs. August was sitting on the armrest of the couch, talking to a few of Iris's classmates. I looked at his face and the hand movements that accompanied words I couldn't hear. He was like a light himself, a light the others turned towards, captivated, and I had the thought that I was not the one in a category of my own; August was. He paused in the middle of some story when he noticed me and sent a smile across the room. I returned it. Then I realized that Hugo was standing behind me and that August was smiling at both of us. I went to join Harriet and her friends.

Harriet and Iris had also received flowers and housewarming gifts. Some of them had been addressed to the entire household. When the party was over and all the guests had gone home, I went over to the table where the presents were piled up. Flowers, chocolates, booze. I noticed a book positioned face down and a glittery gift card glued over the back copy. The card had the words *For Stiller – with the times!*, a pun on the King's motto, written in large, slanted letters.

I turned it over to look at the cover.

Then I tossed the book, along with the card, in the trash can. I tied the bag with several tight knots and walked, barefoot, into the stairwell, where I dropped it in the trash chute. It tumbled through the building all the way down to the garbage room; I could hear the final, heavy thud when it came to rest. The stone floor was cold under my soles. Snowflakes were falling outside the window, landing on frozen streets. I didn't mention the book to Harriet or Iris.

Hugo

August rarely talked to me about Thora, and whenever he did mention her I stopped myself from asking any follow-up questions. I would have liked to hear him explain their relationship to me but he never did. The few times he brought her up it was always in passing, in a tone of voice so neutral that it was clear Thora was an established part of his life – questioning her importance would be tantamount to attacking a family member. At one point, when he inquired about me and Ella, and I finally admitted – half joking, half in earnest – that I wasn't sure if I'd ever truly been in love, he asked me: 'What does that mean?'

I smiled to soften the effect of what I said. 'That I've never felt that strongly about a person?'

'Are you asking me?'

'I don't know,' I said. 'Isn't that what love is? Loving everything about someone?'

August observed me, his face serious as if he was taking my measurements, and then he said: 'I truly love Thora. I always will.'

I blinked. I didn't understand why he was telling me this.

'Okay,' I said.

August smiled.

And I felt I had revealed something about myself – confirmed some kind of suspicion that had been sprouting in August, something I couldn't take back or refute since I didn't know what it was.

I felt like a failure, suddenly tempted to make up stories about great loves I had never experienced. It would have been easy to concoct something from my Berlin years; I had real material I could have elaborated on, but I knew I wouldn't be able to produce the kind of clarity of voice, void of even a hint of irony, that August had when he said he loved Thora.

Thora frequently raised her hand during lectures and seminars. She answered questions, asked questions, commented on nuances and subtexts nobody else in the class had picked up on. There was a kind of calm ruthlessness in the way she took on a book – she didn't tiptoe around the literary canon and she didn't leave unfinished sentences hanging in the air for someone else to complete her thought. I liked listening to her, not because I always agreed, but because I was fascinated by how she was able to cut to the core of the matter. When she was done I always wished she'd look at me. She never did.

In contrast to her, I found it difficult to discuss the books we read. I had no experience at all talking about literature, and it was hard to shake the feeling that the rest of us were using other people's theories and research to avoid having our own opinions, as if we were constantly glancing over our shoulders to check the reaction of an invisible audience. Thora, instead, saw the theories as levers for her own conclusions, indifferent as to whether those levers broke when she used them. She hammered her interpretations into the air when she spoke, forcing us all to relate to the long shadows they cast over the discussions. The teachers appeared interchangeably entertained and displeased by her way of laying down facts, but the uncompromising nature of her expositions irritated many of our classmates.

'If I was a dude, nobody would be annoyed that I say what I think,' Thora remarked loudly during a break.

The hallway was crowded, so I couldn't see who she was talking to. In much of what Thora said there was an ambiguity that made it hard to tell if she was serious or just playing with people's expectations. This created a tension around her that I felt drawn to. Others sensed in Thora an unwillingness to meet them halfway. She never interrupted anyone, but when she did say something she spoke until she felt she was done.

'Does she *have* to be so arrogant?' Ella said to me once after class.

I wondered if Thora was correct, if her opinions would be received differently if she was a guy. I couldn't voice these kinds of musings to Ella – she'd recently read *The Golden Notebook* and *The Faculty of Dreams*, and she'd think I was making an arrogant attempt at feminist analysis.

One day I walked up to Thora at the old café on Surbrunnsgatan. I couldn't say why, maybe it was just out of impatience; I wanted something to happen. I'd noticed her at the café several times before – I liked doing schoolwork there in the afternoons – and every now and then we'd nod at each other across the room before returning to our books and screens without a word. Once we had coffee together when August showed up and insisted on bringing us together at one table.

The café was packed on the day I approached her. There were no free tables. The windows were foggy, scarves and jackets hung over the backs of chairs, and stacks of cups tottered on abandoned trays. Thora was sitting in a corner and took up two tables with her computer, books and notebook. Her face was pale against the dark wooden walls. She was typing with her eyes on one of the books, like she was copying something. Her left hand rested on the pages to stop them from closing.

'Hey,' I said.

The white cup in my hand rattled against the saucer. I wasn't nervous, I told myself.

She looked up.

'Hey,' she said, and was silent for a moment before she added: 'You're bleeding.'

I brought my hand to my nose. 'Shit.'

She passed me the napkins from her tray and I held them over my nose.

'Thanks,' I said and leaned my head back. 'Sorry.'

'It's better to lean your head forward,' she said.

I did as I was told.

'It happens sometimes in the winter,' I said. 'I'm not sure why.'

'Small capillaries maybe.' She dog-eared her page and made a gesture as though inviting me to step into her office. 'You can sit here if you want.'

I plunked down on the chair across from her. The computer screen rose like a protective wall between us. Outside, winter winds tore at pedestrians and the sun ripped open the clouds over the roof-tops, a slow-moving mass forced to separate. A few tables away, two older men were eating in silence as their cutlery scraped against the plates, until one of them said: 'So, you ever think about climate change?'

I looked at Thora's books and notepad.

'What are you working on?' I asked.

'European law.'

I knew nothing about European law. 'Is it fun?'

Thora looped her fingers around the ear of her cup and leaned back. 'It's alright. Not as fun as studying literature.'

When I looked into her eyes I thought: that vast greyness.

'It was nice of you and Tigran to buy flowers,' she said. 'Was it really your idea?'

'Yeah,' I said and put the napkins on the table. The bleeding had stopped. 'My mom says you should always bring flowers and wine to a housewarming.'

'And you listen to her?'

'Sometimes, yes.'

'August's friends don't tend to give me things,' Thora said.

'Do you not have any friends in common?'

'Not really. People generally like August better. I'm used to it. Sometimes I think that I don't care at all about other people's impressions of me. But I don't know if that's true. August says I'm deluding myself.'

She stopped abruptly, as if she'd realized she'd said too much.

The sun disappeared behind a cloud and the café was dim again. The wood-panelled walls, warm and protective, sheltered us. I didn't stir. I tried to puzzle out the meaning of what she'd told me, worried that I'd discover a hidden accusation somewhere in there to attack me.

'Why would you be deluding yourself?' I asked. 'It sounds nice not to care.'

'Do *you* care?'

'About other people's impressions? I think so,' I said, and hesitated before correcting myself: 'Yes, I do.'

'Most people do, probably,' she said. 'But I can't always tell with you. You don't come across as someone who cares, even though I suspect you do.'

'I must be good at pretending in that case,' I said, and I thought that our conversation was like wading into dark water – I didn't know when the bottom would drop.

We headed to the lecture together that evening. Snow crunched under our feet. Thora was wearing a peacoat, and wrapped a long red scarf around her neck before we stepped out the door. Her laptop and books went into a large, stuffed shoulder bag. Now and then she took off her mittens to brush back the hair that blew across her face once we were out on the street. I figured it would be too forward of me to do it for her.

'Can I ask you something?' she said when we got to the bus stop.

'Yes.'

Thora scraped the ground with her foot. Then she looked up at me with such determination that I dug my hands deep down into my pockets, looking for something to hold on to, though all I had in them were old receipts.

'Was that you who left the book at the party?' she asked.

'Huh?'

'The book. About the Stiller conglomerate. Was it you who brought it as a gift?'

'No,' I said. 'I have no idea what you're talking about.'

She looked at me over the edge of her scarf. Large snowflakes got stuck in her eyelashes. She blinked them away. 'Okay.'

'Thora—' I realized this was the first time I'd said her name in her presence and I hesitated, as if I'd touched something private. 'I didn't leave any book at yours.'

'Okay,' she said. 'It doesn't matter. It was probably a friend of Harriet or Iris who did it as a joke.'

We sat next to each other on the bus. Across the water, Haga Park lay like a large, sleeping animal in the middle of the city, its breath ruffling the surface of the bay. I could feel the warmth from Thora's body, wrapped in multiple layers of clothing, next to me. She was better-dressed for the cold weather than I was, and when I commented on it she said, with a smile, that I had moved from Berlin after all, not to mention that I'd grown up in the south of Sweden. I laughed and said nothing about the bitter winds that blew through Malmö and Berlin in the winter.

August was seven years younger than his brother, Samuel, who had lived in London for years. August described him as a businessman with three phones and an inbox that was never not full. To me it sounded like a child's portrait of a working parent: briefcase, suit, office. August told me about the house in Belsize Park where Samuel lived. The orchids in the living room, the gleaming coffee machine, the wine cellar, the dry cleaner where he sent his shirts each week. As if his brother was the sum of his job, his belongings and his consumption.

Samuel came to visit Stockholm a few weeks before Christmas, and August spoke of his impending arrival as if a large storm was blowing in over the city. It was decided that the brothers would have dinner together at a restaurant on Tjärhovsgatan, and August convinced me to come with him. When I protested, he said he didn't like being alone with his brother. He added that Thora was coming too.

'Why don't you want to be left alone with him?' I asked.

'You'll see.'

Thora and Samuel were waiting for us outside the restaurant. If Thora was surprised to see me she didn't let on. Her hands were in her pockets and her face was half buried in her scarf. August introduced me and Samuel to each other and then he went to stand next to Thora. He took her hand and she murmured something in his ear. He kissed her cheek in response. Samuel and I shook hands, his black leather glove slippery against my palm. He was tall and broad-shouldered, dressed in a black coat with his scarf tied in a neat loop around his neck. He shared August's clear blue eyes and straight nose.

August was quiet during the meal. He downed multiple glasses of wine and kept looking up at the clock above the entrance. Samuel didn't comment on his brother's lack of enthusiasm but I saw him observe August, who either didn't notice or studiously looked the other way. Meanwhile, Samuel directed the conversation as if he was checking off topics on a list. He expressed himself well in Swedish, but his sentences sounded stiff and formal, the intonations and silences of English gliding beneath the Swedish syntax.

Samuel started off by asking me a few short questions – when did I move to Stockholm, did I like it here, how long had I lived in Berlin for – and thereafter he turned to Thora and enquired about her time in Paris, if she'd want to move back there in the future.

'I like Paris better than London,' Thora said.

'Truly? Why is that?'

'It's more beautiful, more friendly to pedestrians. And I prefer cafés over pubs.'

'But London isn't stuck in former days of glory,' Samuel said. 'It keeps evolving.'

'By constructing ugly skyscrapers and raising the rents.'

'London is unique. Paris is *ladylike*.'

'No, Samuel, you're wrong.'

They smiled at each other. August gave me a knowing look I didn't know what to do with.

Between the starter and the main course, it became obvious that Samuel's own life was not part of the conversational repertoire he had prepared. August's life, on the other hand, was scheduled as the main act.

'You have to be able to support yourself,' Samuel said.

'Yes, I know that,' August said.

'You can't live off of your paintings.'

'I'm not dead yet.'

'I'm serious.'

'But you would never let me starve, would you?'

'You should have a real job on the side. For safety.'

'I have no academic ambitions.'

'I'm not saying you need to get a PhD.'

'I'm in school right now.'

'You said you might drop out.'

'You're so banal,' August said. 'You think you're educated and cultured because you go to the National Theatre and the Tate Modern on the weekends.'

'We can't all be starving bohemians.'

'I'm not starving.'

'I know that your work is good, August,' Samuel said. 'But it's difficult to support yourself as an artist.'

'Sure, thanks for your job-market analysis.' August turned to me. 'Samuel can't get over the fact that I've never wanted to follow in his footsteps and have a real career.'

Thora looked at August with displeasure.

'That's not true,' she said.

When the waiter gave us the dessert menu, she got up and asked August to come out for a smoke.

'August can be pretty ridiculous,' Samuel said when they couldn't hear. 'He's mad because I invited our father for dinner the other day. Without *forewarning*, as he put it.'

Samuel leaned back in his chair. It was easy to picture him in an office in London's financial district.

He asked if I had any siblings, and when I said no Samuel smiled as if I'd revealed something enviable about myself.

'Seven years is a big age difference,' I said.

'Yes,' Samuel said. 'And I thought I'd be less worried about August as he grew older.'

'But that's not happened?'

'On the contrary.' Samuel's hand rested around his wine glass, and he shook it lightly so that the wine sloshed around. 'He's shallow.'

He looked straight at me when he said it. I didn't ask what he meant since I assumed that was what he wanted.

Thora and August came back in a cloud of warm breath and cigarette smoke, their cheeks red. On his way around the table August put his hand on my shoulder. Thora said she wanted crème brûlée for dessert. Samuel paid for the meal, passing the waiter his card without looking at the bill. Neither Thora nor August said anything, but I, who had ordered my food and drink based on price, sat frozen with my hand on the wallet in my pocket and considered protesting, insisting on paying for myself. Then I caught Thora's eye. She winked and shook her head. I let go of my wallet. My face felt hot.

Once we'd left the restaurant, August grabbed hold of Thora and me and announced that we were going to head to a bar.

'A dive,' he told Samuel. 'Nothing for you.'

'I believe you,' Samuel said.

Thora shrugged out of August's grip. 'Not for me either,' she said.

'As you wish.'

'But August, you already had a lot to drink,' Samuel said. 'Do you really need more?'

August ignored the question. 'Ciao, big brother, thanks for the meal. I'll see you this weekend.' He started walking down the street and gestured for me to follow.

'Thank you for dinner,' I told Samuel.

'My pleasure,' he replied.

'Enjoy August when he's in this mood,' Thora said and wrapped her scarf around her neck. 'Will you walk with me for a bit, Samuel?'

Samuel said yes but didn't move. He looked at August, who was balancing on the edge of the pavement, his arms spread.

'Take care of him, please,' Samuel said with a quiet solemnity that surprised me.

I nodded.

Thora gave me a wry smile.

When I caught up with August he put his arm around my shoulders and sighed. His breath came out in a cloud.

'Thank God that's done,' he said.

'He seemed alright to me.'

'That's because he's not your brother,' August said. 'He has no interest in turning your life inside out to see if it's good for anything.'

It had started to snow, and when we stepped into the warm bar the white flakes in August's hair melted. My socks were wet, and I shivered. It was noisy inside and there was a plastic Christmas tree draped in garlands by the entrance, topped not by a star but by a beer can with a Santa hat taped to it. August found a table while I got beer. The candles on the tables flickered wildly each time the door opened, sending shadows lurching across the walls and intensifying the already chaotic atmosphere. I had to lean over the counter for the bartender to hear me.

'I can see the resemblance between you and Samuel,' I said as I put the drinks down in front of August.

'How do you mean?' he asked.

'It's clear that you're brothers.'

August leaned back and gazed out over the room. His cheeks were red, as if the cold had pinched them hard, and he'd kept his scarf on.

'You should have seen us at the dinner with Dad. We were mostly just sitting there in silence. We have nothing to talk about,' he said. 'One of the few things Samuel and I have in common is that neither of us likes to hear Dad drone on about his favourite topics.'

'What are his favourite topics?'

'How immigrants are destroying Sweden, and why the Left and the workers' movement are doing so badly,' August said and took several large swigs of his beer, as if he needed to rinse his mouth before continuing. 'Dad has no idea what to talk about when he can't rehash those old grievances. He doesn't understand what I or Samuel do for work. So we just sit there. Three strangers around a table.'

I watched him. August seemed so comfortable in Thora's milieu that I'd always assumed he came from something similar. I'd pictured suntanned parents in polo shirts who played golf and rode horses on the weekend, and travelled to Paris and Milan every season to buy designer clothes. Now I saw those clichés dissolve and be replaced by something more oblique; shadow figures that I had a very hard time associating with August, no matter how much I tried. I wanted to know more about Thora and August, I wanted to understand them, but I worried that it would require some kind of counter-offer on my part. I would be fully satisfied if I could get close to them without having them come too near me. I also wondered if this would be an impossible balancing act.

A few days after that, I met Thora at the National Library. It was early in the afternoon and we got coffees and sat down at a free table. Thora was stressed about an exam and told me she couldn't stay for long. I wanted to know how she felt about the dinner with Samuel, but I wasn't sure how to bring it up. In the end, Thora did it for me.

'How did you like Samuel?' she asked.

I took a moment to answer. 'He was nice.'

'They're very different from each other.'

'They look alike,' I said. 'But it seems like August gets upset around him.'

'Fretting about August is the only way Samuel knows to show that he cares,' Thora said. 'He doesn't know any other way. But August finds it infantilizing.'

I tapped the lid of my coffee cup. When I'd first met Thora I had thought that she observed her surroundings with a kind of stand-offish disinterest, but now I saw that she was in fact scrutinizing the people around her with the same acuity she used on the books in our lit class. I looked at the coffee stains ingrained in the blond wood and wondered what kinds of observations she had made of me. What simple sentences would she employ to nail me down if someone asked what she thought of me? I pictured her hammering a nail through a shivering, panting shadow and holding it up for all to see.

'You look tired,' she said.

I sat up straight and let go of the coffee lid. 'Yeah. Sorry.'

She laughed. 'Late night with Ella?'

'No,' I said.

I sounded unnecessarily serious.

Vera and Tigran entered the café and I waved at them. Thora noted my hand gesture, but she didn't turn around.

The National Library functioned as a kind of living room for students, freelance culture critics, retirees and academics. It was the only place in Stockholm where it was the rule rather than an exception to hear the people at the table next to you discuss Foucault or Butler or Merleau-Ponty with the same ease as if they were talking about the weather or a TV show. I'd come to understand that this was where you went to bump into friends and classmates, not to spend a few quiet hours alone in the reading rooms.

Vera and Tigran pulled up chairs to our table. Thora rested her hands on top of her slender laptop, as if signalling that she was ready to get up and leave at any moment. Hoping that she would linger, I asked if she wanted a refill. She nodded in response and I went to get more coffee. I returned to Vera listing every person she knew in the arts who also had a job at the government-run liquor store to make ends meet.

'It's crazy when you think of it,' she said. 'All the young journalists and authors I know work or have worked at Systembolaget.'

'They could start a literature programme to encourage reading among the Swedish population,' Tigran said. 'Suggest alcohol–author pairings. Kafka – absinthe.'

'Proust?'

'Prosecco.'

'Duras?'

'Red wine.'

'And how about Karin Boye?'

'Sherry.'

'Poison,' Thora said.

We laughed.

Thora left for the reading room before the rest of us. Vera and Tigran looked curiously at me but I pretended not to notice. I didn't mention the dinner with Samuel, even though I wanted to hear what they knew about August's brother. I thought it was strange how quickly Thora and August had become a part of my life that I kept to myself, as if there was something about them I wanted to protect. Or maybe I just wanted to protect myself.

Thora was seated off in a corner and didn't look up when I returned to my spot. It was already dark outside and the rows of lamps and computer screens were reflected in the tall windows. If I turned around I could see her screen in one of the windows, including the white documents she was slowly scrolling through. The room was full of people, and still it was as if Thora's keyboard was the only one I could hear.

Thora

January came and I spent almost every day at the university library, clicking back and forth between two windows on my computer – one for literature, one for law school. Hugo hadn't bought any of the books for our class and would often come by to borrow one of mine. It felt strangely intimate that he could see what paragraphs and sentences I had marked, but I also knew the library's lending copies were all out. I finished my essay before him, so I told him he could take the whole pile. He stacked them on top of each other and balanced them theatrically, as if he knew I was watching him slowly walk back to his spot elsewhere in the library.

At the end of the exam period, the university organized a lecture series that culminated in a visit by the Foreign Minister. The noticeboards in the hallways were papered with posters that gave the date and time in red capitals in English – the event was meant to attract international students, and the moderator was a former British diplomat. The day of our final seminar we were looking at the posters as we waited for our classroom to open. Hugo said that all the political science students were going, to nobody's surprise.

'It's just words,' one of our classmates said. 'Also, that propaganda makes the assumption that the government *has* achieved something in the world, but how can they be so sure of that?'

'What is literature if not just words?' Hugo said in my ear.

I smiled, but when they finally let us in I didn't sit down next to him.

Whenever I mentioned Hugo in conversations with August I made sure to restrain myself, since August had started looking at me the way my parents did when I'd been proven wrong, their triumph marinating in the air. There were few people I actually liked debating with, but I'd noticed that Hugo was able to follow my reasoning without slowing me down or misunderstanding me. Sometimes he would question me, but I found myself enjoying a challenge from him. He contributed things I hadn't thought of myself. And when I talked with him I never knew ahead of time where we'd end up. With others, the opposite was often true – conversations followed a path where every line seemed taken from a predictable set of opinions – and this made me so bored I lost interest entirely. I didn't care about winning; I just wanted to discover something new, be surprised, *stimulated*. I wanted to push, and feel that someone pushed back.

A few classmates and I walked to the talk together. On our way there, Harriet and her girlfriend, Bella, caught up with us. Bella was studying national economics and was a member of one of the youth party organizations. Harriet sometimes came home complaining that Bella had spent the whole evening explaining why the roots of the financial crisis had not been fixed and what a large crisis in Italy would mean for the economic system of the EU.

The room was crowded. The front row was reserved for the Foreign Minister's staff and the university representatives. We had to split up in order to get seats, and when Hugo turned up later there were no more chairs. Students kept pouring in, settling on the stairs or leaning against the walls. Hugo was on the other side of the room, level with my row. He didn't seem to have noticed me and I didn't try to catch his gaze. Further down I spotted August's friends Brita and Christian with their heads close together, like they were reading something on the same phone screen. Brita had tied a pink scarf around her hair and Christian still had his coat on, as if he wanted to have the option of getting up and walking out into the winter at any point during the talk. Everyone around me held their phones in their hands and something about the way they gripped them made me think of stone-throwing. I shoved mine deep into my bag.

The murmur in the room quickly died down when the Foreign Minister entered. The former diplomat went up to the podium. Noting that the person of the hour hardly needed an introduction, she nevertheless launched into one before inviting the minister onto the stage. The girl in front of me zoomed in on the minister's face with her phone camera. I watched as she unscrewed the lid of a water bottle and took a few sips while the moderator posed a long, winding question in British English that the minister answered with a brief joke. The audience giggled. I glanced at Hugo, who was smiling but didn't laugh. The British woman said something about *Nordic humour* and asked yet another winding question. The difference in their English established a dynamic that made me uncomfortable. The British ex-diplomat was able to create elegant sentences that she modulated with well-considered silences, while the Foreign Minister's answers were concise, less abstract, and were constructed using a simpler grammar that could be read as either inept or cheeky. I knew that many of August's friends exaggerated their Swedish accent when they spoke English, as some kind of insolence against the Anglo-Saxon dominance. I thought it was silly, though August defended the practice.

It was a short talk. The British woman nodded incessantly, now and then closing her eyes as if her interlocutor's voice was a pleasant musical piece. Once she had finished talking, the minister sat down while the British woman invited the audience to ask questions. She explained that the microphone would be passed around before returning to the podium like a fishing net full of questions for the minister to choose from. She seemed pleased with this simile. The atmosphere changed when the questions began; suddenly everyone was alert. Brita adjusted her scarf. Christian leaned forward. Now and then the minister's gaze fluttered in the direction of her staff in the front row. A blond man shook his head at various points, as if to assure her that she needn't bother with the degree of relevance or truthfulness of the questions. The moderator had stopped smiling and her eyes were now wide open. When I heard my name in one of the questions I suddenly felt acutely aware of the way I'd crossed one leg over the other, and a needling sensation spread over my cheeks like the febrile steps of invisible ants. I did not look at Hugo.

Christian was among those who took the mic. He asked a two-part question about shell companies and arms factories in totalitarian countries. I expected his voice to tremble the way it sometimes did when he got upset in our duels, but he sounded calm. He'd probably practised on Brita, maybe even on August. I looked at his neck where the tag poked out of his jacket collar. When he passed the mic and sat back down, Brita leaned closer and fixed the tag as she whispered something to him. They made me think of two ruddy school kids on a mission to confuse the adult behind the teacher's desk. The room was silent; there were no more hands in the air.

The microphone having returned to the podium, the Foreign Minister said something about maintaining a strong global voice for peace and added that every country had a choice between multi-lateralism and nationalism. A few students grinned. The moderator started clapping her hands, and after a few seconds the audience joined her in applause. When I looked in Hugo's direction I found him looking straight at me, as if he'd been waiting for me to acknowledge him.

Exiting the auditorium surrounded by buzzing voices, I discovered that snow had settled on the ground outside – fragile white flakes on the frozen grass. It was dark already and I felt tired and cold. Everything I valued seemed to sift between my fingers like sand.

A bunch of people went to the café next to the library, and I let myself be swept up by the crowd. We bought coffees and pulled several tables together so everyone could have a seat. The discussions, in the line and at the tables, were unruly, with some students looking excited while others seemed more resigned.

Hugo took the chair next to me and stirred his coffee with a white plastic spoon that seemed small in his hand.

'What did you think?' he asked.

'About our Foreign Minister?' I said.

'Yes.'

I looked at him and thought about how a person can live an entire life without caring or thinking about anything outside of their immediate surroundings. They might express an opinion while reading the paper or watching the news but forget whatever sparked the idea as soon as the paper was folded up or the evening broadcast finished. Tons of people did live that way. Why couldn't I?

'Interesting, I guess,' I said, and warmed my hands around the paper cup full of steaming coffee. 'But it's not like it's anything new.'

Hugo looked at me like he knew I was only giving him the crumbs of my real thoughts.

'I was watching you,' he said. 'During the event. You looked very critical.'

I licked my lips. The coffee was hot in my mouth. 'I *always* look critical, Hugo. Critical resting face.'

I wanted to make him smile but he kept looking at me like he was expecting more, a bigger window into my mind. I wasn't about to give it to him.

'Okay. Sure,' he said when I didn't keep going. 'Critical resting face.'

'It's what's going to make me a good lawyer,' I said.

Hugo looked at me as if I had stolen something from him. It annoyed me; I didn't owe him anything.

Christian and Brita recounted select parts of the Foreign Minister's visit to August. I could hear echoes of their laughter in August's voice when he, in turn, recounted to Hugo and me what Christian and Brita had told him. When August asked for my thoughts I said I had no opinion.

'It's just politics,' I said, because it sounded laconic enough that August wouldn't make me expand. I was afraid of the hole I could sense at the end of any argument taken to its conclusion. It was like slowly cleaning a dirty mirror and finding myself, without any means to dissimulate. Maybe this made me more similar to my parents than I liked to think. Ease above all.

Hugo said that the event had confirmed his feeling that cynicism was the only reasonable way to relate to the world.

'All man-boys are cynics, unless they happen to be neoliberals,' I said. 'It's banal.'

'Ah, you were inspired then?' August said.

I shoved him. 'We can't all be detached artists.'

'The cynic, the realist and the romantic,' August said. 'This will never end well!'

Hugo and I looked at each other with amusement.

Light snow blew across Mariatorget as we walked the gravel path under the naked trees. Snow covered the statue's wings and the fountain had been drained of water. The green in Hugo's brown eyes seemed to move in the light of the winter sun like in a kaleidoscope.

Winter had settled and would not give an inch. Darkness came abruptly in the afternoon, lowered itself like a lid and then screwed shut, and we crouched as the light disappeared in the cracks. We trudged through drifts of snow in the mornings before the ploughs had done their job. Still, it was beautiful. People playing on the icy lake. Frost on the boughs. Pastel sunsets that could silence a whole bus or subway car as passengers fumbled for their phones to snap a few pictures before it was too late. I wondered what they were going to do with those photos.

In the Styrmansgatan apartment we hung more fairy lights in the kitchen and the living room, and I bought pillar candles that I lit first thing after stepping through the door. My bed was next to the radiator and at night I'd press my feet against it, the warmth moving from my toes up through the rest of my body.

August wore a scarf and fingerless gloves in his studio, and Hugo and I worked on our essays in the cold reading rooms of the National Library. We often went to see a movie in the evenings, bringing coffee and candy with us. More than anything I wanted to stay at home in bed and hide under my duvet topped by several layers of blankets. There were mornings I woke up ready to cry at the thought of wading through yet another day of cold and darkness. Some nights August stayed at my place and we huddled close to each other, eventually kicking the blankets off as we slept.

One evening he interrupted the TV show we were watching by asking if I'd slept with Hugo. We'd had a lot of wine, and the question made me laugh.

'Why don't *you* sleep with him?' I said.

'I think he's hopelessly heterosexual,' August said. 'Like you. Also, he's my friend. I don't have sex with my friends.'

'So what am I when we're not sleeping with each other?' I said, and hit pause on the laptop to look at him. 'Your closest acquaintance?'

'You're my *best* friend,' August said. 'That's different.'

During the winter he had been courted by an older man who was a gallerist and liked to buy August cashmere sweaters in a range of colours. August wondered what kinds of gifts he'd have received if it were summer. Linen suits, I suggested. He accepted the sweaters but not the invitation to go on a date with the gallerist; instead he tried to convince him to show his paintings.

Hugo and Ella had stopped seeing each other and Hugo went on dates with girls he sometimes talked to August about but not to me. We never brought up that kind of stuff between us. I was sporadically seeing a law school classmate who told me he was planning to get rich. I wasn't in love with him and I knew I never would be, but I enjoyed his company and liked the way he furrowed his brow and ran a finger across the page when he looked things up in the law books. He wasn't in love with me either.

It was as if I was watching us all from the outside. I couldn't grasp that these were our real lives and that they couldn't be done over again if something went wrong. August complained about already seeing signs that our friends would disappear into traditional family structures in just a few years, due to boredom or lack of imagination, but I still felt like we were just play-acting adulthood. Going over to a friend's house and making dinner, eating together around the table while we drank the wine we'd brought – sometimes I looked around and expected people to start laughing, as if we were kids in a staring contest who would finally have to drop our game faces. But nobody laughed.

And so the days passed.

On Sundays I usually ate dinner with my parents. Per my request, it tended to be just the three of us that winter. I preferred having them to myself when we got together – I liked them better that way, when they didn't have an audience of friends to perform for. Sometimes, while we were cooking and large swaths of comfortable silences spread between us, I was struck by a feeling of missing them even though we were in the same room. I looked at their backs and their faces and their hand movements, which were so familiar to me, and still I felt like I didn't know them. I could tell if it was Aron or Laura opening the door even before they called hello from the hall, and I could sense their mood from the way they entered a room or handled an object – a phone, a computer, a coffee mug, a dish brush – but I had no idea what kinds of challenges they were facing, what they were anxious or excited about.

I was so used to either idolizing or disparaging them that I didn't know how to relate to them as normal people. It was as if our family bond concealed their true selves – what linked us also created a distance, a kind of padded wall, impenetrable no matter how you attacked it. When Laura mentioned her students or Aron his interns, I wondered what they would have thought of me, were I not their daughter but rather a ward they had been charged with. As a child I'd had a recurring dream of meeting Laura on the street, and her walking past without recognizing me. Once, after waking from that dream, I had told her: 'It's only because you're my mom that you love me.' And Laura replied: 'It's only because I'm your mom that you exist.'

I continued to think it was insufficient as a proof of affection. It made it seem like I was the recipient of a love that had nothing to do with me, based only on the social convention that parents must love their children. When I shared these thoughts with Laura she gave me a little smile and said I'd understand when I was older.

'Why do you not like Maggie?' Hugo asked me following a dinner at Aron and Laura's.

It was Friday night. We were meeting up with August and his friends at a club on Södermalm and were walking to the subway. Tigran had checked the weather on his phone at the dinner table and told us he wasn't coming. Outside, the wind grabbed hold of us and I shivered as I bunched my hands in my pockets.

'Why are you asking about her?' I said and pulled the scarf over my chin. 'She's just one of the people my parents have collected.'

'It doesn't seem like you like her.'

'Do *you* like her?'

Hugo smiled as if he recognized my tried-and-true strategy for changing the subject. 'I don't know her,' he said.

'She's an American,' I said and got my subway card from my wallet. 'She's lived here for several years and she doesn't know more than a few words in Swedish.'

We walked through the turnstiles. Hugo stopped a few steps down on the escalator and turned to face me. I rested my hand on the moving banister and felt it shudder.

'Okay. Sure. But those don't sound like legitimate reasons to dislike her,' Hugo said.

The long rows of spotlights overhead were blinding after the compact darkness outside. I couldn't decide between answering him playfully or taking offence.

'I have nothing against Maggie,' I said. 'I really don't. But Laura is different around her. She wants Maggie to like her so bad, and that makes me uncomfortable. Maggie is one of the few people Laura wants to impress.'

Hugo didn't say anything. The clattering of my heels echoed across the empty platform. The station resembled an enormous cavern, with its blue wall and ceiling that had been carved to look like waves.

'What? You don't think it makes sense?' I said.

'Yeah. It's just—' Hugo ran his hand over his neck, a gesture I'd noticed he made whenever he was bothered or embarrassed. 'Sometimes you scare me a little.'

'Why?'

'Because you *see through* people.'

'I only see it because I know Laura better than you do. You would never think of it.'

'Yeah. Maybe,' he said without sounding convinced.

'I don't see through people,' I said.

'I don't mean it as an insult.'

'It's not a compliment.'

Hugo looked down the tracks in the direction of the incoming train and raised his voice over the screeching of the rails. 'I didn't think you cared about what others think of you. Or what I think of you.'

We waited for the train doors to slide open. I got on before him and gave him a wink over my shoulder to indicate that I wasn't looking for an apology. We sat down in an empty four-seat section. I texted August that we were on our way and then I put my phone in my pocket. The lights in the tunnel smudged into long lines as the train started moving.

'Sometimes I think that Mom and Dad take in people like you and Tigran because it makes them feel less bourgeois,' I said after a while. 'If they surround themselves with young people who talk about art and politics they can give someone like Maggie the impression that they're living a bohemian, unconventional life.'

'So Tigran and I are the only thing that stands between them and the bourgeois lifestyle?'

'Yep. It's a heavy burden you must bear.'

Hugo hummed in agreement, as if this was something he needed to think over. Then he smiled at me.

'Or perhaps they're just generous,' he said. '*Kind*.'

'Don't be so simple-minded,' I said. 'It's too easy for them to do things that make them look generous.'

'Because people only ever act generously if it makes them feel better somehow?'

'Ideally it makes them look like something they're not. Unconventional, for example. It's brand management on a small scale.'

Hugo shook his head as if he'd been given a riddle he couldn't or didn't feel like solving.

'I think they're just generous. Even if it doesn't demand much of them,' he said, and then he pointed a finger in my direction. 'And *you* should be nicer to Maggie.'

I waved his finger away.

'I'm exercising my right to not be pleasant all the time,' I said. 'As opposed to my parents, who are always trying to please everyone.'

'You're annoying,' Hugo said.

We got off at Mariatorget. I looked straight ahead, sensing Hugo's sideways gaze, and under his scrutiny my face cracked into an involuntary smile. It was like coughing; once I was smiling it was hard to stop. We were walking so close to each other that I could feel the slight quaking of his laughter when his arm touched my arm.

Hugo

We made plans for a trip to Paris. Thora found cheap flights and convinced August to go, and August, in turn, convinced me to join them. I'd never been to Paris before. In Stockholm, rivulets of melted snow trickled down the gravel-strewn pavements, and tufts of grass emerged where there used to be snow. It was April, and Thora said that in Paris we'd be able to have dinner outdoors. She didn't seem to mind me joining, but I couldn't help but wonder if she'd have preferred it to be just the two of them. Sometimes I was confused about my role in their dynamic, just as I was confused about their relationship, such as it was. There was a quiet intimacy between them, so palpable that the air seemed to grow denser when they were together. I didn't know if I was alone in sensing that, and I didn't feel equipped to determine whether or not it was normal. I didn't want to be the kind of person who had these types of thoughts – and yet, here I was.

'I thought you were a free spirit. Berlin and all,' Thora said. 'Why is it so hard to believe that we're just friends?'

'It's not hard,' I said and tried to figure out how to continue my line of reasoning. Then I realized I was about to entangle myself in a conversation that might be hard to straighten out. I looked at Thora, the freckles over her nose and the black sunglasses that hid her eyes, and thought that she was right and I was wrong.

We were sitting on the benches outside one of the entrances to the main university building. Thora's law book was on the table between us, and the little Post-its in blue, pink, yellow and green that she had stuck between the pages fluttered in the wind. The neon colours looked garish against the sober book – *LAW OF SWEDEN* in gold type on the spine, and the national crest on the cover.

'I can't be the only one who wonders about it,' I said after a while, and pushed my fingers under the plastic lid of my coffee cup. It pinched my cuticles.

'People who ask are usually interested in one of us,' Thora said. 'And usually that's August and they want to know if I'm standing in their way.'

I didn't know where to look, and wished I was wearing sunglasses too. I took the lid off my cup and sipped the coffee. Thora was busy flipping through her calendar to find out which lectures she'd miss while we were in Paris.

'I'm going to need to write a case brief while we're there,' she said.

'What's that?' I asked.

'A summary,' she answered without looking up.

'I'll have to prepare for an exam about globalization,' I said.

'From a Marxist perspective?' she replied sarcastically.

'I think we can choose the perspective. But most people choose liberalism,' I said. 'Our lecturer the other day told us that if we'd been Americans, most of us would have been drawn to realism.'

Thora placed her calendar in her bag and gathered up her hair, holding the black hair tie between her lips. After she'd secured the ponytail she pulled her fingers through it a few times, and I could smell the scent of her shampoo.

'So much for free choice,' she said.

Once we'd cleared airport security we went to pick up something to read, along with chewing gum and three bottles of water. Then we ate an expensive lunch none of us thought was good. We landed in

Paris in the late afternoon, and when we exited the metro the evening air was mild; none of the passers-by wore winter jackets. We hung our own coats and scarves on our suitcases. We were going to stay in an apartment that an acquaintance of Thora's had recommended, and Thora was on the phone with the host while August and I fanned ourselves with our books. We were sweaty after having dragged our bags through the transit system, and the clammy air from the tunnels had made our skin and clothes feel grimy.

An old woman who barely reached my waist met us at the entrance to the building. Thora explained to us that she was the host's mother, there to open up and give us the keys. The woman smiled at us and talked to Thora in rapid French while she waved us through a courtyard and into a narrow stairway. We had to carry our bags in front of us to fit through. The woman showed Thora the apartment, and August and I heard them move from room to room before they came back, and then we all gathered for a few minutes in front of the stove while the woman explained to Thora how it worked. The apartment had a street-facing balcony, and as soon as the woman was gone we flung its doors wide open. Sounds from cars and restaurants flooded in. The wooden floor creaked and bulged in some places, an old building's stress knots. There were two bedrooms with beds that took up almost the entire room, and a bathtub at the centre of the kitchen. There was a sink and a shower in the bathroom. The toilet had its own little room with gold-painted walls.

We decided to go out for dinner after a shower and change of clothing. When I stepped out of the bathroom and found Thora and August getting ready in front of the hall mirror, the feeling I'd had when I saw them through a bus window in Stockholm came back – like I was spying on something that wasn't meant for me. Then Thora and August both looked at me and smiled, and I felt calm again.

Thora was brushing her hair. She had on thin tights and a blue dress with a belted waist. August rolled up his shirtsleeves and now and then shook his head to get rid of the curls that tumbled over his forehead. Thora had painted her lips red and August smelled of clean laundry. I thought they were beautiful, but I didn't tell them. I put on jeans and a black t-shirt with my hair still dripping; I rubbed my head with the towel. Thora lifted a few strands of hair from my forehead when I joined them in the hall to put on my shoes.

'You look like you've been swimming in the ocean,' she said.

That was the first time she touched my face.

As we walked down the street, I glanced at Thora and August and then at our reflections in the shop windows as we walked by. I was surprised to note that I fitted between them, between Thora and August. I looked like I belonged with them.

We laughed at nothing in particular and touched each other more than usual. Thora explained to me the spiral organization of the city's arrondissements, with low numbers in the centre and bigger numbers further out. She drew the shape with her hand in the air in front of her, and I observed her gestures without understanding anything of what she was saying. I asked where the Eiffel Tower was located, and she rolled her eyes and pretended to erase her drawing from the air. August informed me Thora refused to go anywhere near the Eiffel Tower.

'I want to see it,' I said.

'Yes. We have to go,' August said. 'Thora will do her best to pretend she has nothing to do with us tourists.'

We ate dinner at a restaurant near Canal Saint-Martin. Thora translated the menu for us but there were words she didn't know, so we looked up pictures on our phones. Thora showed us how to use a two-pronged fork to tease the meat from the shells of the snails we ordered as an appetizer.

On the way back to the apartment Thora walked between August and me, her arms around our waists. She swayed a little and I felt the weight of her body as she leaned against me.

The beds had been made with all-white sheets. I fell asleep almost as soon as my head hit the pillow. Through the wall to the other bedroom I could hear their muted voices. Then the apartment was silent.

It rained on our first full day. We bought umbrellas in a small tourist shop but the wind grabbed hold of them on our walk along the Seine and turned them inside out. We shoved them into a trash can and went to a café instead. Thora glared out the window as if she could will the weather to change. In a doorway across the street, a woman was sitting on wet pieces of cardboard, wrapped in a blanket with a mug in front of her. *J'Aime Paris*, the text on the mug read, with the first A shaped like the Eiffel Tower. August went outside and placed a twenty-euro bill in her cup before jogging back across the road with his jacket over his head. Neither Thora nor I said anything.

When the downpour finally let up we went to the bookstore close to Notre-Dame, per my request. Thora called me a Hemingway cliché but she purchased two books for herself, while I got none. Afterwards we took the metro to Jardin des Plantes and looked at the skeletons in the Museum of Natural History. August stood in front of the glass cases and drew the bones in a sketchpad while the rain, now back, hammered the skylights. Thora laughed and took a picture of him poking out from the hordes of schoolchildren being shepherded through the space. Then we went to a café that was part of the large mosque near the museum. We drank sweet tea and ate baklava as we sank back into the soft chairs. I was sleepy. In the late afternoon we went to see a movie, a US action film with French subtitles. Now and then August mumbled the French sentences into my ear, imitating, with great flair, the American actors' theatrical delivery. Afterwards we walked to the Eiffel Tower. I photographed the monument and we looked at the lights that studded the darkness. Thora said it was an ugly building made beautiful by night.

The following day was sunny and we had cold sodas and ice cream on the roof of the Musée Picasso. The buildings in the neighbourhood were bright white in the sunshine, and it hurt my eyes so much I had to squint underneath my baseball hat. All the balconies had flower boxes with red geraniums. Thora and August both wore sunglasses, and watching them look across the yard and the rooftops with impassive faces I told them they looked straight out of a French New Wave film.

We took pictures of each other that I figured I'd look at later – in a week, a month, a year – to remember the cautious joy that was kicking in me. It felt like a small animal that might run away at any moment. I wanted to cup my hands around these Paris days and save them somewhere out of time.

On the third evening we met up with some of Thora's French friends at a bar on a square. On our way there Thora pointed out the Bibliothèque Sainte-Geneviève, and said she'd done schoolwork there almost every day of her year in Paris. It was like she was giving us a tour of a previous life, erecting verbal monuments to the person she had been back then – a full year ago. August and I exchanged glances during one of these expositions, until August said, with fake solemnity, that Paris was crucial in Thora's coming-of-age story.

'Une jeune fille à Paris,' he said, and opened his arms as if to embrace someone running towards him.

Thora gave him the finger but immediately hid her hands in her pockets from the two elderly women who passed us. August and I laughed when she all but curtseyed at them.

Thora's friends had met August when he visited her the year prior, and they greeted him with excitement, waxing nostalgic about nights that didn't end before other people woke up for work. Thora rested her hand on my arm when she introduced me to the others, and I nodded at them. They yelled my name without the H. The terrace was lit with round lamps in different colours, and the awning that hung over the chairs and tables framed the view of the square and the fountain at its centre.

I admired how easily Thora and August merged with the lively mood of the table. It was the first time Thora reminded me of Aron and Laura. I felt weird speaking English around them and it was weird hearing them speak English too. August's English was clearly marked by his Swedish, though he seemed to be as unconcerned with his accent and grammatical blunders as Thora's French friends were about theirs. English was not the mother tongue of any one of us, but this didn't hamper the conversation, which moved forward by way of tender linguistic abuses. It had taken me several months before I got over myself making similar mistakes in German, before I stopped hearing every stumble as an insistent, shrill tone that rang in my ears way past the end of the conversation itself.

We went from bar to bar. In one place we played pool, at another we sang karaoke. Thora's friends laughed so much that they cried when August performed a serenade in French. He was a good singer, but even I could hear that the language sounded made-up in his mouth. He took a deep bow when the song was over and passed his hand through his hair. We all clapped.

Thora smoked lots of cigarettes and her voice grew hoarse and cracked when she talked. She told me that she was going to stop smoking, that smoking the way she did was a special kind of self-harm for someone who was a hypochondriac like her. I nodded and told her I'd like for her to have a long life, and she laughed as if the thought of a finite life was a joke I'd just come up with. When she leaned her head on my shoulder and closed her eyes as if she was going to fall asleep, I smelled the cigarettes in her hair.

We were invited to an after-party on the other side of town. I knew it was the other side of town because Thora emphasized this when she conveyed the invitation. August said he wasn't the least bit tired and that he definitely wanted to go.

'I'm going to head home,' Thora said with a look at the French girl with a pixie cut who had been flirting with August all night. August seemed to understand what she was looking at and leaned down to kiss Thora's forehead.

'I don't want you to go home alone,' he said.

'I'll go with you,' I said.

Both of them looked at me. August smiled. Thora got up on her tiptoes and kissed August's cheek. She whispered something to him that I couldn't hear.

August and the others got into a cab and we said goodbye. Then we walked home. I didn't pay attention to where we went, I just followed Thora. The air was cool and the cobbled streets were empty. Moonlight and orange street lights striped the dark river.

'Did you find her attractive?' Thora asked after a while.

'Who?'

'The girl. With short hair. And large breasts.'

'I don't know,' I said. 'Pretty attractive, yeah. I didn't really notice her.'

'Not your type?' Thora said.

I tried to get a look at her face, but she walked a few steps ahead of me, facing the other way. I wondered if she was intentionally avoiding my gaze. She kept her arms crossed, hands hidden in her armpits as if she was cold.

'Why aren't you and August together if you're in love anyway?' I asked.

'Because we need other people. We can be together later if we want. We don't need to be a couple now that we're young,' Thora said. She turned and let her arms fall. Her face stood in relief against the limestone facades, timeless and eternal in the moonlight.

There was a candour in her voice that made me unwilling to ask anything else. I contented myself with nodding and she slowed down and leaned her head against my shoulder. I kissed her hair, a quick and light kiss I didn't know if she could feel.

We didn't exchange more than a few words back at the apartment. I changed my clothes, brushed my teeth and drank a glass of water before going to bed. Thora was in the bathroom brushing her teeth when I told her goodnight. She winked at me in the bathroom mirror, her mouth full of foamy toothpaste. A moment later I heard her turn off all the lights and go into the other bedroom.

There was the sound of sirens from a police car or ambulance from somewhere far away. Someone passed on our street with a speaker blasting music. I didn't know how long I'd hovered between sleep and wakefulness when I heard a creaking of the floor outside my room, and the crack of the door slowly widened.

'Hugo? Are you asleep?'

'Almost,' I said.

Silence.

I turned to face the door.

'Are you okay?' I asked.

'Yes.'

Silence.

I didn't know what to say. I tried to discern her shape in the dark.

'Can I sleep here?' she asked.

'Yes,' I said, and looked up at her. Neither of us moved. 'I'm sorry. I didn't know you wanted to.'

I moved away from the centre of the bed to make space for her. She lay down on her back next to me, but not so close that we touched each other.

'Thank you,' she said and turned onto her side, with her back towards me.

I looked at her without saying anything, uncertain. Then I moved closer. I put my arm around her waist and felt her body lean closer into me, her legs mimicking the shape of my legs, bending around my knees. I pushed my other arm under her pillow, moved her hair and rested my face close to her neck. She interlaced her fingers with mine.

'Goodnight,' she said.

When I woke up the next morning Thora was no longer next to me. I sat up in bed and looked at the light that pushed through the blinds. There was still a shallow indentation in the mattress from her. I rested my hand in it for a few seconds before I got out of bed.

I found August in the kitchen making coffee and slicing up oranges. He looked up from the cutting board as I entered the room and told me that Thora had popped out to the bakery for croissants.

'Ah,' I said. 'Got it.'

The morning light made me disoriented.

'Did you have fun last night?' I asked. 'When did you get back?'

'It was amazing. We watched the sunrise from a roof. You don't get those kinds of after-parties in Stockholm,' August said and plunged the coffee press. The grounds swirled in the canister. 'I came home around six. You and Thora were still asleep.'

I looked at August. He looked untroubled. I was about to say something, but in that moment Thora came back and I closed my mouth again. I felt overwhelmed by the sun and Thora and August and wished I could crawl back into my darkened bedroom.

August asked if I wanted coffee.

'Yes. Please,' I said.

'Good morning,' Thora said and held up the bag of croissants. 'Fresh out of the oven.'

I looked at her and she looked back at me with a question in her eyes. I smiled at her and then she smiled too. It felt weird that it was her breathing, her heartbeats I'd fallen asleep to last night. I thought about all the people who slept in doorways and under bridges all over Paris and wondered why I couldn't be more grateful for the life I had.

Thora

My cousin Lydia had lived in Paris for several years. She was more than a decade older than me, and was Grandma and Grandpa's first grandchild. Her mom was British and she'd only been with Jacob, Lydia's dad, for a short while. When Jacob came to visit Lydia in Paris she brought him along to the bars and the nightclubs. During my year in Paris, Lydia sometimes invited me to parties and dinners at her place, and since I was inevitably the youngest guest I had always made an effort to seem older than my years. I later learned that Lydia had described me to her friends as one of her 'baby cousins'.

I messaged Lydia and told her I was in Paris with two friends, and she replied with a dinner invite. Hugo and August accepted the invitation when I asked so I let Lydia know and we set a time for the meal. We decided that I'd pick up wine and Lydia would take care of the food.

That morning we went to a photography museum in the Marais. I was restless and would have preferred to take a stroll instead, but Hugo and August wanted to see the exhibition. A guard checked visitors' bags at the entrance. From the street, the museum looked small; inside, an old staircase with a carved wooden banister opened up to floor upon floor. The top level held a large showcase of war photography, and that's where I headed while Hugo and August lingered elsewhere. The rooms were dim, each photo lit by a lone spotlight. I paused at each of them to read the card. My feet seemed naked in my sandals and I pressed my thumb against the vein in my wrist. A narrow room was dedicated to a set of black-and-white photographs of people and buildings in Hiroshima and Nagasaki after the nuclear bombs. It was crowded in there, but nobody spoke, not even the children. Something about the photos allowed for both an accusation and an appeal, and I didn't know what to do with that.

Stepping out onto the sunny street after our visit, I felt shaken in a way I didn't want Hugo and August to see. I put on my sunglasses and took large swigs of water from the bottle in my bag. I didn't ask the others what they thought about the exhibition, ignoring their enthusiastic discussion. As a vague discomfort took hold of my stomach, I realized I was about to have my period. When the blood came I wanted to go home and take a hot shower. Instead I led the way to a restaurant where we sat down. I asked the others to get me a Coke and a Caesar salad and then I went to the bathroom, put in a tampon and swallowed a painkiller. I dabbed my face with cold water before returning to Hugo and August.

'You alright?' August asked when I sat down.

'Yes,' I said.

They looked at me and I tried not to calculate how many more times in my life I would have to experience this dull ache in my stomach and lower back. I was glad I'd put on black jeans that morning.

'Cramps,' I said and poured the Coke into a glass.

My knees touched theirs under the round table.

We were sitting in a glassed-in courtyard where trees in large pots stood between the tables – a garden with no seasons. A chandelier, lit even though it was the middle of the day, hung from the glass ceiling. The cutlery was wrapped in linen napkins, the chairs were softly cushioned, and the waiter wore a black waistcoat over a white shirt, the cloth gleaming in the sunlight that filtered through the roof. A breeze came from somewhere and made the leaves flutter. Hugo and

August still hadn't put down the menus, which were the size of American newspapers with the restaurant's name embossed in gold on the front.

'Did you not order yet?' I asked.

'I don't think I'm that hungry,' Hugo said.

'We haven't been able to decide,' August said.

There was an almost imperceptible edge to his voice, subtle enough that Hugo didn't react – he kept looking at the menu – but knowing every shift in August's voice, I heard it and I looked at him, questioning. August shook his head, and when Hugo looked up from the menu August immediately broke eye contact with me and reached for the water pitcher.

'Just pick something,' I said. 'I for one am hungry.'

The waiter came to take our orders. Hugo turned to him and I noticed that his neck was red. Just as the waiter was leaving I added a bottle of wine to our order.

'I've been here before,' I said. 'With Dad. Good food. Good wine.'

'Yes, it looks like the type of place Aron and Laura would patronize,' August said.

I pressed my knees hard against his under the table. He pressed back.

'We're too old to eat grapes and baguettes for lunch every day,' I said and glanced at Hugo, who had his phone out. I wanted to make him smile but he didn't; his fingers moved over the screen with a restlessness that didn't match the rest of his body language, his indifferent face. His neck was still red.

'Thora,' August said, serious.

I felt myself blush.

'I'll take care of the bill,' I said and moved to cross my legs, far from August. 'Jesus.'

Hugo put his phone on the table. I saw August and Hugo exchange a look. I wondered what they'd talked about when I wasn't there.

Hugo leaned his elbows on the table without looking at me. Right then I wanted to put my hand on his, but instead I leaned back with my hands on the armrests. Across the table August looked at me, as if he was curious against his own will about where I would take the conversation next. Sometimes he made me feel like a child, a child trying to hide something from a parent who knew precisely what was going on, but for the sake of the child's growth chose to stay out of it.

'I don't judge people for not having money,' I said.

Hugo tapped his fingers on his phone. 'But you assume that everyone *has* money,' he said.

His screen lit up with a notification. I wondered who was messaging him.

'No,' I said, and paused a few seconds to suck all the juice out of the word. 'For example, I have never assumed that you have money. You don't look like someone who has money.'

Hugo's gaze immediately flicked up to my face, uncertain. Then he smiled.

'Was that why you got so little food?' I asked.

'No,' he said and rolled the cutlery out of the linen napkin. 'I'm just not that hungry.'

The waiter came with our orders and we leaned back in our chairs to give him space to put the plates on the table. When he walked off August told me: 'You never know when to drop it.' Then he and Hugo picked up their knives and forks and started eating, seemingly unperturbed. I wanted to throw my water at them, but I filled their wine glasses instead.

'We're going to have dessert too,' I said. 'And coffee.'

We ate in silence. It reminded me of being at the table with Aron and Laura after an argument, trying to dodge Aron's black gaze and Laura's refusal to acknowledge me until I'd apologized. I didn't know who was punishing whom with their silence. It was only once we got to the dessert, cracking the crème brûlées with the backs of our small silver spoons, that the mood returned to normal again. I paid while Hugo and August went outside to smoke. When they came back in again I was standing up with my bag over my shoulder, and pushed in my chair.

'Ready?'

Hugo nodded; August smiled at me.

As we left the restaurant I did not turn around to check if I'd left a bloodstain on the upholstered chair.

On our way back to the apartment, August insisted on stopping at a grocery store to buy potato chips. He made his selection from the numerous shiny bags on offer while Hugo and I watched him, standing in the aisle in silence. Back in the apartment, August poured the chips into bowls, opened a cheap bottle of rosé and invited us to gather in the living room. I was sleepy, as if from a long journey, and didn't have the energy to protest August's demand that we try all the flavours. We sat on the couch, with August joking and Hugo laughing politely, and I picked one chip from each bowl August offered me. He stretched his arms and gave a big yawn.

'We're so happy,' he said. 'Did you ever think about that?'

Hugo and I sat in silence with August in between us, as if we were both pondering the question.

'Sometimes,' Hugo said finally.

I took a handful of chips.

August leaned back into the couch and rested his hands on his stomach. His breathing was even, growing heavier, and his hands rose and fell slowly. I looked at his feet; his socks didn't match.

'We'll never be happy in this way again,' he said. 'All we need to do is take care of ourselves, and nobody we love has died.'

Hugo hummed something in response. August closed his eyes. I tried to catch sight of Hugo's expression, but with August in the way I couldn't see more than his hair and his nose, and it seemed excessive to lean back or forward. Instead I sank deeper into the couch and rested my head on August's shoulder. August was always warm, not like me, with my fingers that were so cold people jumped in fright if they happened to touch them. August ran his hand through my hair. I dozed off against his shoulder.

The living room was dark when I woke up. A street lamp shone outside the window. August was still sleeping. Hugo had left the couch.

Lydia lived on a backstreet in Montmartre, in a building where the stairs were askew and uneven, as if the building wanted to shake off anyone who set foot on them. I'd been to her place several times during my year in Paris, and was well acquainted with the serpentine way from the metro. From the outside, the building was unadorned and resembled a two-dimensional theatre set. But inside, the view from Lydia and her boyfriend Julian's apartment had often made me so distracted that I'd stopped listening to the conversations around me. It wasn't easy to tear your eyes from that immense blue sky and the grey city. Down below, Paris lay so vast that it was hard to see where the eaves ended. And in the midst of those milky-white buildings the Eiffel Tower rose, glittering at the fall of darkness. The apartment had three small rooms: bathroom, kitchen, and a larger space that served as bedroom, living room and dining room in one. Lydia and Julian didn't have much furniture but they did have lots of books stacked on shelves and all over the floor. During my time in Paris, Lydia had passed me old, thumbed novels by Cora Sandel and Isaac Bashevis Singer in Swedish translations, and I'd underlined sentences in *A Young Man in Search of Love* and tried to trace Alberte's footsteps through Paris. She'd slipped me books ever since I was little, and I'd always found it easier to take to what Lydia liked than what my parents liked.

Lydia worked in a bookstore and Julian made his money as a barista and baker. I had told August about Lydia and Julian and their apartment – to me, their life and their home were inseparable – with badly concealed fascination over a way of life that didn't include striving for a career or a larger apartment or more stuff. The idea of a life where work was not the sole source of meaning was so foreign to me that I kept having to stop myself from asking Lydia and Julian what they were going to do *after* all this.

'We could live that way,' August had said when I first told him about them. 'We could live that way and be happy.'

August said it was Stockholm's fault that we all thought there was only one way to live; the city squashed anyone who didn't embrace that life, whether because they couldn't or because they didn't want to. I wasn't sure I agreed, but there was many a time that I had left Lydia and Julian's with the sense that other modes of life had been kept from me.

Lydia had made spaghetti and spicy tomato sauce for dinner. We took the pasta from a large serving bowl and ate from smaller bowls. Julian had brought home baguettes from his job, and we dipped them in the sauce.

Hugo and August sat next to each other, and it was like I'd lined them up for Lydia's assessment as they complimented the food, admired the view, drank the wine. I knew that Lydia and Julian thought of us as something in between children and adults, whose problems could never match the scale of their own.

Lydia seemed perpetually enclosed by a cloud of smoke and laughed so loudly that Hugo jumped several times. Every time she got up to refill the water pitcher or get more wine from the kitchen, I noted her resemblance to Karla and Laura – tall and broad-shouldered – though she dressed in old men's pants and faded button-ups and t-shirts that were similar to Julian's clothing. I assumed they shared their wardrobe. Lydia didn't wear make-up or jewellery.

The two of them were talking about spending a few months in Greece, and there were Greek dictionaries and language learning books in a pile on the floor by the desk.

'It's cheap to live there,' Julian said.

'We figured we'd profit off the financial crisis,' Lydia said.

'Like vultures,' Julian said.

'Would you be feasting on the corpse of Greece or capitalism?' August asked.

'Capitalism, I'd like to think,' Julian said.

I twisted spaghetti onto my spoon and leaned over my bowl so I wouldn't splash tomato sauce all over my clothes.

'I don't want to spend my life shut inside an office,' Lydia said. 'So much better to live cheap on a Greek island. Work under the open skies.'

'What does Jacob think about this?' I asked.

'He says it's a phase, a social-critical phase,' Lydia said. 'That it will pass.'

'Like a cold,' Julian said.

Lydia pushed her chair out and walked to the bedside table, where she picked up a book like an heirloom she would sell to the highest bidder. I let out a sigh when I recognized the cover.

'I still haven't read it,' Hugo said.

'You should read it,' Julian told me.

'I don't need to,' I said and sloshed the wine in my glass. 'I already know it's going to make me depressed.'

'It might make you want to *do* something,' Hugo said and looked at me across the table.

He was smiling, but it was a smile I didn't like, as if he was holding a long stick with a toy dangling from the end and expected me to play with it.

'What I do or don't do doesn't matter,' I said.

Lydia returned the book to the nightstand and sat back down again.

'Thora took us to an expensive restaurant today,' August said.

'I *bought you lunch* today,' I said.

'Lydia and Jacob took me to the opera once,' Julian said, and scratched his chin. His cuticles were white with flour.

'How was it?' Hugo asked.

'Terrible. I had nothing to wear and Jacob teased me about my sneakers when everyone else had brogues on.'

I smiled and said: 'You're ungrateful.'

Julian laughed and I wished Hugo would have laughed too. Lydia disappeared into the kitchen again. She didn't like talking money, even though it was understood that our family was the reason she and Julian could live in an apartment with a real kitchen rather than a studio with a cockroach-infested kitchenette. I felt like pointing it out but I knew it would only produce groans all around; neither Hugo nor August would appreciate the contribution. I observed the way they looked at Lydia and wondered if they were comparing us in search of family traits. August had looked my way a lot during dinner, but Hugo had barely met my gaze. I couldn't tell if the discomfort I felt in my stomach came from my cramps or something else that had to do with the contrast between his warm breath on my neck last night and his impersonal manner in the morning.

Later he turned to me, when August was in the kitchen with Lydia and Julian. 'Are you okay?'

'Yes,' I said, confused by his concern.

'Are you mad at me?'

'Why do you ask?'

'You haven't been talking a lot.'

I was nauseous and I could feel the blood trickling out of me. I crossed my legs and looped my right foot behind my left calf.

'Not everything is about you,' I said.

'No, I know—' He stopped. It sounded like he was going to say something more but he remained silent.

I looked at him and saw, almost imperceptibly, how something in his face closed, like he was pulling a zipper up over himself.

'Are *you* mad at *me*?' I asked, and tried to soften my voice.

'No, I just—' He shrugged and gave me a forced smile that annoyed me. His complaisance made me want to go hard, provoke a reaction, any reaction. I didn't care what he thought of me, as long as I knew what he was thinking.

'How do you like them?' I asked, and tilted my head in the direction of the kitchen. The tap was running but I could hear August's voice and the laughter of Lydia and Julian.

'Lydia and Julian?'

I nodded.

'Nice, I guess. Why?'

'Lydia can be pretty self-absorbed. Her friends here think that she's from an *artist family*.'

Hugo looked at me with a mildly amused expression, but he didn't say anything.

'What?' I said and moved my finger through the flame of the candle, back and forth. There were dried wax stains all over the table.

'Don't you think that you're pretty self-absorbed yourself?'

Before I could produce an answer, the others were back from the kitchen.

We had eaten the food and drunk the wine. The table was littered with crumbs from the baguettes we'd devoured. We decided to go to a club in Pigalle where Lydia's friend worked as a bartender. She and Julian flung worn blazers over their shirts, and in the hall August put a hand on my lower back and murmured into my ear that we should start dressing in matching clothes. I leaned closer to him and he hugged me from behind, his arms on my collarbones. When Hugo came back from the bathroom he was looking at the floor instead of at us, searching for his shoes in the light shed by the bare light bulb in the ceiling.

We walked down rue Lepic. In some places the pavement was so narrow that we couldn't walk side by side. August ended up between Lydia and Julian, and I saw him gesticulate excitedly but I couldn't hear what they were talking about. Walking close to Hugo, I wondered if our silence bothered him.

'Can't you tell me what you're thinking?' I asked.

Hugo looked at me. I didn't know what I'd expected but the cold in his eyes made me flinch.

'Why should I?' he said.

His voice was calm but his jaw was tense. I could see the muscles moving under the skin, as though struggling to free themselves.

'Because that's what you do when something bothers you?' I said, making an effort to match his calm.

He didn't answer. Instead he turned his face away from me, all neck, ears, nose, jawline. I wanted to reach for him, rest my hand against his cheek and feel the hint of stubble, but I didn't do it. I was worried he'd push it away.

When we got to boulevard de Clichy, I walked away from Hugo and joined Julian as we waited for the light to change. He asked if I had any plans to move to Paris and I told him I didn't know what I wanted to do.

'You don't need to do what your family wants you to do,' Julian said.

'Did Lydia instruct you to tell me that?'

'Non, ma chérie,' he said, and put his arm around my shoulders. 'I thought of it all by myself.'

We were approaching our destination but I wanted to keep walking, wanted to continue down to the water and then follow the river, by myself in the darkness.

The club was situated in a basement that had previously been someone's home. Large doorways connected the rooms and the parquet had been scratched up by heels. A DJ booth had been installed under a chandelier in the largest room and gilded mirrors covered the walls almost up to the high ceilings, creating the impression of an enormous hall of reflections. A soft red light, whose source I couldn't locate, suffused the rooms and distorted the colours of clothes and make-up and hair.

Lydia introduced us to her friends. They had monopolized a leather couch in one of the rooms. I didn't catch any of their names but

I kissed their cheeks and saw their mouths move, just as I felt my own mouth move without hearing any of the sounds it made. I stuck to August, who either was able to hear what the others said or was just good at pretending. Hugo plopped down next to some French girl and struck up a conversation with her as though the noise didn't bother him either. August took my hand in his and I followed him into the larger room where we joined the bodies on the dance floor.

'I don't know if I like Hugo anymore,' I told August.

August smiled.

I glared at him and he leaned closer.

'What's that?' he said.

I shook my head. 'Forget it.'

He looked inquisitively at me.

I made a dismissive gesture and he kissed my cheek. His smell was so familiar – I'd be able to locate him blindfolded in a room full of people.

Lydia and Julian pushed through the throng and joined us. They were already sweaty and had left their blazers by the couch. I avoided them, leaving the dance floor and heading to the toilets instead, which were located in a corridor close to the entrance. The line was long. When my turn came I covered the seat with toilet paper and sat down. I bunched my hands in my lap and looked at them, then stretched my fingers out again. Someone waiting outside the door was speaking a language I didn't recognize, barely audible over the music booming through the walls. Washing my hands, I briefly glanced at my own reflection; I didn't like the way I looked in the red light.

On my way back to the dance floor I passed the room where Lydia's friends had gathered. Hugo was still next to the French girl on the couch. His hand was on the inside of her thigh. They were making out. I wrenched myself away and returned to the dance floor where I found a sweaty August. He tried to get me to dance. Instead I got on my tiptoes with a hand on his shoulder to make myself heard.

'I'm going to go,' I said.

He grabbed my wrist. 'You're leaving already?'

'Yes.'

'I can go with you.'

'No. Stay. I want to walk by myself for a bit.'

August frowned, trying to get a read on my face.

'Text me when you're home,' he said.

I hugged him.

Then I left the club without saying goodbye to anyone else. I walked past the Opera and down to the water. I knew the way, recognized the facades and the shop windows. It started to rain and I took cover in a long tunnel of columns, inhaling the smell of wet asphalt. I went through a mental list of people I knew in Paris, and finally texted Alex. He replied just a few minutes later asking if I wanted to come over. It was 1 a.m. I said yes. He lived close to Les Halles, in an apartment paid for by his parents. He was from Amsterdam originally and we'd been in the same French class.

'I had no idea you were in town,' Alex said when he opened the door.

'I leave tomorrow,' I said.

He leaned down and kissed me.

'Red wine lips,' he said.

'I'm on my period,' I said.

He paused.

'No worries,' he said and went to get a towel that he spread on the bed.

His breath was ragged as he put on a condom, and I looked at him, unsure of who was using whom. I had to get better at doing things without ascribing meaning to them. When I stepped out the door it was still raining, but I decided to walk anyway. My feet were aching from my stiff sandals, but my body felt strangely soft, as if sex with Alex was better after the fact.

Hugo and August were sitting at the kitchen table when I got home. August got up as soon as he saw me.

'Where have you been?' he said.

'Walking around.'

'You left the club several hours ago.'

My shoes were wet. I spread my toes and felt my heel throb with a blister.

'I'll take as long a walk as I want to,' I said.

'Why didn't you pick up?' Hugo said.

'It was on silent,' I replied without looking at him.

I took off my shoes and left them on the floor as I went into the bathroom to dry off. August followed me. Hugo stayed in the kitchen.

'Do you not understand how worried I was?' August said.

I pressed the towel over my face. When I took it away, it had mascara and lipstick stains all over it.

'I'm sorry,' I said. 'I didn't mean to worry you.'

August moved his hand through his hair as if to stop himself from saying something. He leaned against the door frame with his arms crossed and watched me as I brushed my hair in front of the bathroom mirror. Water was dripping onto the floor and the sink.

'Where were you?' he asked.

I paused, arm still raised. I looked at myself in the mirror and wondered if that was really what I looked like.

'August,' I said. 'I'm tired.'

'I'm going to bed,' he said.

I reached out for his hand and rubbed my thumb over the back of it. He gave me a small smile before walking away. I locked the door and took a shower. As I washed my hair and scrubbed my limbs, blood and dirt mixed in the drain. The straps of my sandals had dyed my feet, and the colour didn't go away when I rubbed them.

Hugo was still up when I stepped out of the bathroom wearing my robe. He was at the kitchen island with his laptop open but closed it when he saw me. I poured myself a glass of juice from the fridge, then leaned against the counter.

'You have a hickey on your neck,' I said. 'Nice.'

Hugo didn't move. 'Do you know how terrified August was that something had happened to you?'

'Who even gives hickeys? Is she fourteen?'

'I don't believe that you didn't see our calls.'

'Did you give her one too?'

'You just left without saying bye.'

'You were busy.'

We looked at each other. I drank up and put the glass in the sink. Then I walked past Hugo without saying anything and entered the bedroom where August was already snoring. I got into bed next to him but I couldn't fall asleep. I lay awake all night.

Hugo

We packed our bags the next morning. August put on music; Thora and I didn't speak to each other. Once we'd cleaned and finished packing, August suggested going out for lunch since our flight wasn't leaving until late in the afternoon. Thora said she needed to do some schoolwork and demonstratively slid her computer out of its case. August made a few attempts to convince her to come while I stood mute in the hall until he finally gave up. The two of us took the metro to a restaurant he'd looked up on his phone, reading me the reviews. I told him it sounded good. It turned out to be further away than we'd thought, and without Thora we had no sense of direction. When we finally did find it we were both sweaty and hungry. We got a table outside and ordered using a clumsy mix of French and English. The waiter smiled tolerantly.

August smoked several cigarettes in a row, something I had rarely seen him do in the middle of the day. He felt hungover, he said. I tried to think back to isolate the exact moment when things had gone wrong between Thora and me. It was like moving a finger over the passage of time to locate a bulge in order to smooth it out, but right then everything seemed lumpy. I got angry when I remembered the expensive lunch in the Marais, I got angry when I thought about Thora's obvious ease in contrast to my own insecurity, but most of all I got angry when I thought about how much I wanted Thora and

August to lean closer and give me some kind of stamp of approval, a promise that they'd never stop liking me.

It was a cloudy day, heavy with humidity. The trees slouched over the streets. Exhaust fumes lay sharp in the air, irritating the nostrils. Both August and I sneezed. A man next to us had a small fan connected to his phone and closed his eyes while it whirred. We looked at the man and then at each other. We smiled.

The waiter came with our food.

'I don't know what happened last night,' August said when the waiter had left.

'I don't know either,' I said.

August was sitting with one leg crossed over the other and slowly twisted his foot, flexing the joint. He hadn't started eating yet.

'Are you sure of that?' he said.

'Are you saying it was my fault?' I said.

'I'm not saying that it was anyone's *fault*.'

'Thora is mad at me.'

'And you're mad at her?'

I sighed. I looked at the people walking by. Their faces were shiny and their armpits were stained with sweat. Some fanned themselves with newspapers.

'I don't know,' I said. 'Maybe.'

'It will pass.'

I stirred my glass and took a drink of my soda, sucking on an ice cube for a few moments before crushing it with my teeth. The cold radiated in a shiver. I swallowed.

'We're not going to hurt you,' August said.

I looked at him. His blue eyes were probing, and to look into them was to subject yourself to scrutiny.

'Why do you say that?' I asked.

'Is that not what you're afraid of?'

'Why would I be afraid?'

'Aren't you?'

I took a deep breath and was about to produce a loud *no* before I stopped myself.

'You can't promise that,' I said instead. 'Nobody can promise something like that.'

'And you'd rather not take the risk.'

'What do you mean? I'm here, right?'

August didn't reply.

'I don't want this to be hard,' I said after a moment of focusing on my food in silence. 'I want it to be simple.'

'And what if it isn't?'

'You're making it hard. The two of you are *choosing* to make it hard.'

'You're so suspicious of us.'

I didn't know what to do with my hands. I wasn't hungry anymore. I wanted to get up and leave.

'We don't want to hurt you,' August said, his voice low. 'And even if Thora can be pretty clueless sometimes, she doesn't mean it. Quite the opposite.'

'I don't know what you want me to say.'

The phone fan whirred. One of August's cigarette butts was still glowing in the ashtray. I'd put my cutlery down. Looking at the street I wished I could meld with the anonymity of the passers-by.

'I didn't mean to make you uncomfortable,' August said. 'And I'm not trying to say it was your fault that Thora just took off like that.'

I was silent for a long while, twisting my hands in my lap. Then I said: 'I think I'm going to walk around by myself a bit. Before we leave for the airport.'

'Okay,' August said.

'I don't want to fight with either of you.'

'Okay,' August said again.

I didn't move.

'You can go if you want,' August said. 'I'll pay.'

I wanted both to apologize and to snap at him. Instead I just said thanks, forcing a smile before I left.

'I'll see you later,' I said.

August nodded.

I walked back to the trafficked main street and then followed the canal until I reached Place de la République. Thora and August's voices were an unintelligible noise in my head. It blended with the sounds of people yelling, calling, talking to each other in French and Arabic, with the sounds of cars honking and sirens blaring from ambulances and police cars, until everything imploded into a silence that throbbed at my temples.

We were polite to each other on our way to the airport. We handled our language carefully, as if the courteous mood risked being punctured by one ill-chosen word. I assumed Thora and August had come to some mutual understanding while I was on my walk, so I made an effort to listen attentively whenever either of them said anything. We didn't talk about anything in particular – we commented on the weather, the dilapidated buildings outside the train window, the number of people on the train, whether the flight would be on time or not.

Every time they looked the other way I snuck a glance. I wondered if this performance of neutral politeness was what would smother everything of substance, dissolving it into nothingness. The thought made me so depressed that I wanted to put my forehead against the window and give myself over to something – or someone. But I just sat still in my seat, suitcase pressed between my legs, and agreed with August's reminder to buy water and chewing gum before boarding.

Back in Stockholm I signed up for extra shifts at the restaurant. I'd used up a good chunk of my savings in Paris and wanted to make up for it. The job required me to be agreeable, but it didn't require me to think or feel. August texted me to ask if I wanted to hang out, and it was easy to tell him I couldn't – I was working. I didn't hear from Thora, nor did I get in touch with her. And since our literature class had ended we didn't see each other at university either. I spent my time with friends who required less of me, and I dated girls who laughed at my jokes and came when I made an effort.

I had a recurring nightmare where I was trying to text Thora and August only to have the message come out as distorted emojis and words taken out of any context. I seemed unable to string together real sentences; no matter how hard I tried, the only result was a hodgepodge of graphics and misspelled words. The panic of not being able to make myself understood lingered even after I woke up.

I applied for a phone canvassing job at an aid organization, since waiting tables made me so tired I could barely focus on my studies. Many of my classmates had similar jobs at comparable organizations. They said it looked good on a CV, a motivation that appeared morally dubious to me. Then again, it didn't seem noble enough to tell the interviewer I wanted a job just for the money. So I said I hoped to do something meaningful and help other people, and left brimming with self-loathing. I wanted to call up August and ask why it was considered ugly to work just so you could afford rent and groceries and subway fares and textbooks. I felt deceitful pretending that work was what gave life meaning, and yet that seemed to be the expectation at a job interview. But I didn't call August; I'd resolved not to get in touch with him. Instead I brought it up with Tigran, who said that the alienation of work must be obfuscated by superficial ambitions of improving the world. He added, impassively, that if he couldn't get a job in academia or at a museum after completing his PhD, he planned to make his living as a cleaner or a truck driver, writing for art and culture publications on the side.

'At least in that scenario nobody is going to ask me to pretend I'm saving the world,' he said. 'It makes it easier to retain a sense of self-respect.'

A few days later I was offered the job, and all but left the restaurant. I was told I had a good phone voice: low and calm. The latter surprised me since I felt anything but calm, especially during my first few shifts. The people I got on the line sighed loudly when I told them my reason for calling; they interrupted me mid-sentence to ask if I was soliciting, then told me I was calling at a bad time. We weren't allowed to ask why they'd picked up if they were so busy. It was important to remember to thank them. During one of my shifts, a soft-spoken woman asked: 'I'm sure it's good to help them, but what kind of life can the people we're saving expect in these countries?' The conversation made me feel gross and I didn't know what to do with myself other than furiously scrub my hands with soap during my break. I learned to keep a smile in my voice without actually smiling. Whenever I got someone who was nice and ambivalent about how much they could spare of their pension or salary, it made me so surprised that I lost track of the script.

I spent my breaks smoking in the courtyard, scrolling through pictures I'd taken of Thora and August in Paris on my phone. Only two of them included all three of us. We'd asked a passer-by to photograph us standing in front of a yellow wall, and he'd snapped a shot before we'd turned to face the camera, capturing our backs. The next photo showed us leaning against the wall, smiling at the camera. I zoomed in on our faces, feeling like I was holding my hand on a hot burner to see how long I could stand it.

After my shift one evening I walked over to August's studio. The sky was pink and there was a pebble in my shoe that kept poking my heel, but the discomfort wasn't enough to motivate me to stop, take the shoe off and remove the stone. On my way there I bought three sunflowers and a loaf of cinnamon bread from the grocery store. When I got there August wasn't in but his friend was, and she told me he had been at ad school all day. I put the flowers and the loaf on August's desk and left.

He called me the following day while I was in class. I saw his

164

name light up the screen and walked out of the room to pick up. I could feel my classmates watching me; I didn't care.

'Hey you,' August said. 'Thanks for the flowers.'

I took a deep breath.

'I'm sorry for being MIA,' I said, clutching the phone hard as my eyes trailed over the red stripes painted on the walls and floors of the hallway.

'It's okay,' August said. 'Do you want to come over this afternoon and we can eat that loaf? I'll tell Thora too.'

'Yes. Thank you,' I said. 'Sorry.'

'Don't worry about it, Hugo,' August said. 'I'll see you soon.'

The sunflowers were in a zinc pitcher on August's desk when I returned to the studio. The coffee machine was gurgling in the corner and I was surprised when August hugged me. Thora wasn't there; August said she'd told him she needed to study for an exam. He didn't look at me as he said it, but I tried not to give her absence too much meaning.

We stayed at the studio until it got dark, and then we went on a long walk which ended with August apologizing for what he'd said in Paris.

'It didn't come out right,' he said. 'It made it seem like I was cornering you. I didn't mean to do that.'

I told him there was no need to apologize. I was silent for a moment, watching Riddarfjärden's water crease in the wind.

'You and Thora are so used to having each other,' I said. 'But I'm not used to it. Having someone else, in that way.'

I looked at the ground. Our steps were synchronized. August squeezed my hand for a few seconds.

A few days later I ran into Thora by chance, at a café on Drottning-gatan. It was a popular spot for people to hunker down with their laptops, and I'd brought my own to go over a few articles for a seminar. Thora was sitting at a table close to the till; we locked eyes while I was in line. After ordering, I went over to her.

'Can I sit here?' I asked.

'I guess,' Thora said.

I didn't know how to interpret that, but when she moved her computer to make room for my stuff I took the chair across from her.

We hadn't seen each other since the Paris trip. I asked how she was. Fine, she said. She didn't look or sound angry, but her manner was reserved, as if she was just too polite to ask me to leave.

'I'm sorry I haven't been in touch,' I said, initially concentrating on a stain on the table, but then I turned my gaze to Thora. She looked back at me with an inscrutable expression, pressing her fingers over her lips. Then she lowered her hand.

'You really admire August,' she said.

'Sorry?'

'You do,' she said. 'You're much harder on me. You look down on me because you think I look down on others. But August can be difficult too. All of a sudden he has this idea that he's dying from some illness, and he'll call me in the middle of the night so I can tell him that the birthmark on his arm is not skin cancer, that his headache is not a brain tumour, that his cough is not lung cancer. And then he'll spend a couple of days making the rounds with various doctors and borrowing money from his brother to see a psychologist who tells him exactly what Samuel and I said: *you're not sick, it's just anxiety*. There are times when I almost think he'd actually prefer to be sick – at least then he wouldn't have to deal with the uncertainty.'

'I don't look down on you,' I said. 'If there's anyone that I look down on it's myself.'

'How silly,' Thora said.

I couldn't tell if she was making fun of me. I shrugged. She looked down at her computer and brushed something off her keyboard.

'You make me feel so lonely sometimes,' she said, and ran a finger down the narrow space between the keys.

I sat motionless in my chair. I didn't know what to say. Whenever I hadn't seen Thora and August for some time, I got used to small talk and forgot how to discuss difficult things. She looked out the window as if she longed to be there, in the pale sunlight.

'I don't mean to,' I said. 'I don't want you to feel that way.'

'Okay,' she said.

I tried again, with the sense of rummaging through a cupboard that didn't have what I needed.

'I don't know what you want me to say but I didn't know you felt that way. That I made you feel that way.'

To my surprise Thora laughed, and then she leaned across the table with a strange gleam in her eyes.

'Good lord, it's not like there aren't *other people* I can be with.'

She took one last drink of her coffee and then she started to pack up her belongings. I wanted to get some indication that things were fine between us but she wouldn't look at me. I followed her out the door even though I'd planned to stay at the café to do my school-work. Halfway down Drottninggatan she told me she was meeting up with some friends. She got her phone out and opened the travel app while I watched her, trying to think of something to say. Her sudden cheer made me feel uncomfortable.

'I think I'm going to take the bus from T-Centralen,' she said without looking up. 'The subway is so crowded at this hour. Where are you headed?'

I didn't answer.

She put her phone in her pocket and sighed. 'It doesn't matter,' she said.

'That you're mad at me?' I said. 'It matters to me.'

'It doesn't feel like you care,' she said. 'And I'm not about to try to convince you to care.'

'Of course I care,' I said.

She adjusted her shoulder bag as if she was pressed for time. I could tell she wanted to leave.

'Thora, what do you want me to say?'

'I'm not about to stand here and tell you what to say. If you can't come up with something on your own then that speaks for itself.'

'What do you want from me?' I asked.

'Nothing,' she replied. 'And I have to go now.'

'Sure. Okay.'

Thora turned on her heel and went down the hill towards Sergel's Square, leaving me looking after her with tears burning my eyes. When I tried to wipe them away, my hand came back dry. I walked the other way, in the direction of Odenplan.

Thora

That spring, August landed a first-hand rental on Crafoords väg, near Sabbatsberg Hospital. It was through the city agency's waitlist for young people, widely understood among August's friends as the only way to get a lease in Stockholm. For August, it marked the end of a raft of temporary situations he'd hustled between ever since graduating high school. He'd always lived among other people's furniture, with his suitcases within close reach. He still hesitated to buy furniture, but I convinced him to get a kitchen table, a few chairs, and a large shelf we spent a sweaty Sunday assembling and mounting on a long wall. The apartment was small and shabby, but it was high up, with a view over Stockholm. With the windows open it was as if the river and the streets and the buildings and the people all came closer, like the city wanted to climb over the windowsill with all its sounds and lights.

There was a housewarming party in May. The guests all arrived with gifts: frying pans, pots, chopping boards, cutlery, an electric kettle. I gave him a set of striped coffee cups with saucers. Looking at the presents piled up in the little kitchenette, I thought of the furniture I had spent hours on end moving around in my doll's house as a child: a miniature representation of adult life. It all seemed so ephemeral that the smallest bump might cause the wall-mounted shelves to crash and the building to topple.

August's friends had made themselves comfortable wherever

they could find a spot: on the bed, on the floor, on the rug, leaning against the wall. Hugo was sitting between Elif and Brita, a plate of food balanced on his lap. August had arranged a spread of bread, olives, grapes, cheese, hummus and tzatziki on the table. Several of the guests had brought food contributions too, primarily various kinds of pasta salad. The apartment was so small that there was no way for me to pretend not to notice Hugo. We said tentative hellos.

I felt adrift in the company of August's friends. I wasn't in the mood to get pulled into a debate where opinions were accessories on a par with a new sweater or the white powder in the cracks of a cell phone screen. There wasn't much of a difference between my parents' friends and August's friends — they just happened to select different backdrops for their performances. August's friends oriented their political discussions around the two divergent camps of taking a stance or not taking a stance. Aron and Laura's friends focused on identifying and describing various factions, distancing themselves from the debate itself by assessing the way other people took their positions — so they didn't have to declare an opinion of their own. I wasn't sure which approach I preferred.

I wondered if August ever had the same thought. He came over and sat down next to me and I wanted everyone else to go and leave us alone. August gently rubbed my back. Seeing Hugo's smiles and excited gestures made me upset. Could he really be that cheerful?

I stood up to put my plate in the sink and August came with me. As I scraped my leftovers into the trash and rinsed my plate and fork I could sense his gaze boring into my neck, but he didn't say anything until we were alone in the narrow space between the entrance, the kitchenette and the bathroom door.

'Why are you acting so dismissive with Hugo?' he asked.

'I'm not dismissive at all.'

'You told me you miss him.'

I shrugged.

'I think you're being ridiculous,' August said.

'So let me be ridiculous,' I said.

August looked at me like he was trying to think of something that would unsettle my equilibrium. I crossed my arms.

'You're so severe sometimes,' August said. 'Nobody is up to your standards.'

There was a lump in my throat, but I kept my gaze steady, defiant. I tapped my fingers on my arm.

'I don't need to be accountable to you,' I said. 'You're always out to make me seem petty. And you're way harder on me than anybody else.'

August closed his eyes and moved his thumb and index finger along one eyebrow each, then let them meet in a pinch around the bridge of his nose.

'It's because I care more about you than anybody else,' he said. 'But you'd rather make yourself miserable than risk coming across as weak.'

'If that's so then it's my own problem. Not yours. Not Hugo's.'

'It will make you lonely,' August said. 'My brother's like that. Clams up whenever something is hard, and views every relationship like a competition.'

'Come off it,' I said. 'You're making a big deal out of nothing.'

I gazed into the room where August's friends were gathered. They were laughing, talking loudly; different faces with the same excited expression, as if they were afraid they'd miss the punchline of a joke or a story because they'd allowed their facial muscles to relax.

August sighed and straightened his back. 'Do what you want. I'm only telling you what I'm seeing.'

'Sure. Thanks,' I said. 'Very generous of you.'

He gave me a look and then joined the others, leaving me alone by the kitchenette. I looked around: the pile of presents, the empty wine bottles and beer cans on the counter, the dirty dishes in the sink.

I slammed the door when I left, assuming that August would blame it on a draught, if he even noticed.

I could never stay mad at August for long. Whenever we went a few days without speaking, it was as if the world was out of sync. I could focus on schoolwork or go to dinner parties at Aron and Laura's, where I listened to their friends and colleagues talk about stuff I didn't care about. But then, in the midst of lunch or coffee with a friend, this gnawing sensation, like a hunger, would make itself known. It would take me just a second or two before I realized where it came from. With a bit of effort I could redirect my thoughts away from August, but no matter what I did his absence lodged itself in my body, like a dull muscle pain.

My parents' friend Joel hired me to work a few hours a week at his law firm. Their office was situated near Strandvägen and my job was to man the reception, picking up the phone and welcoming clients. Joel said he'd be able to give me more stimulating tasks when I was further along in school. I alternated with another law student, and we split the days between us so that we could both make all our lectures and seminars. There had to be someone at reception every weekday between 9 a.m. and 5 p.m. It was a small firm, and there were times when several hours went by without any visitors. I sat behind the desk with my laptop and my books, reading and taking notes and chatting with classmates I had group projects with. Whenever someone entered I stood up, framed by the orchids on the desk. Those orchids were part of the job too – Joel said something about how the well-being of the flowers reflected the firm's ability to 'cultivate' long-term relationships with its clients. I thought he was joking, but when I smiled ironically he just looked at me and asked if I knew how to care for orchids.

'I can look it up,' I said.

When he walked off, I thought that August would have laughed at this exchange.

Every so often Hugo and I would pass each other in the corridor on the way to a seminar or a lecture. He was easily recognizable from a distance; he often kept his hands in his pockets and was so tall that he had to lean down to hear what the other person was saying. His face tensed and his eyes widened when he listened attentively, as if this made it easier to follow the conversation. We didn't say hi. We didn't seek eye contact. The corridors were crowded with students and professors and I had no idea if Hugo even noticed me walking past him. It was as if we didn't know each other – as if we never had. That fall he'd be eligible for an apartment in the student housing system, and that meant we wouldn't see each other at Aron and Laura's anymore. But I figured these things happen all the time. You get to know someone, spend some time together, and that's that. A seemingly endless flow of people that make no significant mark on your life.

These things I told myself. While scribbling notes in class with my stomach churning.

August always liked to say that we met on an island in the archipelago as kids. This was not true. The first time we met was on a steamboat leaving Stockholm. August claimed to have no memory of that boat ride, but I remember seeing August with his dad and older brother. It had been the early days of summer, shortly after the semester ended, and I was shot through with the nostalgia I associated with pale purple lilacs, classmates in their summer best and seasonal hymns sung on the last day of class. I spotted August the moment I stepped onto the boat with Aron and Laura. Then I proceeded to observe him from a distance in an effort to determine whether he was more likely to be a friend, rival or enemy. We caught each other's eyes a few times across the tables full of picnic food and coffee thermoses, between rain jackets and bare legs and arms with goosebumps, and I would never forget how the directness of his gaze struck me. He wouldn't look the other way.

I still couldn't make him look the other way.

*

Though I couldn't stay mad at him for long, I wasn't in the habit of seeking August out to apologize. Every time I had the impulse to call or text him, it seemed to me like the apology would require me to apologize for myself, something I could not do. I drafted messages in my notes app, and deleted them after just a few sentences. If I didn't erase the words I continued to feel their weight in my bag or my pocket, a constant reminder of how impossible it was to find the ones I wanted. It seemed to me that August should know that I missed him without me having to tell him.

Sometimes I caught sight of Hugo and August together in the city. I avoided the National Library since I risked running into them there. I thought that maybe August had replaced me with Hugo. When Aron asked how August was doing, I shrugged and told him to ask his lodger. My father looked at me with something like compassion and suddenly I wanted him to put his arm around me so that I could ask why I was the way I was, if I'd always been this way, even as a child, and if that was not the case, then how and when I'd become the person I was today. I changed the topic instead. I knew how trivial my problems were, and I didn't want that knowledge confirmed by a reassuring smile from Aron.

'The world is going to shit,' Harriet said one evening. 'And you're moping about a guy. *Two* guys.'

'I'm not moping,' I said.

'Isn't the world always going under?' Iris asked. 'You can't stop living just because of that.'

'I'm not *moping*,' I repeated. 'I just have a lot of work to do before the end of the semester.'

Harriet and Iris looked at each other. I took the law book from my bag and dropped it on the kitchen table so that the fruit bowl and my coffee cup clattered. My cousins left me alone in the kitchen. I didn't know whether to laugh or cry. Instead I opened multiple browser tabs and read the news on Swedish, French, British and US websites. I caught myself marking and screenshotting various quotes

I wanted to post in the group chat between Hugo, August and me, and when that impulse grew too strong I closed the tabs. I looked at my desktop image, the folders and documents spread out over it like stickers. Then I shut my computer. In the hall I yelled to Harriet and Iris that I was going for a walk. They called back asking me to get milk. I didn't respond.

It was early evening. I texted August and asked where he was and then resolved to do one loop around the block before looking at my phone again. He was at his studio. I told him I was out on a walk and asked if we could meet at the St John's Church stairs. I started heading in that direction without waiting for his answer. When the message came in I sped up. He wasn't there yet when I arrived, so I sat down on the stairs and waited. A few minutes later he appeared, hands in the pockets of his jacket. He looked at me for a few seconds before sitting down next to me.

'You took your sweet time this time,' he said.

'So you noticed?'

'Of course I did.'

'I'm sorry,' I said.

I spoke slowly, and emphasized each syllable in the apology like I was afraid to drop it from lack of practice. Some words were so heavy and lingered in the silence that followed – I was scared of the contrast between their smallness and the large meaning they carried.

August took my hand in his.

There was light in the windows facing the park, and the people who lived there appeared in silhouette when they walked past a lamp or a TV inside their apartments.

'It's true,' I said with my eyes on the figures inside the buildings. 'If it weren't for you, I'd be alone.'

August put his arm around my shoulders and pulled me close. I smiled without looking at him. I didn't need him to say anything, neither protest nor confirm. I knew that both Aron and Laura would have something to say about how much I needed August. Independence was the only virtue they'd encouraged in me. And yet, it was easy for me to admit that I needed him. It meant permitting myself to rest, to ask for help. It made me feel good.

We went to the studio and lay down on the red velvet couch under a chequered blanket. August put on a documentary and we watched it while he told me about things that had happened while we weren't in touch – how bored he was with ad school, the internship he was going to do that fall, Samuel's emails urging him not to drop out – but I was so tired that I only caught snippets. With my eyes closed I thought, unbothered by the banality of it, that as long as I had August close, nothing could ever hurt me.

I woke up early and tucked the blanket around the still-sleeping August. Then I stepped out into the sunlight and birdsong. The subway took me to campus, where I got a coffee and a warm cinnamon bun, which I had time to eat before my first class at 9 a.m. While the lecturer pulled up the PowerPoint I got my phone from my bag and wrote in my notes app: *thriving while the world is going under?* Then I removed the question mark.

A Friday on the threshold of summer at Aron and Laura's, a bright evening. All the regulars were gathered around the table and I couldn't help but think about the fact that, as we were discussing various interpretations of Adorno and Žižek in my parents' dining room, the ice caps kept melting and the oceans kept rising. That simultaneity was dizzying, and all I could see were bottomless chasms that made me want to close my eyes, hard. It was surprising how easy it was, turning away, forgetting. The trees were green and the breeze was warm and the city would soon be redolent of lilacs.

Hugo was sitting across the table from me, and whenever I was sure he was looking the other way I snuck a glance. August was at his dad's for dinner and sent me a steady stream of updates. I told him to put his phone away. He replied that they were just watching soccer anyway, and then added, a few seconds later, that they couldn't watch the news since they'd immediately get into an argument. I noticed that Hugo picked up his phone now and then too, and I wondered if August was texting with him as well.

Later, after the guests had left and I'd said goodbye to Aron and Laura, I stood alone in the hall, looking at my own reflection in the mirror. The blue evening light cast billowing shadows on my face, like I was standing over a swimming pool. My freckles had come out from underneath the powder I'd applied several hours earlier. My lipstick had worn off. I looked into my own eyes, unsure if the dare I saw there sprung from within me or from the unaffected solemnity of the reflection.

I knocked on Hugo's door, and when he responded I pushed it open. He was at his desk, several open books arranged around his laptop. The small desk lamp made an orb of light around the table while the rest of the room lay in semi-darkness.

'I thought you'd left,' he said.

'I was about to leave,' I said and immediately corrected myself, shifting my weight from one foot to the other: 'I'm on my way.'

He didn't move, watching me with something like anticipation. I looked at the books on his desk.

'I have an important exam due on Sunday,' he said.

'The last one before summer?'

'Yeah.'

'Do you have a lot of work? I can leave you alone if you're busy,' I said and backed towards the door.

'No. It's okay,' he said.

I stayed, but I didn't know what else to say. I looked around the room in search of something to comment on, then I sat down on the edge of the bed. My legs were bare and I put my hands on my knees. It wasn't cold, but there were goosebumps all over my skin.

'August says I'm too hard on you,' I said.

Hugo was facing me, his arm resting on the back of his chair. He laughed softly.

'Wow, okay,' he said. 'I didn't know.'

I hummed quietly and smoothed the bedspread with my hand. Then I stood up and went over to the desk, leaning back against it with my hands on the tabletop. Hugo looked at me. I smiled. The computer screen went to sleep. Hugo slipped his fingers over my knee, a light, cautious touch. I didn't move. I wished there were something on the table I could hold on to. He got up from the chair and put his hands on my hips. I could smell my parents' laundry detergent on his t-shirt. I pushed myself back so that I was sitting on the desk and put my legs around him, pulling him closer.

When we lay down on the bed he reached into a drawer for a packet of condoms. I rested my head on the pillow and watched him put one on. He smiled, as if he sensed my gaze on him in the darkness and knew he was doing something I found amusing. His breathing was even, heavy.

'Is this okay?' he asked.

I wasn't sure what he meant but I replied yes.

Later, we fell asleep the way we had that night in Paris. I could feel his breath on my neck, and when I turned my head to face him he rested his lips against my cheek and jawline.

The next morning we went for breakfast at a café nearby. I didn't want to come up with a way to explain to Aron and Laura that I'd stayed the night. We left through the back door while Tigran was in the shower and my parents were in the kitchen. I could hear the coffee maker and the egg timer over the sound of the radio.

We ordered a big breakfast: croissants, yoghurt, eggs, fruit salad. Our feet played with each other's under the table. I slipped out of one sandal and moved my toes over Hugo's ankle; that was as far up as I could reach. We drank coffee and read the paper, commenting on the predictable statements that shaped the op-eds, and the similarly predictable choreography that moulded the debates in the arts section.

'It's as if everyone got a package deal on opinions,' I said. 'Readymade thoughts for each camp and every moment.'

'I think they call it consistency,' Hugo said.

'All I want is to be surprised, just once.'

Hugo looked at me – his face half amused, half inscrutable.

'Is this what we do now?' he said.

'What?'

'Hanging out in cafés, being brats.'

'Isn't that what we've always done?'

'Hanging out in cafés, being brats *together*.'

'I guess so,' I said, not understanding what he was getting at.

'Will August mind?'

'No.'

'How do you know?'

'I just do.'

I smiled, but Hugo didn't smile back.

Hugo had on the same white t-shirt as the night before, and I thought I could smell him through the coffee aroma.

'I'm not good at these things,' he said.

'What things?'

He opened his mouth, paused, seemed to be gearing up for something.

'I like being with you,' he said, finally. 'And I don't like to think that I make you feel lonely. That's not how I want it to be. Sometimes it's just so hard for me to be close to you. I don't know how to explain it, but it's not your fault.'

I didn't speak. It sounded like he'd planned what he was going to say, spent some time thinking it through over the course of the morning, perhaps even overnight? I held my coffee cup on the table. He touched the back of my hand, like a question. I looked at him.

'I don't know why it's that way with you,' he said.

'Maybe because you love me.'

I didn't know why I said it.

The words came to me so suddenly that they seemed snatched from a different context, far from morning crowds and the clamour of cups and coffee machines. Those words didn't belong in that moment, and I wanted to say something sarcastic to patch up the leak in the hull and stop the boat from capsizing. With Hugo I often had the feeling of crossing an invisible line I wouldn't have crossed with anyone else.

I wished he'd give me at least the hint of a smile, a window through which I could wriggle out of what I'd just said.

'Yes. Maybe,' he said with a solemnity that surprised me.

He frowned, as if he'd just remembered something, but he didn't say anything else.

'It's all forgiven and forgotten,' I said, and understood from his face that he was as confused by my ambiguity as I was by his.

Hugo

The city emptied out in July, but we stayed. At night you could bike in the middle of the street because there were no cars about. We paused to catch our breath on the crest of the Västerbron bridge as we looked at the water, the sky, and the city that hovered in between like it had grown out from the point where the two met.

I worked four days a week that summer. Sometimes I was so bored that I just stared blankly at the grey wall of my cubicle. It undid time even as it passed. I heard myself talk whenever someone picked up, but as if from a distance, muffled by a thick wall. I got so used to the sound of the phone ringing that it merged with what I thought of as silence. I'd wake up in the middle of the night, wondering where that sequence of sounds at a perfectly uniform pitch had gone. But work left my mind the minute my shift was over. I'd bike to docks and rocks where Thora and August were laid out on wet towels, reading and napping in the sun. Thora had done one month of full-time work in June and was now on holiday, while August had intermittent free-lance projects, squinting at the screen in the bright sun with a drawing pad to hand. Thora complained that he was being embarrassing, and when he turned to me for an adjudication I replied diplomatically that I'd have worked outdoors too if I could.

One evening Thora took us to a secret bar at the Royal Swedish Opera. Her cousin Iris had a side job as an usher there and stood waiting for us by a statue in the foyer, dressed in the Opera's black uniform with mandarin collar. Thora and Iris kissed each other's cheeks in an exaggerated greeting, as if to match the excess surrounding us, and then Iris curtseyed theatrically before August and me. The two cousins were of the same height and wore their hair in similar pageboy styles, and when they walked side by side, with August and me in tow, they looked like sisters. We went up the stairs and passed through doors that had to be unlocked, long corridors, storage spaces and large rooms crammed with props and costumes, until finally we arrived in a room full of gilded mirrors and enormous chandeliers. Thora winked at me over her shoulder as if she'd just proved the existence of something I'd doubted. In a corner some stagehands were serving beer and hot dogs; ketchup and mustard bottles shared space with plastic containers of fried onions on a grand piano. The open balcony doors looked out on the palace and the parliament.

'The top brass recently discovered the existence of this room,' Iris said with a despondent sigh. 'So now they're planning to make it a members' champagne bar. It's our last summer here.'

We sat down on a hard settee with gold brocade upholstery. August got us beers and hot dogs and then there we were, beneath a mirror, and we laughed as we took each other in, warm and sun-kissed after a full day by the water. Thora rested her hand on my knee and I thought about how I would never be able to take her to a secret spot decked out with eighteenth-century furniture. It was strange how the world both shrank and expanded in the company of Thora and August. I felt more alive with them, even as I realized how starved I'd been before I met them – ignorant and starved of beauty.

The mirrored room was dusky, but outside the sky was bright and blue. Later we went to smoke on the balcony and watched the moon high in the sky. It was almost full. I could hear the water swirling under Strömbron. Lit by the moon, August leaned over and ran his finger over the bridge of my nose.

'You're peeling already,' he said.

*

For me, summer had always come with a sense of obligation, like I had to fill the time. Thora and August didn't seem to suffer from the same syndrome. As a child I used to be the only kid who stayed home in our Lund suburb through the holiday, while others went abroad or to their summer houses in Gotland and the Swedish west coast. I still associated the season with the smell of warm asphalt and entire days going by with me laid out on the lawn, hands behind my head, listening to the sound of my mom's fingers clattering over her keyboard through an open window. I didn't like this sudden dissolution of everyday routines and the emptiness which expanded in its wake. It was why I'd signed up for so many shifts at work, even though I told Thora and August that it was because I needed the money. I did need the money, but I pretended to hate working in the summer when in reality I didn't. It would've been worse to be adrift without anything to do.

It had taken me several years to admit to myself that I liked routine. In Berlin everyone I knew tried to live as impulsively as possible – because they were afraid they'd stagnate, or because routines were synonymous with everything they wanted to disavow. I had acted the same way even though I longed for the illusory comfort that comes from doing things in approximately the same order, in the same place, at the same time.

So I worked four days a week, went everywhere on my bike, and spent many evenings and nights at Thora's. We often had sex before I went to work, and when I arrived at the office it was hard to tell if my pulse was racing because I'd biked there or because it was only a short while ago that I'd willed myself not to come too fast. I liked seeing Thora lose control when I made her come, but I wasn't sure if the reverse was true for her. I didn't know how or when Thora had told August about us. In fact I didn't even know whether she'd told him or let him figure it out on his own. I didn't say anything, I couldn't think of a phrasing that didn't sound like an apology or a request for permission, or both at once. As with so many things that made me uncomfortable, I just let it be and hoped that things would work themselves out without my involvement.

August had started dating one of his classmates. He and Eliel performed the story of their meet-cute for Thora and me, and described finding each other like coming across one sober person in the midst of a huge crowd on drugs. Eliel said, in his wide-eyed way of speaking, that the school force-fed them Silicon Valley ideology, which was basically neoliberalism tricked out in hippie language. Eliel said that at first he had thought there must be something wrong with him, when he couldn't shake the feeling that the school was trying to indoctrinate him by way of inspirational Post-it quotes. Things like *MOVE FAST AND BREAK THINGS* and *FIND YOUR BELIEVERS*. But working on a group project at the end of the spring semester, one of the tabs on August's browser had caught Eliel's attention. It was an article titled 'The Californian Ideology', which Eliel proceeded to look up online. *And then* . . . Eliel said with a flourish in the air. August smiled and looked first at Thora and then at me. We smiled back.

Thora said it was nice that Eliel shared a name with a character in the Alberte trilogy, and the next time we met him, she gave him a paperback collection of the series. August apparently interpreted this gift as a stamp of approval. He squeezed Thora's hand and kissed her cheek.

One evening, Eliel asked me about Thora and August's relationship. We were at a bar, August was ordering and Thora was in line for the bathroom. It was the first time Eliel and I had been alone together.

'Are they in an open relationship?' Eliel asked with a contrived nonchalance that suggested he had harboured this question for a long time.

'I'm not sure,' I said, pretending to think it over. 'No. They're childhood friends.'

'I *like* Thora,' Eliel said, thoughtfully. 'But it's easy to get jealous. Don't you think?'

Eliel was leaning forward with his hands clasped around an empty glass. He had a long face and eyes that seemed to register everything that happened around him, ready to approach anything that might come his way with a sense of mild confusion.

'I don't think you can compete with Thora,' I said.

'Can *you* compete with August?'

'I don't think of it that way.'

It was true. I didn't.

He raised his eyebrows but didn't say anything.

Eliel never asked about Thora and August again. But I wouldn't have had anything to add even if he did.

The first time I realized that I loved Thora and August was shortly after that conversation. There was nothing special about the day, aside from my realization. We were drinking coffee at a sidewalk café on Swedenborgsgatan, watching the pedestrians and talking about things without ever reaching a conclusion – we were just putting words to our thoughts to see if they had wings. I didn't know anyone else I could have these kinds of conversations with; they were the closest you could get to actually inhabiting someone else's mind, with all its associative webs and riddles. So much of what I did, heard and read each day filled me with a sense of futility that was sometimes intense enough to be paralysing. It wasn't that those feelings went away when I was with Thora and August – but they became more bearable, less lonely. Listening to them talk that afternoon, I realized that I cared more about them than myself. It was the first time I'd understood my own well-being as dependent on the well-being of someone else.

I didn't tell them. I didn't actually know if this was what was known as love; I had never heard anyone talk about it that way. It was a powerful intoxicant that made my thoughts clear instead of muddled, and it was precisely that clarity that made me feel dizzy and scared. I couldn't help but wonder why love was so exalted if what it represented was this collision with something unknown that

I experienced as more powerful than me. I didn't know what to make of that feeling; it seemed too big to carry around in my daily life, but also impossible to put aside. I tried not to think too much about it.

I would have expected some kind of reaction from Aron and Laura, an indication that they'd noticed that Thora acted differently around me now. But neither of us said anything to them and Aron and Laura didn't ask. Thora said they didn't care what she did, which I doubted, though I didn't protest. I didn't get Thora's relationship with her parents; but then again I probably couldn't have explained the relationship I had with my parents either. I regularly talked to my mom on the phone, and my dad's primary mode of keeping in touch was sporadic photos of a tree struck by lightning, or a cloudy sky with birds in a V formation, or graffiti on a Copenhagen facade. He never called me. Sometimes I'd react to the photos with a thumbs up. Thora suggested that I send my own pictures back, but I never did. When she asked me about my parents I realized that, in contrast to a lot of people our age, I had no ready-made narrative about my upbringing to offer. I didn't know how to tell the story of myself. Sometimes I was surprised by how readily others would produce a chronicle of their lives, a long guard rail reaching through the years, making everything that had happened seem intelligible and significant. I thought of childhood as a shapeless mass of time, so remote that it couldn't be more than vaguely associated with me.

I found it awkward to meet Aron or Laura's gaze whenever Thora caressed my back or took my hand in front of them. Innocent gestures; still, they made me uncomfortable, much to Thora's amusement. I preferred sleeping at hers. Breakfast on mornings when she'd stayed in my room were unbearable, though I seemed to be the only one in a rush to get it over with. Aron and Laura were as absorbed by the newspaper as ever, while Thora scrolled on her phone or bickered with her parents over who got which section first. The sound of the toast coming apart between my teeth was deafening.

Every so often Laura would look at me as if she was about to share her thoughts on our relationship, but she never did. At most she'd ask how my parents were doing, and I'd tell her they were fine, which as far as I knew was true. Sometimes I tried to look at the Stiller family through the eyes of my father, but it was almost impossible. I began this thought experiment imagining he'd probably mock the pale pink gerberas in the library, and then he'd ridicule the fact that this apartment actually contained a room called 'the library', and he'd keep going this way, one scornful observation after the other until he'd braided a full wreath of scorn around the Stiller family. Then I remembered that Aron and Laura were actually old friends of his. I'd sometimes heard him joke that he'd defend a dictator as readily as a human rights warrior – as long as they were his friend. And my mom would respond: 'That just means that you're easy to corrupt.'

The biggest reaction towards our relationship came from Tigran. I saw him struggling to hide his astonishment and shrugged at the wordless questions in his eyes. Tigran shrugged back at me, as if the situation might make more sense if he imitated my body language.

'Well, okay then,' he said and pushed his glasses back up. 'I can't say that I'm not surprised.'

'I'm surprised too,' Thora said.

'Thanks for that,' I said.

Later, when we were alone, Thora told me that the only person who wasn't surprised was August.

A few days before the start of the fall semester, I went online to buy used copies of the books I needed for university, but some of them were impossible to source that way; I could only find them in new editions in a real bookstore. The new books had glossy covers and felt flaccid when I flipped through them, the pages reluctant to separate. Before paying, I paused at a shelf of softcovers to find something to read that wasn't for class. The book about the Stiller conglomerate was under non-fiction; by now it had come out in paperback, much cheaper than the bound edition. I hesitated in front of the shelf, wondering if I could still plausibly claim that the Stiller family had nothing to do with me. But I didn't buy the book. To whom would I need to explain myself? It could only end with me and August's friends agreeing that hypocrisy was rampant, just as I agreed with them that wars, starvation and poverty were all terrible phenomena. I wondered if knowing what was going on in the world was worth anything if all it produced was theorizing and opining in bars and cafés. But I wasn't sure. I rarely was. The constant uncertainty was like standing in rapid waters, trying to steady myself on the sand which moved just as much as I did.

That semester I was studying foreign policy, and the first class consisted of the professor clicking through a PowerPoint about international law – lots of slides with Latin headers. Keyboards clattered in the room like persistent hail. We wrote down the differences between treaties, customary law, general customs, case law and doctrine. At the end of the class the lecturer encouraged us all to read Hobbes and Spinoza. I recounted the whole thing to August later that afternoon. He nodded to confirm that he was listening, but he was quiet and didn't laugh as I'd expected when I described the way the students who were going into the military stood up each time they answered a question. After a while, August cleared away the dirty dishes and rinsed his brushes. Paint poured down the drain in thick streams. He explained that he was heading out to see his dad.

'I bought him theatre tickets for his birthday,' August said. 'And the play is tonight.'

'Nice,' I said and picked up my backpack from the floor, hung it over my shoulder.

'It was stupid,' he said. 'I don't know what I was thinking. That's the kind of gift Thora can give her parents. I can't.'

We walked together in the direction of the theatre. It was out of my way but I wanted to catch a glimpse of August's dad. August lit a cigarette and wrapped his black coat around him without button-ing it. He shivered. Suddenly he made a tortured sound and tossed his cigarette on the ground while pressing a hand over his face.

'I should have bought him a book about World War Two or something, the way Samuel did,' he said.

'It's just a play,' I said.

'I'm an idiot,' August said. 'My therapist told me not to do this. I didn't listen.'

I looked at him, surprised.

August exhaled heavily through his nose. 'I'm sorry,' he said. 'I haven't been doing so well lately.'

'What do you mean?'

'Some kind of depression,' August said while he lit a new cigar-ette and kicked away a stone that rolled into a puddle. 'But it will pass. It always does.'

'I had no idea you're seeing a therapist.'

'It's no big deal,' August said. 'I have tons of friends who have therapists. They like the way it makes them feel like world-weary Americans.'

'When did you start?'

'In June. But I've seen therapists before. Samuel pays.'

'Why didn't you tell me?' I asked. 'That you weren't doing well?'

August looked at me and then at his hands, as if he was choosing his words carefully.

'I didn't know if you wanted to know these kinds of things,' he said. 'And I didn't know how to bring it up.'

'I thought you were happy,' I said. 'This summer. You seemed happy.'

I could tell how stupid it sounded but it was the first image that came to me – August stretched out on a sun-warm rock, eyes closed, face relaxed, the water in his hair glittering in the sunlight. I'd even looked at him and wished, enviously, that I could be as content with myself as he was.

'I'm sorry,' I said. 'I just mean—'

'No, it's true,' August said. 'I did seem happy. I'm good at pretending.'

Neither of us said anything else. We stopped to wait for a green light.

'I do want to know about stuff like this,' I said. 'I want to know if you're not doing well.'

'I really only talk about it with my therapist and with Thora. And a little bit with Samuel since he foots the bill.'

'How about Eliel? Do you talk to him?'

'I *talk* to him.' August smiled. 'Just not about these kinds of things.'

I smiled too, but couldn't quite get my face to fit the smile.

'It's not like you talk so much either,' August said when we crossed the street. 'About how you're doing.'

'I'm fine,' I said.

August looked sideways at me.

'It was about time that you and Thora got it together,' he said.

'I was worried that you would be upset about it.'

'I know,' August said. 'Thora told me.'

I laughed. 'You two, I swear.'

'Eliel thinks we're deviant,' August said and took a long drag of his cigarette before he put it out.

We said goodbye at Nybroplan. I wished we could've spent the rest of the evening together. Before we went our separate ways I told him I was sure his dad was pleased about the present. August shook his head but didn't protest. I crossed the street in the direction of the quay but then turned around just as August sat down on the theatre steps. I stopped where I stood, by the water. Buses, cars and trams passed by, heading out to various parts of the city. The water sloshed against the hulls of the boats tethered to the quay. The street lamps slowly came on, their light bringing out the gold on the statues outside the theatre. August got up when an older man walked up to him. The man was wearing a blue windbreaker and dark jeans. He was as tall as his son. August leaned in and they gave each other a brief hug before both put their hands in their pockets. I wanted to get a better look at August's face, but I didn't dare get any closer. When they disappeared into the building I left the quay and walked home.

Thora

I brought Hugo to Carl's party. It was one of the first big events of the fall, but August wasn't interested. I called him earlier in the day to try to convince him to come. He laughed, but told me he just wanted to hang out with Eliel at home.

'It's too cold to go out,' he said. 'And too dark and too wet.'

'It's October,' I said. 'It's always dark and wet.'

I accused him of having turned into a couch potato. 'It's Eliel,' I said. 'He's a bad influence on you.'

'Thora.'

I sighed. 'Fine, okay. But I'll miss you.'

'You'll have fun without me.'

'We should go somewhere warm and sunny. To Spain. Or Greece.'

'I wouldn't be good company there either,' he said.

'I always like being with you.'

I could tell it made him happy to hear it. I missed him. Even though I was at home, talking to him, I felt the ache of an amorphous homesickness, the phantom pain of something that had never been and never would be. I glanced out the window. The leaves lay brown and trampled on the ground.

'I'll talk to you tomorrow,' August said. 'Enjoy.'

A few minutes later, he texted me with a request for outfit pics; Carl had started to demand his guests show up in evening wear. He claimed he was tired of constantly being surrounded by people in jeans and sneakers. Waiting for Hugo at the subway station, I took out my phone to photograph him when he appeared on the escalator. He raised his eyebrows; we weren't in the habit of photographing each other.

'It's for August,' I said. 'He asked to see what you're wearing.'

I didn't tell him I thought he could have made more of an effort.

We walked to the tram station huddled under my umbrella. Office buildings reached for the sky, and shop windows showcased mannequins arranged in unnatural postures and ads with models sprinting on the shorelines of white beaches.

'Last time there was a party at Carl's we biked there,' Hugo said.

'It was summer,' I said, shaking rain from my umbrella and collapsing it as we stepped under the tram shelter.

'We didn't know each other back then,' he said.

I looked at him and smiled encouragingly. He returned it, but with something guarded in his eyes.

'You didn't like me back then,' I said.

I wanted him to protest and tell me how much he liked me now, laying the foundation for the story about us, one we could fill out and adorn together, a project for the two of us. But he stayed silent. When the tram came we sat down across from each other.

'I don't fit in with them,' he said.

'Well, you're wearing sneakers,' I said.

'You know what I mean.'

Slowly, the city slid past. The tram was pretty empty, but at the other end of the car there were a few people in evening wear made comical by the harsh overhead lighting. I didn't know them, but I assumed they were going to Carl's party too.

'But I fit in?' I said.

'They're your friends,' he said, and paused for a few moments before continuing: 'Last year August said that you don't actually like them but you want them to like you.'

I pursed my lips. The plastic bag with our two wine bottles lay in my lap and they clinked when I moved. I felt Hugo watching me and I wondered how he interpreted my expression.

'Of course he'd say that,' I said.

'Is it not true?'

'Does it matter? It's just a party.'

'I don't know what to talk to them about.'

'Their clothes,' I said. 'Talk to them about what brand their clothes are.'

Hugo made a face but stayed silent. When we got off the tram and headed in the direction of Carl's house, he took my hand. It surprised me; we didn't usually hold hands. But I didn't comment on it. He didn't let go until we were in the hall, where Carl, dressed in a tuxedo, welcomed us. He hugged me, slapped Hugo on the shoulder and then stepped back as if to inspect our outfits. I noticed him lingering on Hugo's shoes, though he didn't say anything. When we were alone again, Hugo glanced at me as if he was expecting me to chastise him.

'I told you that you could borrow a pair from Aron,' I said. 'He has tons of dress shoes.'

'I don't want to borrow your dad's shoes,' he said, calmly.

'Why is it so hard to accept gifts? You're getting to be as silly as August's friends.'

'I fit in better with them,' he said.

'Is it really that important – to fit in?'

He looked at me as if what I'd just said revealed something significant about me. I didn't like it.

'It's so easy for you,' he said.

'To fit in?'

'Yes.'

'Sure, yeah,' I said and headed towards the kitchen.

He followed me. 'It's a compliment. I wish I were more like you.'

I uncorked one of the wine bottles we'd brought and poured a glass without looking at him. Instead I said hi to the people who had entered the kitchen after us. Hugo got himself a glass. I had the thought then that I liked us best as a couple when we were alone together, detached from any context. We stood silently next to each other, leaning against the counter. I took several sips of wine, feeling Hugo's eyes on me. After a while I put the glass down, took his hand and led him to the living room where everyone was dancing. Through the window I could see a row of cressets lit on the terrace, their flames fluttering in the wind.

When we went outside for a cigarette, Hugo told me he'd applied to go on an exchange to England that spring semester. He sounded surprised, as if this was something that had happened to him without his involvement.

'Oh,' I said. 'Nice.'

His hand rested on my lower back. 'I probably won't get it,' he said.

'You have good grades,' I said. 'You'll get it.'

'Not as good as you.'

'You're not in competition with me,' I said. 'I haven't applied.'

Hugo moved his hand to my waist. I watched the dance floor through the windows. Rectangles of light in the dark autumn night.

'Are you upset?' he asked.

'No.'

'It's just a semester. Not even four months.'

I nodded, slowly. 'I hope you get it.'

His hold on me hardened. I turned to face him. His eyes scanned my face, as if he wanted to find something he could hold on to there as well. I got on my tiptoes and kissed him, intending a brief peck, but he pulled me closer. He never kissed me that way around other people. His face was red, like he was already drunk.

'I don't know what's wrong with me,' he mumbled into my hair. I could hardly hear him.

'There's nothing wrong with you,' I said and took a step back to get a better look at him.

He didn't respond. I wondered if he thought I'd been too loud. With August I often knew what he was feeling and thinking, but it was mostly impossible with Hugo, and I had the sense that he would push me away if I tried to understand him better.

When we stepped back into the house we went our separate ways, immediately, as if we'd agreed not to talk to the same people at the same time. Now and then I looked for him in the rooms I entered, and I had the sense that he was looking at me too when I had my attention elsewhere, but we never caught each other's eyes.

We didn't stay long. On the subway home he was quiet but friendly whenever I said anything. I didn't ask what was on his mind; it felt like a wordless act of resistance, though I suspected he didn't even notice.

We went to bed as soon as we got home. I washed off my make-up and undressed before turning off all the lights. Hugo held me close. I felt him getting hard. Quivering, I opened my legs as he caressed me. I tried not to make a sound. A shiver went down my spine and I spread my toes under the covers.

I woke up before him in the morning. The sheets were stained, creased and damp with sweat, a silent testimony that made me blush. I went to the bathroom, where I peed and took a long shower. When I came back the bed was empty. I wrapped myself in my bathrobe and secured the belt tightly around my waist. Hugo and Harriet were both eating breakfast and laughing at something in the kitchen. They only briefly looked up when I came in. Harriet turned up the volume on her computer, for the podcast they were listening to. I sliced a banana into a bowl of yoghurt.

'Anyone else making this joke, it wouldn't be funny at all,' Harriet said. 'It can't be repeated.'

'It's the phrasing,' Hugo said. 'The way he says it.'

They stopped talking and kept listening, heads bent. I opened the fridge and took out a carton of milk. Hugo and Harriet laughed again as I poured myself a cup of coffee and sat down at the short end of the table, staring at the laptop on the windowsill. The screen was black and I could see the contours of myself, Hugo and Harriet reflected in it. Blue sky, the trees in the courtyard yellow and red. I forced myself not to look straight at Hugo because I didn't know what my gaze would convey. It was difficult to reconcile the image of this person laughing in the light of the morning with the person who'd muttered into my hair the night before that something was wrong with him. I pulled my legs close to my chest and balanced my coffee mug on one knee while paging through the newspaper. A few minutes later, the podcast ended and Harriet got up and closed her laptop. She tucked it under her arm on her way out of the kitchen, announcing she was taking a shower. She and Hugo were still smiling, the last joke lingering in the air.

When Harriet had left, Hugo looked at me and I realized that her presence and the voices from the computer had created a neutral barrier between us, which collapsed now that we were alone. I lowered my feet to the floor. Our private world was back, the silence uncovering an intimacy that stayed hidden in the company of others. I thought of Harriet's girlfriend, Bella, currently asleep in Harriet's room, and wondered if it was the same for them, if they also had a private world that went from visible to invisible and back again, at pace with the jerky dance we all perform in the company of others. Suddenly I feared that Hugo would deny that such a world existed for us, but I didn't know how to make him admit it to me.

'Did you sleep well?' he asked.

We looked at each other.

He blushed and coughed.

'I'm not mad at you,' I said. 'I was just surprised that you wanted to study abroad. I didn't know it was something you wanted.'

'Okay,' he said and paused for a few seconds. 'Thanks for telling me.'

'Have you had enough of Stockholm after just one year?'

'No,' he said. 'I didn't really think much about it when I applied. The classes seemed fun. But I don't think I'll be accepted anyway.'

'I'm sure you will be.'

'In that case you'll have to come visit,' he said, his voice cautious, like he was asking a question.

I nodded and he looked relieved.

Later that afternoon I went to the pharmacy and bought the morning-after pill. I was nauseous the rest of the day. Hugo insisted on paying. I didn't protest.

Hugo

The gallery was packed at August's opening. Even though it was November the door was wide open to the street, and passers-by peeked in, curious about what had drawn the crowd. The gallerist talked loudly and with great animation as he gesticulated at the paintings on the walls. August wove through the crowd, shaking hands, hugging, cheek-kissing the guests. He laughed and said things I couldn't hear over the din of voices. It was the first time I'd seen all of August's friends in one place. Thora pointed out some of them, told me their names and how they knew August. Now and then he circled back to me and Thora, and every time he turned his back to the room, the mask of laughter fell away. He rubbed his eyes.

'Do you think people like it?' he said.

'Yes,' I said.

'Absolutely,' Thora said.

'I'm not sure.' He searched our faces.

'I like it,' Thora confirmed, and looked at me before she turned back to August. '*We* like it.'

'Yes,' he said. 'That's the most important thing, that you like it.'

'Your gallerist seems happy,' I said.

We all looked at the man in the double-breasted blazer, who moved his wine glass through the air as he spoke. He was the only person with a real glass; everyone else was holding little plastic cups. Once he'd pulled in some laughs he moved on to the next group.

'He's definitely hoping he'll get to blow August at the end of the night,' Thora said. 'Or the other way around.'

I took a sip of my wine to avoid responding. I didn't like hearing Thora talk about sex. It embarrassed me and aroused me against my will, and I suspected she knew that.

'At least he finally let me show my work here,' August said.

'Eliel seems to like him,' Thora said.

'I think he'd like to exhibit here too,' August said.

Thora and August exchanged a long glance and then he shrugged. I didn't say anything. I was used to their silent conversations by now. Instead I looked around and spotted Vera and Tigran on the other side of the room. I slipped through the crowd, as Tigran waved and Vera turned around, one hand cupping her elbow and a finger moving across her lips.

'We were just talking about you,' she said.

I looked between them. 'Yeah?'

'We were wondering what Aron and Laura think about your thing with Thora,' Vera said. 'Not to mention: what does Karla think?'

'They don't care,' I said. 'Why are you talking about this?'

'I think Tigran needs someone to talk to,' Vera said. 'You know. To process your new relationship.'

'Sure,' I said.

We were silent for a moment.

'Vera thinks it would have been more interesting if you'd slept with Laura,' Tigran said.

'Sorry to disappoint you.'

'Sleeping with Laura is Vera's wet dream,' Tigran said.

'And yours is sleeping with me,' she replied.

The blush crept down to Tigran's neck. I finished my wine and crumpled the empty cup.

When Thora materialized next to me I saw Vera and Tigran look at each other as if to agree on an approach. Vera removed her hand from her lips; they were painted red like Thora's but in a darker shade, more purple. I'd made a habit of regularly rubbing my hand over my own lips since Thora's lipstick smudged when she kissed me. I'd look at the red colour on the back of my hand, feeling marked by her, both inside and out. Depending on my mood this could make me feel good or bad.

'Hey,' Thora said.

Her arm touched my arm.

'We were just talking about you,' Vera said.

'Really?'

'This must be so great for August,' Tigran said.

'Every artist's dream,' Thora said. 'Basking in the admiration of friends, acquaintances and strangers.'

Thora had a tendency to say things that sounded sincere and ironic all at once. I'd come to understand that she employed that ambiguity in situations where she felt insecure, but I knew that Vera and Tigran interpreted it as arrogance.

'So I hear you're studying to become a lawyer?' Vera said.

'Yes,' Thora said. 'My big childhood fantasy.'

Vera and Tigran smiled stiffly. I realized they didn't know what to say. Thora looked at me. I felt it was my job to lighten the mood but all I could think of was that Thora knew me as someone else than the person Vera and Tigran knew. I wasn't sure who I was to myself – maybe just a gap, a void.

Mercifully, August came to join us, followed by Eliel and the gallerist, and Thora left the group. She didn't announce it, just silently disentangled herself and walked away. Nobody commented on it, but I noticed Vera and Tigran looking after her. The gallerist asked what Vera and Tigran thought of the show. August put his hand on my back. I caught Eliel's eye and immediately looked away. It really did feel like I was a void, only filled in by other people's gazes. After a while, I too backed away from the group. August's hand slipped from my back and I turned around, searching for Thora. Finally I saw her standing on the street outside. Her arms were crossed over her chest, her shoulders pulled up, and she was talking to a man it took me a few seconds to recognize: August's dad.

It was cold outside. Thora's hair was loose and blowing in the wind. She was wearing thin tights and a dress with three-quarter sleeves. August's dad was bundled up in a jacket, scarf and hat. I hesitated in the doorway before I went to join them, offering her a cigarette as an explanation of my presence. She shook her head.

'Gustav, this is Hugo,' she said. 'A friend of August's.'

I didn't offer my hand since Gustav didn't take his out of his pocket. We just nodded at each other. I lit the cigarette. I had to click the lighter several times, protecting the flame from the wind, before a spark appeared.

'Another friend.' Gustav laughed softly.

'Don't you want to come in?' Thora said. 'It would make August so happy to see you here.'

'No,' Gustav said. 'He'd be embarrassed.'

'I don't think so at all,' I said.

Gustav looked at me. His eyes were clear blue. August's eyes in another face: sunken, creased by wrinkles, grey stubble. As if August's smooth skin, soft gaze and high cheekbones had come at the expense of his father's face. Gustav coughed like I'd made a joke. Out of the corner of my eye I noticed Thora fidgeting.

'I don't have time,' Gustav said. 'I should be getting home, I just happened to be passing by.'

Thora stood on her tiptoes, placed a hand on Gustav's shoulder and kissed his cheek. It was like witnessing a collision of two worlds, but Gustav smiled at Thora. The two of us watched as he headed towards the crosswalk and then he was out of sight.

'August's dad, huh,' I said.

'Yes.'

'Did he really just happen to walk by?'

'I don't know,' Thora said. 'Probably not.'

She came close to me and I put my arm around her. She was shivering.

'Do you want to go inside? You're freezing,' I said.

Thora was still looking down the street in the direction Gustav had walked. 'Are you ashamed of me?' she asked.

'What? No,' I said, quickly. Too quickly. 'Why are you asking?'

'I just am,' she said with an unconvincing lightness in her voice.

Her hair blew across her face. She brushed the strands behind her ears, but they immediately came loose again. The cold was biting my cheeks and I clenched my jaw to stop my teeth from chattering.

'Why?' I repeated.

'Before,' she said and tilted her head in the direction of the gallery. 'With Vera and Tigran.'

'I'm not ashamed of you,' I said.

'Okay.'

I could have told her that sometimes I was ashamed of myself. If shame was the right word. But I didn't say anything. I just looked at her, and she smiled at me, and I told myself that everything was okay, so I kept silent. We went back into the gallery, into the warmth, the crowd, the clamour.

I was accepted to a university in Brighton and I broke the news to Thora and August together, while watching them intently for their reactions. There was a curious allure in leaving the two of them, who were so rooted in Stockholm; in finding out if my absence would be noticeable to them. The only form of power available to the weak: temporarily removing myself. They both beamed when I told them, which I found disconcerting, but after I'd repeated several times that it was just four months, they laughed and Thora pressed my hand under the table. August took out his phone to look for cheap tickets to London in the spring. He said we could stay with Samuel for a few nights – that way we wouldn't have to pay for a hotel.

We were at the café on Surbrunnsgatan. Drifts of snow glimmered in the sunshine outside. For a second I was about to tell them that I'd turn down the offer, that I wanted to stay in Stockholm with them, but then I realized I hadn't enrolled in any classes in Stockholm. If I said no to Brighton there'd be a hole that would have to be filled with six months of phone canvassing and restaurant jobs. So I didn't say anything. I just squeezed Thora's hand. I could feel the pulse in her wrist, like a tiny creature twitching under the skin.

During our final foreign policy seminar, the class was split into two opposing groups. One was asked to make a human rights argument for the legality of the US attack on Afghanistan, and the others represented the rival side. I had been tasked with presenting the first group's case. I read out the statement we'd written, which made repeated reference to proportionality and preventive self-defence. Following the second group's arguments, silence ensued. We looked at each other. Some giggled, while others who took the role-play exercise more seriously folded their hands on the table. A few seemed barricaded behind their laptops, glancing at the professor like they were hoping for guidance. The debate started haltingly, but things took off when a girl in my group distanced herself from the role she felt she'd been forced into by the professor. I was surprised by the intensity of her reaction. It made me wonder whether there was something ugly about how easily I was able to toy with reality, twisting between positions while maintaining a cool distance. Most of my classmates didn't share that detachment; they were fervent when they presented their arguments, evidently emotionally attached to them.

Eventually the professor cleared her throat and noted that we were meant to use human rights arguments, not political ones. That made everyone silent for a few moments as they tried to remember the parameters of the human rights framework. It all ended with one of the students questioning the relevance of separating human rights from politics if governments were able to interpret and use human rights exactly how they saw fit anyway. The professor smiled and said that the human rights framework stood and fell with that word: *exactly*. Confused looks shot around the room.

The following day we took the final in-person exam of the course in a barely heated classroom while snow fell outside the window. One guy tried to hold his pen through a mitten, inspiring sniggers from those around him. I was bundled up in a scarf, trying to warm my left hand on my coffee cup while writing with my right. I wasn't used to writing by hand, and my wrist started protesting already after the first essay question. A few hours later, when I turned in my paper and left the room, I realized I'd just completed half of my bachelor's degree.

*

A couple of days before the start of the spring semester I took a plane to London, followed by a train to Brighton, where I checked in at a youth hostel in the city centre. The bunk beds were full of students on their backs and bellies scrolling through housing sites. An oppressive atmosphere suffused the dormitory, all of us in silent competition over the few centrally located rooms with low rent, though nobody wanted to admit it. I found a café with fast Wi-Fi near the hostel, and sat down to respond to the listings. I wrote a short introduction about myself, to paste into each email, attached my acceptance letter from the university to prove I was a student, and then looked for English-language templates on how to contact landlords. I wasn't sure how formal I should be. I couldn't bring myself to use *Dear*, even though Thora claimed it was standard.

On the third day I got a reply from a thirty-year-old Brit named Ian, whose entire listing had been written in lower case. It was a Sunday and I took the bus to a narrow, three-storey building close to the university. The room was on the top floor, small and furnished with a bed, desk and a chest of drawers. Rent was low. Ian explained that the building had been one single home, but it was now split up into three apartments, one on each floor.

'No garden access for us, that is to say.'

'Okay,' I said.

When I looked out over the narrow concrete yards lined up next to each other, I figured it wasn't much of a loss. I took the bus back to the hostel, got my suitcase, checked out and moved into Ian's apartment that same evening. I paid the first month's rent and the deposit in cash, and sent a picture of the room to Thora and August with the comment: *wall-to-wall carpeting*. Ian showed me how the gas stove worked and where the mousetraps were. The next day was the first day of the spring semester.

I video-chatted with Thora and August often. I liked seeing their faces and hearing their voices, even though I didn't have much to tell them about my life. It was hardly different from my university life in Stockholm, aside from the fact that my classmates were younger and more liable to raise their hands when the professors asked questions.

I told them about the building I lived in, the stairs that creaked, the wardrobe where Ian grew the weed he sold to our neighbours, the carpets with mysterious stains, the slanted ceiling I invariably bumped my head on whenever I got out of bed. August laughed at that last bit, while Thora frowned and asked if I regretted going to Brighton. I didn't, but I said I missed Stockholm, assuming that she'd understand from this that I missed her and August. She immediately launched into a colourful description of the signs of spring all over the city. I took it as hyperbole; it was only February, after all.

I wondered if Thora and August were sleeping with each other while I was away. The thought of them together made me both aroused and upset. At lectures I found myself with throbbing temples, picturing the two of them entwined, naked, images that appeared in my field of vision without warning, and before which I was defenceless. I suspected that they talked about me, that they compared their respective observations of me. At some point I started to think that part of the reason I'd left Stockholm was to give Thora and August a chance to discover that they were better off without me. Whenever I convinced myself that they were sleeping together, I went to parties with my classmates and made out with girls who laughed at the way I pronounced my name, asking me to repeat the H and the U. By the time they began attempting to produce the Swedish H with their British mouths, I knew I could lean in and kiss them. By the next morning I'd usually changed my mind about Thora and August – convinced instead that they were definitely not sleeping together – and I'd go home suffering from nausea and a headache that I didn't even try to get rid of. I'd lie in bed watching the damp stains that had spread from the corners of the ceiling with a lump in my throat so large I thought I'd never be able to eat again. I wanted to cry, but I couldn't.

Other than that, I spent the days in lectures, and the afternoons and evenings sitting in cafés and pubs or walking along the seafront and onto the pier, swept along in a steady flow of tourists, with the gulls screaming overhead. The birds sometimes swooped down to steal a hot dog or a hamburger. When I reached the end of the walkway, I'd open my eyes wide against the wind until they burned and teared up from the sea foam splashing up the struts of the pier. Then I'd turn back home and spend the rest of the night smoking weed with Ian and his friends.

We made plans to meet up in London over the Easter holiday. Thora and August booked their flights and sent me screenshots of the tickets, as if they felt I needed proof that they truly were coming. The night before they arrived, I stuffed a backpack with some clothes, my laptop and a few books. It was the middle of the day when I arrived at St Pancras, and I spent a couple of hours strolling aimlessly. I didn't know the geography of London; I knew the names of a few places but I didn't know where they were situated or how far apart they were, and I didn't bother checking the map on my phone. Instead I set out in a random direction, thinking to myself that in the present moment I was as free as I'd always thought I wanted to be. I had everything I needed on my back, enough money in my bank account to sustain me for a while, and there was nobody waiting for me anywhere, nowhere I had to be. It was the middle of the lunch rush and the chains were chock-full of people in line, scrolling on their phones. Now and then they looked up from their screens to check if they were any closer to the till.

I toyed with the idea of going back to the station and buying a one-way ticket to France, riding the train through the tunnel beneath the Channel to Paris and continuing on east through Europe, perhaps to the verdant valleys of Slovenia or Albania. Then I thought of Thora and August, of the way their names seemed etched into me now, and I imagined those inscriptions burning like coals, splintering like glass in my flesh, if I went too far away from them. I realized that what I'd wanted to prove with my move to England was that I didn't need them. Needing them seemed at odds with freedom, such as I'd understood it. And with this realization freedom became elusive, a memory or dream that couldn't be put into words.

Samuel's home was a short walk from the underground station in Belsize Park. Like my building in Brighton, his house was made up of three narrow floors, but Samuel owned the entire place and there was no water damage, no mousetraps anywhere. Samuel told me he'd renovated the house a few years ago – torn up the carpeting and put in wooden floors in every room except the bathroom, where the matt tiles were heated and felt like sun-warmed rocks beneath my feet. The first thing I noticed upon entering the hall was the carved banister leading upstairs, and a flower arrangement on a half-moon-shaped table by one of the walls. It was as if Samuel had deliberately given August a scene to cut out and show to his friends in Stockholm, a picture to illustrate how different they were. Personally, I wasn't so sure that the brothers were as different as August liked to claim.

'If you were rich you'd have a table for flowers too, don't you think?' I said to August later.

We were sitting on a wooden bench in Samuel's garden, drinking coffee. There were small puddles on the ground but the grass was green and daffodils were coming out in the beds, tree crowns overhead.

August and Thora had arrived just after me, and Samuel had let us in right before he had to run off to a dinner meeting. He explained that August knew the place and could show Thora and me around. It made me imagine the house as a living being, temporarily placed in August's care. There were two guestrooms, and a pull-out couch in Samuel's office. Thora had immediately parked her wheeled bag in one of the guestrooms and announced that she was going to take a shower and nap for a bit before dinner. Then she'd closed the door. I had looked at that closed door for a moment before telling August I didn't mind sleeping on the couch, after which I went downstairs, leaving my stuff in the office. I figured this would make it easier for Thora and August to find each other in the night if they wanted to.

The office was bigger than my Brighton bedroom, with tall ceilings and walls lined with bookcases. A dark wooden desk stood by the window, but there was nothing on it; the room didn't give the impression of being in frequent use. The window looked out on the gardens, which weren't cemented but lush and free from brightly coloured plastic furniture. All the buildings on the block were red-brick with white window frames, and they looked as rooted and natural where they stood as the trees surrounding them.

'You're saying that what differentiates me from Samuel is that he has money and I don't?' August said.

I nodded and took a sip of my coffee.

'If I were rich,' August said slowly, 'I'd live somewhere warm where there were always flowers I could pick.'

I looked at August, who had tilted his head to face the sky. He smiled, eyes closed, as if he knew I was looking at him. The tiny bubbles in my coffee glittered in the sun. A moment later Thora came out, and sat down on the bench with a cup of coffee in her hand and her hair wrapped in a towel. Her white silk shirt felt soft against my arm. I wished I knew if I could touch her.

'Where are we going to eat tonight?' she asked, her face also tipped up to the sun, eyes closed.

I sat between them, my hands around my mug, thinking that in their company I regained my contours. I had stepped out of my anonymity, my role as an exotic-enough exchange student, and turned into a person I might like, despite it all.

*

August had made a list of museums he wanted to visit, and we started on it the following morning. I'd lain awake most of the night listening for footsteps outside the door to the office. The house remained silent. I hadn't bothered to draw the curtains, so I lay on the pull-out couch looking at the dark sky. No stars were visible, only the shapes of branches and clouds. I slept fitfully. When I woke up in the morning, Thora and August were eating breakfast in the kitchen. It was Friday and Samuel had already gone to work. August said he hadn't been able to take the Easter weekend off.

'To be honest I'm not sure he even tried,' he said. 'But he threatened to spend some time with us tomorrow.'

Thora looked up from her phone. 'Promised,' she said. 'Not threatened.'

'Freudian slip,' August said.

Thora raised her eyebrows and returned to her reading. Her fingers moved slowly across the screen while minuscule changes in her face gave clues to her thoughts on its contents. I was standing by the kitchen counter, waiting for my toast. A comfortable silence emanated from Thora and August, like a pet curled up under the table.

We took the Northern line down to Leicester Square and walked to the National Gallery, which was at the top of August's list. London, which had seemed so shapeless when I'd wandered around the day before, already felt more graspable now that I was walking next to Thora and August.

August had brought pens and a sketchpad and informed us that he wanted to walk around the museum by himself for a while. The idea of being left alone with Thora made me nervous, as if August's absence would upset the balance of our dynamic, but I didn't protest, I just asked Thora what part of the museum she wanted to see. She shrugged and I suppressed a sudden pang of irritation.

'Old or new?'

She smiled. 'Everything here is old, isn't it?'

I flipped through the guide they'd given us at the ticket counter, and she put her finger on an arbitrarily chosen page.

'Botticelli,' she said. 'Let's do the fifteenth century. It won't be as crowded there; everyone wants to see the Impressionists.'

I gave her the brochure and let her lead the way. She told me that she'd been to the museum once before, years ago, with Aron and Laura, and that she'd fallen asleep on a bench in front of a Caravaggio. When she woke up, the painting had taken up her entire field of vision, plastered itself over her eyes. The dramatic light and the grave gestures and facial expressions had made her cry.

'How old were you?' I asked.

'Not sure,' she said. 'Eight, nine years old maybe.'

I looked at the children passing through the rooms and tried to imagine Thora at that age.

'So you hadn't met August yet?'

'No,' she said and looked quizzically at me, as if it was a strange comment. I didn't know why I'd said it, maybe because I found it difficult to picture Thora and August without each other.

'Hey,' she said and touched my arm. 'You're so quiet.'

'Sorry,' I said. 'I didn't sleep well last night.'

'Are you not happy to see us?'

'No, I am,' I said. 'Of course I am.'

Thora gazed at me with her head cocked to the side. I looked into her eyes. The lump in my throat was so big that I wondered if she could see the outline of it, like a second Adam's apple. At one point in Brighton I'd gone to the bathroom and opened my mouth to see if it was actually visible, but I didn't find anything.

'What?' she asked.

I shook my head.

'Nothing.' I kissed her head. 'I'm glad you're here. I missed you both.'

She didn't move for a few seconds.

'So why don't you show it then,' she said and turned her back to me, but she smiled over her shoulder.

That night Thora came to me. She lay down next to me on the pull-out couch and I turned to her, rested my face against her chest. She caressed my hair. I started to cry. She didn't say anything. She kissed my forehead, moved her fingers through my hair. I tried to quell my cries but they just came out as violent tremors instead, until my ribs ached and I could hardly breathe from sobbing.

'I'm sorry,' I mumbled eventually.

'It's alright,' she said.

I wanted to tell her that she could leave, that she didn't have to stay. But I still couldn't quite speak.

Thora slept next to me all night. I woke up in the morning and looked at her. After a while she opened her eyes. We considered each other in silence. There was a question in her eyes I didn't know how to answer, so I leaned in and kissed her. She asked if I had a condom. I got out of bed and opened my backpack, and she undressed while I took one out. I lowered myself on top of her and, as she pulled me inside her, the images of her and August naked together came flooding back, like memories that weren't mine but were no less colourful, vivid. Real. I imagined August watching us through a keyhole or window, just like I'd watched Thora and August in my fantasies. I closed my eyes, and when I heard her gasp and moan and mumble my name it felt like I'd dissolved, I no longer knew where I started and ended. There were no boundaries left between me and them. I saw Thora wrap her legs around August; saw the sweat trickling down August's back, his muscles contracting as I watched myself kneel behind August, and I didn't know if it was Thora or August that I was pressing into. I felt August come inside me, August's hands on my hips, Thora's hands on my face, heat emanating from me and into me.

Afterwards I took a cold shower. I dried off with one of Samuel's soft cotton towels and put on jeans and a fresh t-shirt. Back in the office Thora was still naked in bed, one leg under the white cover and the other on top of it. One arm was on the pillow, over her head; the other arm rested on her tummy. She'd spread her fingers, nails painted red, across her belly, like the petals of a white flower. Her eyes were closed.

'Are you sleeping?' I asked.

My hair was wet, dripping onto my shoulders. Thora didn't stir. The hand on her belly rose and sank with her slow breaths.

'I love you,' I said.

She was as still as before, eyes closed. I shut the door carefully and went downstairs, where August and Samuel were eating breakfast. For a moment I saw myself as if from the outside. I thought of Thora sleeping on the pull-out couch in the home office, the discarded condom in the trash can, the words I'd just spoken. Maybe it was the sight of Samuel at the table, wearing suit trousers and a button-down shirt and with a watch on his wrist and a cloud of aftershave around him, that established a sense of normality, making it all seem distant already. It was a relief.

'Is Thora still asleep?' Samuel asked while I poured myself a coffee.

'I think so,' I said.

I sat down next to August and spread marmalade on a piece of toast.

'You've become as British as Samuel,' August said.

'Just for now,' I said. 'To fit in.'

When Thora joined us in the kitchen a while later, she'd put on make-up and a dress, cardigan and black tights. I noticed she'd removed the nail polish, and when she walked past me I caught a waft of acetone. She yawned and asked if there was coffee. August poured her a cup. She smiled at the three of us, as if there was a joke she was keeping to herself. When I looked into her eyes the smile took on a different tone, like a colour that deepened when it came into contact with a darker shade. I wondered if she'd only pretended to be asleep.

We took a long walk on Hampstead Heath that day. Thora, August and I raced about on the big hills, collapsing into walls of wind, while Samuel walked, dignified, behind us, supported by an umbrella he'd brought even though there wasn't a cloud in sight. We had lunch at a café near Kenwood House, and afterwards went to the gallery to look at the art in the old rooms. Through the windows we could see the surface of the ponds rippling in the wind.

We lingered in front of Vermeer's painting of a girl playing the guitar. Samuel explained that it had been stolen once in the seventies, and that the thieves had demanded food be distributed in Grenada or they would destroy the painting.

'But they never distributed the food,' Samuel said. 'They didn't take the threat seriously.'

'Why not?' Thora asked.

'Because people are less important than art,' August said tartly. 'Anything else would be inconceivable.'

Samuel frowned. 'I thought you were the artist here?'

'That doesn't mean I'm doing something meaningful,' August said, and took the umbrella from Samuel. He leaned on it and spun around.

'Life has no meaning,' Samuel said and walked past his brother.

The rooms seemed to straighten to attention when Samuel passed through. August looked at Thora and me, and put one hand on his hip while he knocked the umbrella against the old floor.

'Come on,' Thora said and took August and me by the arms.

Thora

On our last day in London I woke up before Hugo. For a long while I lay still on the pull-out couch, and watched pink clouds float past in the sky as the light in the room changed with the rising sun. I looked at the objects around me. The spines of the books, the sheets, the rug, the condoms, the water glass. Hugo's breathing was even and heavy, and I imagined hearing August breathing at the same slow pace through the wall. Hugo was sleeping on his belly, with his face turned away from me. I was between him and the wall and I had to climb over him to get out of bed. With my striped pyjamas on, I slipped my feet into a pair of slippers that Samuel had put out; they were too big for me, but the wooden floor was cold and draughty. Holding on to the door handle, I turned to look at Hugo.

'I love you too,' I said.

I waited for him to stir or open his eyes. I wasn't sure if it was disappointment I felt when he didn't. The spines of the books, the sheets, the rug, the condoms, the water glass. The silence. A sunray fluttered through Hugo's eyelashes, over his cheek. I went down to the kitchen and put on the coffee before measuring oats and water into a pot. The porridge slowly cooked as I stirred it with a wooden spatula. Outside the window, the sky was blue again and the spring flowers brightened the garden. I wondered if there would still be snow on the ground when we came back to Stockholm. For as long as I could remember I'd pictured the months of the year in the shape of a half-moon, with January at the base and December up top, and each new year meant a plunge through a dark vacuum to the base of the shape, where it started all over again. April was somewhere right before the rounding of the curve.

Samuel entered the kitchen already dressed in a fresh button-down and trousers, and I felt like a child in my pyjamas with the bowl of oats in front of me on the table. When I told him so he smiled and asked if Hugo and August were still sleeping. I nodded. He poured a cup of coffee and sat down across from me.

'How are you?' he asked.

'Good,' I said.

His silence seemed intended to make me keep talking.

'How are *you*?' I asked.

'Good,' he said.

I felt a strange tenderness towards Samuel – there was a sensitivity to him that was similar to August's, even if August didn't see it himself and would deny any resemblance if it were pointed out to him.

'You know that you don't have to take care of him, right?' Samuel said. 'When he's down.'

'Because it's not my responsibility?'

'Exactly,' Samuel said, emphatically. 'It's not your responsibility.'

'August takes care of me too,' I said. 'We take turns.'

'Yeah, and that's nice,' he said. 'But you should really focus on taking care of yourself. Put yourself first.'

'But you don't do that. You watch out for him.'

'That's different. He's my brother. I didn't choose him.'

I looked at the table, the cups, the bowl of oats, the spoon, my own freckled hands, the watch around Samuel's wrist. I decided to test out an idea that had rooted itself in my mind and seemed to have grown strong before I'd even realized I'd adopted it as truth.

'There's nothing wrong with needing other people,' I said.

Samuel gave a little smile. I couldn't tell if he agreed or if he just couldn't be bothered to object. When my phone lit up with a notification he got up to smoke outside. I stayed put, watching him through the window as I wondered if the opposite truth had taken root and grown strong in him a long time ago.

It still felt like winter in Stockholm; the sun didn't warm the skin the way it had in London. On Walpurgis Night, August and I went to see the bonfire in Rålambshovsparken, and then we walked over Västerbron to Södermalm. The city smelled of fire and smoke, and drunk teenagers were spread out all over the cliffs on Långholmen – a sight as old as the spring tradition itself.

We discussed Hugo's idea of spending the summer in Berlin. August was in favour; he liked the idea of trying out Berlin bohemia. He'd recently got a job at a small advertising firm and spent more time than ever talking about *being an artist*, as if he was grasping for something he feared would elude him now that his days were dedicated to developing graphic identities for corporate clients. Sometimes he messaged me quotes from his meetings with executives in the business of selling shoes, clothes, coffee, textiles, all of whom wanted August's help in finding their 'identity'.

I was more sceptical about Berlin, but I couldn't figure out why.

'We can't be there all summer,' I said. 'I want to spend some time in Stockholm too.'

'We can go for July. Stockholm is boring and empty then, all tourists.'

'But where would we stay?'

'We'll leave that to Hugo, he knows the town,' August said, and he looked expectantly at me, ready for yet another objection to tackle.

I didn't say anything, just looked out through the guard rails that had been mounted on the bridge to prevent people from jumping. The water, far below, was shiny, like silver-black asphalt; the sky above it swaths of pale pastels. August found my hand and I let him take it, his fingers warm and soft.

'What are you thinking about?' he asked.

'I don't know,' I replied truthfully. My thoughts had no more substance and weight than the smoke smudging the sunset.

We met up with Eliel and some of his friends at a crowded bar where I couldn't hear much of what anyone was saying. I didn't mind. I was sitting next to August and he put his arm around me. I looked at the faces of the others and smiled when they smiled, laughed when they laughed. When I came home later that night, my hair still smelled of the Walpurgis bonfires.

Hugo came back to Stockholm at the end of May, but I didn't see much of him during the daytime. He was working double shifts in order to afford the month in Berlin. I told him that August and I could cover his part of the rent, and he said he didn't want that, that it would make him uncomfortable.

'But I'd be happy to,' I said. 'And I know the same goes for August. He makes good money at that firm. He says he doesn't sell himself cheaply.'

I expected Hugo to laugh, but he didn't.

'Yeah, but—' Hugo stopped and frowned. 'I wouldn't feel happy if you paid for me.'

'Because I'm a girl and you're a guy?'

'What? No,' he said. 'Because . . . I don't know. It just feels wrong. Uncomfortable.'

After that I didn't bring it up again, and I didn't tell him I thought he was working too much. In the evenings he'd come home to me, his voice hoarse and his eyes tired as he imitated people he'd called over the course of his shift. He was good at doing accents and often made me and my cousins laugh.

He didn't say much about his semester in Brighton and I wondered if he'd slept with a lot of British girls, if he'd even fallen in love. He was quiet the way he had been in London. I wondered if he regretted crying in front of me. I could ask August anything, tell August anything I wanted without fear that he'd leave me, but with Hugo I wasn't so sure. I pressed up close to him at night and he held me, interlacing his fingers with mine as I listened to his breathing until I drifted off.

One evening I couldn't sleep. I tossed and turned until he grabbed my hand and asked me to be still.

'I can't sleep,' I said.

'You drink too much coffee,' he said.

'I like drinking coffee after dinner.'

I lay still for a few seconds and his hold on my arm loosened. I turned over again, kicking off the covers.

'Thora,' he said. 'I have to get up early.'

'Sorry.'

I tried not to move, but it was like forcing yourself to stop coughing. Hugo looked at me.

'Count sheep,' he said.

'It doesn't work.'

He rubbed his eyes. 'So recite a poem then. Any poem.'

'To you?'

He nodded and closed his eyes. He'd pulled the covers all the way up past his chin, so that all I could see was his nose, eyebrows and forehead. I turned to face him and slid my hands under my pillow. I saw his closed eyes crease into a smile, and I moved so close that I could feel the warmth of his breath on my cheek and lips. I leaned even closer and mumbled into his ear the only lines of poetry I could recall right then. The words felt like more than sounds – fragile, living things wrapped in the warm humidity of my breath, which lingered in the silence after I'd finished. I pulled away a few inches. His eyes were open, he was looking directly at me, and that look sent me lurching as if the room had suddenly tilted, a sucking feeling in my gut. The sensation was so powerful I thought I'd never experience anything like it again, that I'd never again touch those flapping wings of his being, or whatever the thing was that existed inside of him and made him the person he was – that thing I could feel moving inside of me too.

Hugo

The nights were so bright that the gossamer blue that lowered itself over the land as the day finally faded seemed unnatural, like it came streaming in through a crack to another world. August and his friends arranged a Midsummer party with an all-black dress code. I had worked late the day before, so I slept in, and when I woke there were several messages from Thora and August on my phone.

Thora and her parents were at a Midsummer lunch at Karla's, and Thora was asking me to bring her a black dress. In a string of messages, she described in which closet in her old room I'd be able to find it. August had texted to ask how much booze I'd bought, if I had time to stop at the liquor store to get more and, in the third message, he said not to mind since apparently the liquor stores were all closed for the holiday. His fourth message asked what bus Thora and I were going to take to the party. I slid my finger over the text boxes while still in bed, and then went to take a shower before responding. I got dressed and ate a bowl of cereal standing in the kitchen with the radio on. Before leaving I put Thora's dress in my backpack. Then I started walking towards Humlegården. I texted Thora as I approached the street where Karla lived. She asked if I wanted to come up for a second, and before I'd even replied she sent me the door code, like a dare. I didn't want to see Thora's relatives but I couldn't think of an excuse not to go.

I took my shoes off in the hall only to discover that everyone else

239

had kept theirs on. Shiny brogues, heels. I considered retrieving my sneakers from the hall, but then Harriet spotted me and took my arm while asking if I wanted something to eat, and I let myself be ferried into the kitchen in my socks. Thora was nowhere to be seen. Iris waved at me; Aron smiled; Laura nodded; the rest of Thora's relatives blended into one indistinct mass, much as they had the first time I encountered them at Aron and Laura's that summer when the Stiller scandal broke. It had been a long while since I had thought of that book, but when I saw Thora's family gathered again, all a bit tipsy, I remembered the air of ridiculousness that had characterized the fuss of those summer weeks. Nothing could get to them – and they knew it. I hadn't discussed the book with Thora or asked August if he'd read it; I couldn't think of anything to say that wouldn't sound like an accusation masquerading as something else, an accusation I felt might just as well apply to me. Everything was a pose, and what did not begin as a pose would inevitably end as one – a perverted result of being aware of the immensity of the world's injustice and hypocrisy. It was something I thought a lot about, but I never mentioned these ideas to anyone since even I recoiled from them. There was no setting where I could imagine them making sense: not at the university, not at work, not among friends.

Serving plates with leftovers from lunch were all over the counters in Karla's kitchen. The coffee maker stood in a corner, blue-white cups and saucers stacked nearby. The hum of voices rose and sank at even intervals from the living room, and everywhere I turned there seemed to be a different bouquet in a large vase. Harriet handed me a clean plate from the cupboard. I wasn't particularly hungry, but I served myself two eggs with caviar, a piece of smoked salmon, and two slices of bread with cheese. Harriet was telling me about her final exam, sighing loudly about how much more school she still needed to do.

'I have no idea what I'm going to do after I graduate,' I said and tried to cut a piece of the smoked salmon with my fork. 'So I'd love to switch with you.'

'You could become a civil servant? Work at some government agency?'

'Yeah, maybe,' I said.

'Thora is the careerist in your relationship though, right,' Harriet said.

'I don't know,' I said, and realized we'd never discussed our post-university plans. 'Is she?'

'The expectation in our family isn't exactly for anyone to end up as a case manager at some regional government office,' she said drily.

'Ah, of course,' I said. 'It's hard being a Stiller.'

Harriet peered at me over the frames of her glasses.

'You're just like August,' she said. 'It's funny that Thora is drawn to you both. Maybe she likes the challenge.'

'What's August like?'

Harriet smiled as if it was a rhetorical question, but I really did wonder how he appeared to everyone else.

Thora entered the kitchen with Karla just when I noticed there was a small hole in my sock, right at the big toe. Karla nodded at me and put her hand on Harriet's arm without saying a word. I tried to hide the hole behind my other foot. Thora had on a pair of black sandals and she brightened when she saw me, but didn't come closer until Karla had poured herself a cup of coffee and passed through the double doors into the living room.

'We were just discussing whether you're a careerist or not,' Harriet said.

Thora tore off a piece of the bread on my plate and rested her head on my shoulder. 'Isn't everyone in our family?'

'Bella thinks that we're a group of overachieving capitalists who contribute to war and climate change.'

Thora straightened her back and brushed the flour from her hands.

'Bella is making a good point,' she said.

'Hugo, what do you think?' Harriet asked.

'Sounds like an accurate description.'

Thora gave me a shove.

'But I don't know what it says about me,' I said. 'That I spend my time with people like you.'

'It means you're worse than us,' Thora said. 'Because for you it's a choice. We have merely been born into it.'

She looked at the floor, at my feet and then back at my face. I had the thought that we wouldn't talk this way if it was just the two of us.

Thora went to change into the dress I'd brought, and while I was waiting for her in a corner of the living room with my plate and my glass of champagne, Laura joined me. I could tell she was drunk from the way she wished me happy Midsummer – her voice, dripping with sarcasm, indicated that she didn't want to be there, in her mother's turn-of-the-century apartment full of flowers, with ceiling medallions and relatives all dressed in white. I tried to inject my reply with the same kind of sarcasm. She gave me a little smile and scanned my outfit, raising her eyebrows.

'Dress code,' I explained. 'For August's party.'

'Right,' she said. 'Thora did mention something about that.'

She tapped her fingers on her champagne flute. I was so used to seeing her in motion, on her way out or deep in conversation with someone, that it was strange to have her standing next to me, quiet and observant, as if the people in the room were as foreign to her as they were to me.

'I hope you are happy living with us,' she said.

'Yes,' I said and checked that there wasn't food in the corner of my mouth. 'I am.'

The amused sparkle in Laura's eye was so reminiscent of Thora's way of looking at me that I blushed.

'Do you know what it is about August that Thora likes so much?' she said.

'No?'

She swept her gaze over the room as if to encourage me to look for the answer somewhere beyond us, but I stayed focused on her.

'His capacity for wonder.'

I frowned.

'Like children,' she continued, coolly. 'They're like children.'

I wanted to ask what she meant by that, but right then Thora came to get me, now in her new outfit. She twirled and curtseyed in front of Laura and me. I almost pointed out their likeness, but stopped myself since I had a sense that Thora wouldn't have appreciated the comparison.

While Thora took leave of her relatives, I put on my shoes in the hall, and then we walked along the water to the bus station at Slussen. Thora read me the route to the party several times, like she wanted us to memorize it. Every café, restaurant and shop we passed was closed. The streets were devoid of people, except for a few tourists who seemed confused by the quiet. An American couple came up to us and asked where everyone was. The sunlight was white and sharp.

It took two hours to get to the party. The bus dropped us off at the turn-off to a narrow country road. Music was booming from the house August and his friends had rented. Thora looked annoyed, as if it was my fault she'd been lured this far from the city. I laughed at her. We'd been drinking on the bus and I was vaguely tipsy and carsick, the ground undulating softly. August came to greet us with a flower wreath on his head.

'There's a lake too,' he said, indicating the forest with his hand.

Smaller and larger groups of people were spread out in the garden, their black clothes contrasting with the greenery. Fairy lights hung from the trees and the breeze pulled smoke over the lawn from the fire pit, where hot dogs and vegetables were being grilled.

People asked me about Brighton. I'd got that question so many times since returning to Stockholm that I now had a canned, concise statement that summarized my stay. Whenever Thora or August were listening I tried to think of something new to say, because repeating the same things they'd already heard made me feel like my dad, who was forever recycling jokes and anecdotes, not worried in the least that they were getting worn out.

Late that night, Thora, August and I headed down to the lake. We were drunk and high and laughing at nothing. Thora got on her knees on the dock and tested the water with her hand. It wasn't that cold, she said, and stood up, slipped out of her sandals, sweater and dress, until she was naked except for her bra and panties, arms hanging down by her sides.

'Come on,' she said and dived in. Soft curve, feet stretched out.

August looked at me with a glimmer in his eye. We followed suit. Arms and legs stretched out on the surface, we floated beneath the bright night sky. Afterwards we dried off, sharing the towel Thora had brought from the house. We walked back up the jetty to the flat rocks at the edge of the lake, where August wanted to lie down – he said everything was spinning. The three of us got onto our backs, Thora in the middle. She mentioned ticks and August said he was vaccinated. I was silent. I felt as if we were floating at the level of the light in the sky. The wind rustled the treetops. If I strained, I could just make out the music from the house. Eyes closed, I felt Thora's hand on the inside of my thigh, but when I opened my eyes she was facing August, and August was supporting himself on his elbow, kissing her. A current of electricity jolted through me. Thora turned around, sought my gaze. I kissed her and she smiled and caressed my thigh. Then August leaned over Thora and pressed his lips onto mine. Thora giggled when he reached down and pulled her up to his chest without breaking our kiss. Our breathing was louder than anything else, leaves got in our hair, we laughed when someone's arm or leg fell asleep and had to be straightened to activate the circulation. The tree trunks and the ground were darker than the sky and soon everything was warm, wet; ants scuttled over our arms, mosquito swarms hung in the air. Afterwards we got dressed in silence, smiling while brushing twigs and pine needles from each other's clothes and hair. It was a short walk back to the house and the fairy lights in the trees, and I glanced back at the grove, which seemed darker from afar than close up, and then I looked straight ahead. I already felt strangely disconnected from the person who'd lain with Thora and August on the ground, though their taste was still in my mouth.

We stopped at the edge of the garden when the others, who were still dancing on the lawn, came into view. I saw Eliel jump up and down in the centre of the group, a flower crown hanging off the side of his head. A lot of people were singing along to the music. The sun was coming up behind the roof and the tables were full of empty beer bottles and cans that rolled off whenever a gust of wind blew in from the lake.

'Our Midsummer night's dream,' August said, with an edge to his voice. He smiled at Thora and me over his shoulder as he went to join Eliel and the others.

Thora and I locked eyes.

'Guessing I look terrible?' Thora said.

'No,' I said and moved a few strands of hair from her face. 'A bit tousled maybe.'

She smiled. Her eyes were shiny, like she was running a temperature.

'You too,' she said.

'Yeah, I know,' I said. 'I feel it too.'

She stood on her toes and kissed my cheek, and I held her tight.

We took the first bus back to the city in the morning, the seats filled with revellers. The driver laughed when he saw us lined up on the side of the road, all dressed in black with wilting wreaths. Many closed the curtains over their window seats and fell asleep; others looked out at the view, yawning as they played with the thin white wires slithering up to their ears. I scratched at a mosquito bite on my arm. Thora fell asleep with her head on my shoulder. I woke her once we arrived back in Stockholm.

Thora

I couldn't help but compare Hugo's mom with Laura. I looked at Rakel and thought that the clothes Rakel wore were not clothes Laura would wear; the way Rakel expressed herself was not the way Laura would express herself; and the books that filled Rakel's apartment were not books Laura would choose to read. I also kept looking for ways in which Hugo resembled Rakel. It made me pause when I noticed how much they seemed to enjoy each other's company – this was a part of Hugo I hadn't known before, and I wondered if he'd consciously kept it from me. Rakel and Hugo joked with each other, talked fast and made lots of references to people and things I had never heard of. Hugo looked at his mother with a tenderness modified by a measure of indulgence – as if he didn't dare to look at his mother with tenderness only – and I couldn't help but think that it was exactly how I wanted him to look at me.

Lovingly.

A silly thought. I pushed it away.

The sun had been setting over the town and the cathedral when our train stopped at the station in Lund. The cobblestone streets were shiny after a flash storm and the sky was lit in pink and blue. The wheels of our suitcases clattered on the pavement. Rakel's building was split into four apartments that shared a backyard, and Hugo explained that everyone who lived there was an academic.

'Low-income academics,' he added after a short pause, apparently having realized that this was important.

'Are there wealthy academics?' I asked.

The pavement was so narrow that he had to walk a few steps ahead of me.

'Laura,' he said.

I looked at his neck without saying anything. August would have thought of something funny to say if he'd been there, but he'd stayed behind in Stockholm, coming to meet us in Berlin as soon as his vacation started. I thought of Copenhagen, just a short train ride away across the Sound, of hotel rooms with white sheets, cafés and bars full of nameless men, the freedom of superficial conversation where nothing warranted interpreting, twisting, turning.

I liked Rakel instantly, which was a relief. I wanted to like her, I'd set myself on liking her, so I was happy when I saw I wouldn't have to make an effort. When we arrived at her house she hugged us both, then tasked Hugo with keeping an eye on the food simmering on the stove while she gave me a tour and explained that I could choose between sleeping on the couch or the cot. To me the house looked more like student housing than a professor's home, an observation I blurted out without thinking. Rakel laughed and said she'd take it as a compliment. There were just three rooms: a small bedroom, a bathroom and a long, narrow space – the largest room – which functioned as kitchen, living room and office in one. Books were piled on the floor, sharing space with posters in frames leaning against the walls and green plants in large pots on the floor and on tables. This room also had a set of stairs out to the garden, where lush trees grew with laundry lines strung between the branches.

'Not as big as Aron and Laura's home,' Hugo said.

'In Hugo's mind I think that everyone lives in enormous apartments or mansions,' I told Rakel.

'I'd imagine that has more to do with his own feelings of insecurity than with you,' Rakel said in a soft voice.

I gave a brief laugh, not sure if Hugo had heard his mother's words.

'He has it in common with his father,' Rakel said.

'What do I have in common with my father?' Hugo asked, loudly.

Rakel waved her hand dismissively.

During dinner, I poked Hugo with my foot under the table; he smiled at me while the light from the candles flickered over his face. We ate and drank red wine and laughed a lot, and my cheeks were still blooming red by the time I fell asleep on the couch, which had been made with soft, washed-out cotton sheets.

We slept two nights at Rakel's. We spent the day walking around Lund, seeing the parks and the used bookstores and the university campus. It was relaxing to let Hugo take the lead; in Stockholm I was always the one in charge. It was warm and sunny, and we talked loosely about going for a swim somewhere but we never got to it. We bought soft-serve ice creams with sprinkles and ate them sitting on a bench while cyclists swished past. I admired the campus, feeling nostalgic for a university experience I would never know, full of climbing ivy, student clubs, and book piles transported on bikes. When I shared this with Hugo he looked at me with scepticism, telling me I'd be over that life after one month.

The second evening, Rakel asked if we were a couple. Her voice was playful, as if she was making a joke she wouldn't need to finish to laugh at. Neither Hugo nor I laughed. We were cooking, garlic frizzling in the frying pan and water boiling in the pot.

'No,' I said. 'We're friends.'

Rakel glanced at Hugo.

'It's complicated,' he said.

'Maybe you're making it complicated,' Rakel said. 'It seems like your generation tries to make everything as complicated as you can.'

'It's not complicated,' I said.

Rakel patted my shoulder before she reached for a spice jar. I wondered what Hugo's face would show me if I turned to him, but

I focused my attention on the cutting board and the knife and the onion which I was chopping into small, even bits. My eyes were burning.

'I didn't know we were friends,' Hugo said later that night, him on the cot and me on the couch.

'What did you think we were?' I asked.

'More than that.'

'I figured you wouldn't want to introduce me to your mom as a friend you sleep with.'

For a second I wondered if I'd gone too far, but he just laughed quietly. I turned onto my side. Hugo's legs were too long for the cot and his ankles hung over the floor. He hadn't taken his socks off. The laundry lines in the garden were hung with white clothes that glowed in the summer darkness, and I could see them flutter in the wind from where I lay.

'I've always assumed you don't want a girlfriend,' I said.

'Why?'

'Am I wrong?' I said.

He didn't respond.

'My mom likes you,' he said instead.

I smiled though he couldn't see it. The sheets smelled of floral detergent.

'I knew she'd like you,' he continued.

I looked at the ceiling. 'What if your mom is right. Maybe we are making things more complicated than they need to be.'

'You mean our generation?'

I laughed, hands on my belly. I felt full and sleepy.

'Or maybe we're just complicated people,' I mumbled.

'You and I?'

'Yes,' I said. 'Or just stupid.'

'Probably,' he said.

Early in the afternoon the next day, we took the train to Copenhagen. We got food and something to drink from a store near the central station. Walking down the aisles, picking up fruit and chocolate and triangular sandwiches in plastic packaging, Hugo told me that his dad lived in Copenhagen with his new wife.

'I don't know if I've mentioned that before,' he said.

I broke off four bananas from a larger bunch and set them in the basket.

'I think you've mentioned it at some point,' I said. 'Don't you want to see him now that we're here?'

'No,' he said. 'Our train is leaving soon anyway.'

'Okay,' I said slowly, expecting him to say something more, but he just shrugged. 'Maybe on the way home then.'

'Sure, maybe,' he said without enthusiasm, and I understood that we wouldn't.

It took just over seven hours to get to Berlin. We switched trains in Hamburg, where we got coffee in large takeaway cups, burning our tongues on it. I photographed the landscape outside the train window and sent the pictures to August. Each time, he answered within a few minutes with pictures of the open office where he worked, a desert of white walls and whiteboards and uncomfortable-looking furniture in bright colours. The train compartment was small and stuffy. The fruit peels in the trash bags that hung underneath the windows shrivelled as the hours passed. I retreated into myself, as if sleeping with my eyes open. When Hugo said something it felt like I was waking up from a deep, wordless coma, and responding required me to first find my footing in language again.

We arrived late at night. Berlin was warm and loud and crowded. Hugo took my hand and led me through the masses of people, down into the underground where tourists in shorts and caps surrounded large maps of the subway system.

The apartment Hugo had found us had a railroad layout. We opened the windows to air out the weed smell and then we went to the convenience store on the corner to get wine, chips and cheap cheeses, which we ate on the balcony while watching a TV show on

Hugo's computer. I felt like a part of me had stayed behind in the stuffy train compartment, still gazing out over the flat European landscape with its pale fields and old cities.

Our first days in Berlin were tranquil. We slept a lot, took walks, lay on blankets in the park, and made dinners that took a long time to prepare and a short time to eat. We drank beer at sidewalk cafés, where Hugo tried to teach me German, frequently to the delight of the people at the tables next to us since my pronunciation was so bad that even Hugo couldn't keep from laughing. I exaggerated the French influence and enjoyed seeing the corners of Hugo's mouth twitch.

Then we began hanging out with Hugo's Berlin friends, and the quietude evaporated as the days grew hotter. We bought fans and dunked our sheets in cold water before going to bed, and even so I woke up several nights in a row from the sensation of the heat pressing down on me, and had to retreat to the bathroom to rinse my wrists in the stream of rust-brown water. I missed Stockholm, but I didn't tell Hugo.

At a bar one night I ended up next to one of Hugo's closest friends from his Berlin days; at least, that was how he introduced her. Her name was Bianca and I could tell from the looks of mutual understanding that passed between them, and from the way she touched Hugo, that they'd had something together when he lived in the city. It made me curious despite myself, and I noticed that she was just as curious about me. She sat down close to me, leaned her elbow on the table and gave me her full attention. She was wearing a striped t-shirt under an apron dress and she kept touching the straps to stop them from sliding down over her shoulders. She was tanned and told me she'd spent a few weeks with her family by Lake Constance. She smiled at me and I smiled back.

'We miss Hugo here,' she said. 'I really thought he was one of the long-timers. But I guess all expats go home sooner or later.'

'Hmm,' I said.

'He's so funny, right?'

'Right.'

Bianca rested her chin on her hand. 'Always joking. And very self-confident. He listens to what you say.'

I sat on my hands and looked down at my feet. My cheeks were warm. I was still smiling.

'But he doesn't tell you what's actually on his mind,' Bianca continued, pensively. 'You have to guess. Sometimes it's like he's elsewhere, right? Like he doesn't let you in.'

Bianca caught Hugo's eye over the table and then gave a short laugh, as if he'd conveyed a joke. I looked past Hugo, over his shoulder, out towards the street and the blinking neon signs in the shop windows on the other side of the road. I didn't like having to wonder if I truly knew Hugo, or rather if the version of Hugo I knew was the truest one.

With the sense of stepping into the ring for a wrestling match, I turned to Bianca again and asked: 'Were you in love with him?'

Bianca looked at me, seemingly taking my measure for a few seconds before she responded.

'I don't know. Yes. I guess I was, at least for a while,' she said with a forthrightness that made me feel strangely moved. 'Before I understood that he's the kind of person you're better off loving from afar.'

Bianca smiled and I blushed. It felt like admitting defeat.

As we walked back to the apartment later that night, Hugo asked what Bianca and I had talked about.

'You, of course,' I said without elaborating.

It annoyed him, but I wasn't withholding out of spite. I was afraid of judging him too harshly if I said anything.

I wasn't sure I liked the Berlin version of Hugo. He was a different person around his friends in this city. I'd often heard him talking about wanting to fit in but I'd never experienced him making an effort to do so before. In Berlin the adjustments he made to his personality were so glaring that the more he laughed and smiled, the less I laughed and smiled. I wondered if it meant I was an ungenerous person – that I'd have preferred him weeping and depressed to this eager display of enthusiasm. He hardly drank, but he took drugs when we were out with his friends and I hated his cloudy eyes when he was high. He got excited over nothing and gesticulated wildly while calling everything *cinematic*. I crossed my arms, he pulled me close, I wriggled out of his embrace and tried to find someone to talk to who wasn't out of their mind.

Several times I left a bar or a club without telling Hugo. On those nights I'd walk around alone, sticking to large, well-lit and populated streets. I thought of calling August but I knew I'd start crying if I talked to him, so I didn't. I looked at the men I passed on these walks – tall men, short men, skinny men, fat men – but I didn't look into their eyes. As soon as Hugo realized I was gone, my phone screen would light up incessantly until I switched to airplane mode so I could listen to music without interruption. When we met back in the apartment he'd be upset, but he seemed incapable of starting a fight and I remained stubbornly mute, and would turn to do the dishes or change the sheets. We had sex instead of talking and it made me feel empty inside, neither happy nor unhappy. In bed one night Hugo told me he loved me, and it made me cry though I couldn't explain why – not to him and not to myself.

In the daytime, when it was just the two of us, he was different. He sought my eyes more often, as if he wanted to get a read on me, get a sense of my mood, understand me – in order to grant my wishes? Or defy them?

'I'm sorry,' he said, out of the blue, on one of these days.

'For what?' I said.

And when he didn't answer and I finally looked at him, there was something pleading in his eyes that I didn't know how to protect myself from.

'I don't know that I like Berlin,' I said and smiled.

He didn't return the smile.

'Sometimes it feels like I'm trying to make you stop liking me,' he said.

'Why?' I asked.

The mascara had clumped on my eyelashes. I regretted having gone through the trouble of putting on make-up. It was late afternoon and the air was quivering over the tram tracks, the café full of people having conversations in German, Arabic, English. My legs were crossed and I could feel a drop of sweat trickle from the back of my knee down my calf. My head hurt like I was at the bottom of a lake and would need to push up through a great mass of water to breathe fresh air again.

'Because it feels like I'm misleading you,' he said in a voice so clear it didn't match the words.

I looked at him and wondered if self-awareness was worth anything at all, if all it yielded was carefully worded observations of your own behaviour.

'You're not misleading me,' I said. 'You're not smart enough to mislead me.'

Hugo looked at me, silent for a few seconds. Then he laughed. I did too, strained at first, but soon I was bubbling with laughter and I realized how much I'd missed it. I wished so badly to hold on to the ease of that moment, the lightness I had imagined for our summer days, that I ignored the implications of what he'd said. Instead I swallowed down two painkillers with a sip of iced coffee, and then we walked down Görlitzer Straße hand in hand.

Hugo

By the time August joined us in Berlin, Thora and I had been there for just over two weeks. Thora told August that it felt like several months – *like forever* – and I wished there'd have been laughter in her voice when she said it.

In bed, one of our first mornings in Berlin, she got on top of me, palms on my chest, and said: 'I like you like this.'

'Because you're in control?' I said. She must have felt how hard my heart was beating.

'No,' she said with a frown. 'Because I feel close to you.'

I didn't say anything. I spent so much time craving her reassurance, and yet in the moments when she offered herself to me, I had the urge to shake my head and reject it.

When August asked how things had been, I told him that they had been good. I felt this to be true. It was difficult for me to imagine a happiness that wasn't muddy. Pure joy always seemed too short and flighty to stick. I *was* happy with Thora. The weeks in the Kreuzberg apartment had made me toy with the thought of what living with her would be like. I enjoyed waking up to the scent of fresh coffee in the kitchen, finding her at the table, deep in an article or book with her feet pulled up on the chair. I liked going to the grocery store with her, then unpacking the bags and cooking something together. I liked watching her remove her make-up at night, swipe cotton pads over her face, rinse, moisturize, brush her teeth, brush her hair and put it up. But now and then something happened between us, seemingly insignificant arguments that would leave me with the vertigo of having missed a step on my way down a precipitous set of stairs.

Introducing Thora and August to my friends in Berlin was like witnessing a slow collision between two worlds, two different kinds of life, where I myself was the sole common denominator. I felt obligated to make sure everyone was having a good time, and as a result I was constantly on edge, nodding, humming along. Thora said she hadn't known I had so many female friends in Berlin, and I couldn't tell if it bothered her or if it was just an observation made in passing. Some of them were girls I'd slept with – and though I didn't tell Thora, I got the sense that she made the connection on her own since she made such an effort to be nice to them, even when I heard them say things she'd normally roll her eyes at. Liese would loudly discuss the differences between being drunk and being high, or Madison, in her broad-vowelled American English, would refer to Europe as a single country or complain about the lack of air conditioning, and Thora would keep her indulgent smile. She rarely looked me in the eye when we hung out with my friends, and I tried to avoid thinking too much about whether the collision between my two lives felt louder and more violent to her or to me.

A few days after August's arrival, Eliel joined us with two friends in tow, Jens and Natalie. They had bought last-minute tickets but couldn't find a hostel with vacancies, so they spent three nights on blow-up mattresses in the Kreuzberg apartment. Then they were getting on the train again, headed to Budapest and Prague. Thora was not pleased at their sudden appearance and accused August of being too nice. I heard them arguing in one of the bedrooms while Eliel, Jens and Natalie were lined up on their bellies on the floor in the living room, watching a TV show, apparently unaware of the drama. I too felt their presence as an intrusion, but I had no desire to

yell at August, who was the mediator between the two groups. I'd
seen him look at Eliel with irritation several times, glances Eliel
apparently pretended not to notice. I remained in the kitchen, doing
the dishes and trying to ignore the feeling that somehow I was the
reason for Thora and August's quarrel, even though I had nothing
to do with Eliel's friends. The sound of their voices through the
closed door reminded me of fights between my parents when I was a
child.

Thora left the bedroom, immediately put her shoes on and then
slammed the door as she left the apartment. August came into the
kitchen a minute later, grimacing.

'I should have given her a heads-up,' he said and filled the kettle.
'She doesn't like having other people sprung on her. And she's right
that I'm not good at saying no.'

'She'll live,' I said.

August got a teabag and dropped it into a mug, twisting the string
around his finger until it turned white, at which point he let go and
watched the blood flush back into the tip. Steam from the kettle rose
towards the ceiling.

August smiled. 'I'm glad she has you.'

I put a plate in the dish rack. I still wondered what Thora and
August said about me when it was just the two of them. I felt his eyes
on me, and when there were no more dishes to rinse, I said: 'I think
she'd be doing fine without me too.'

'It's been empty without you guys in Stockholm. Eliel was upset
because I just walked around thinking of you all the time.'

The kettle clicked. August poured the water and a few drops of
milk into his mug. The milk swirled around until the tea settled into
a smooth, steaming brown surface.

'He seems jealous,' I said tentatively.

'Yes,' August said. 'He is. You'd think that someone with that
many tattoos would be less conventional.'

Thora returned an hour later with two bottles of red wine which she opened and placed on the living room table as if to signal a peace treaty. She kissed August's cheek and then sat down on the floor, leaning against my legs. I stroked her hair as Eliel glanced restlessly between her and August.

On their third and final night, we all went to a bar in Neukölln together at August's suggestion. Our group took up the entirety of a long table, near a large fan that whirred in a corner and made the posters on the wall flutter. Over several rounds of beer we discussed topics like: why all architects seemed to work in the same style; why public service media only offered temp jobs; why Swedish newspapers reported on US politics with such interest and detail.

'I mean, it doesn't really affect us that much,' Natalie said, 'if the US has a Democrat or a Republican president.'

'Maybe it affects us in ways we don't even know,' Eliel said.

Thora sighed loudly but didn't say anything. Despite myself I admired her ability to express her boredom so openly. Sometimes I made such an effort to appear interested in things I didn't actually care about that I almost fooled myself. August was more oblique: he'd often be quiet until he started nodding in affirmation, a reaction that spurred the speaker's own enthusiasm. I wasn't sure if he understood how much he shaped the conversation with these subtle signs of agreement. He never had to raise his voice to be heard. I envied the effect he had on his surroundings, the way he made others feel relaxed, but I also found it hard to reconcile this easeful, jovial character with the other, more shadow-like side of him – the depression and self-doubt which I knew existed but had only caught glimpses of. My inability to see the whole of August increasingly felt like a betrayal.

After some time, Jens turned the conversation to what we were all studying. Thora was the last to speak, her turn coming when August and Eliel were out buying cigarettes from a convenience store down the street. I got the sense that Jens had been hoping for a moment to question Thora, and I wanted to put my arm around her, but we were on opposite sides of the table and in any case I wasn't sure it was a gesture she would appreciate.

'Law? What kind of law?' Jens said.

'I'm not sure yet,' Thora said. 'International law maybe. Human rights.'

Jens raised his eyebrows. 'Human rights?' he repeated, smirking. 'Thora Stiller?'

'Yes.'

'As in the Stiller conglomerate?'

Thora looked directly at Jens.

'Yes,' she said.

'Kind of ironic,' he said and leaned back. 'A Stiller in human rights.'

'Thora has nothing to do with the Stiller conglomerate,' I said.

'I'm assuming that she – or the two of you – are living in central Stockholm in an apartment paid for with Stiller money. And Thora, I'm guessing you have a trust fund you can dip into whenever you need.' Jens paused for a moment and spun his beer glass on the table. 'But I guess you could defend human rights in countries where Sweden isn't doing arms trades. A compromise.'

Natalie typed something on her phone. I tried to catch Thora's eye but she just looked at Jens, unruffled. The black wings of her eyeliner were still sharp but her lipstick had worn off, leaving red marks on her beer glass. Her thin hoop earrings looked like the slightest touch could break them.

Natalie pushed her phone away, screen down. 'Honestly,' she said and leaned her face into her hand, 'what does it even mean to be a good person these days? Everyone's a hypocrite. For example, we *flew* here.'

'I'm just curious,' Jens said.

'I've never said I'm a good person,' Thora said.

'Why would Thora have more responsibility than anybody else?' I said.

265

Thora looked at me and shook her head, as if she wanted to disperse my words. My face felt warm. I bit down hard but didn't say anything else.

Jens smirked again.

When August and Eliel came back, August asked what we were talking about. Natalie had returned to her phone. The fan was swivelling back and forth and I felt the wind at my neck, but I was still sweating.

'Future dreams,' Jens said.

Thora and I walked home together while the others took a taxi to a club. Trees stood in dark rows along pavements littered with cigarette butts and empty beer bottles. Long lines snaked from the food trucks and the smell of warm asphalt and cooking oil hung in the air. I looked at my sneakers. Cigarette ash had smudged into grey lines on the fabric. Thora's feet looked naked in their sandals against the dirty pavement. Her eyes slipped over the people waiting outside the dimly lit venues. Her silence felt loud, demonstrative, and I braced myself for her anger.

'Don't mind that stuff,' I said. 'What Jens said.'

'Why not?' she said, her face half turned away from me. 'He's right, after all. He's even right about the apartment.'

'He only brought it up to feel morally superior.'

'I know. But that doesn't mean he's wrong.'

'Are you going to let him tell you what you should do with your life?'

'It *is* hypocrisy,' she said. 'And the worst thing is that it would suit them perfectly. They'd love to have a human rights lawyer in the family.'

The light from the neon signs reflected in her eyes. She smiled at me but the smile chafed against the hardness of her gaze.

'You know, I could join them on their travels,' she continued. 'Come up with arguments for why their business actually promotes human rights. And sit next to some royalty on the plane, drink champagne to celebrate the completion of a deal with a *non-democracy*—'

'You're exaggerating,' I said, and took her hand to try to make her slow down. She snatched her hand back and adjusted her shoulder bag as if she thought I was about to rip it from her.

'Let me be,' she said.

I reduced my pace. 'I honestly didn't know that you cared about where your family's money comes from. You've never brought it up before.'

'What am I supposed to say? That I think it's bad? That I'm ashamed but there's nothing I can do?'

'I don't know,' I said. 'What do you want me to say?'

'You don't have to say anything.'

As we entered the apartment, Thora tugged impatiently at the straps of her shoes. 'You always think everything is about you.'

'Okay.'

'I don't mean it in a bad way,' she said. 'But you always assume that something is wrong between us just because I'm quiet.'

'Maybe that's because you're annoyed with me so often.'

She looked up and I was struck by the force in her gaze.

'I can't be made responsible for your insecurity. You don't like the fact that I don't need you,' she said with a new sharpness. 'You want me to be like your girlfriends here. Pleasant, high. *Uncomplicated.*'

I tried to look calm. It took me a few seconds to realize that I was holding my breath. I exhaled deeply and then opened my palms, empty before her. I pictured her tossing our relationship away like it meant nothing.

'I've never believed that you needed me,' I said, and turned my back to her.

We woke up to find the air mattresses gone from the living room and a note on the kitchen table thanking us for the hospitality. August and I went out for breakfast. Thora didn't want to come; I heard her running the bath as I locked the door.

Sun flooded through the tall café windows. The white tiles on the wall gleamed. Some of the patrons had kept their sunglasses on indoors, and others squinted at their computers in an attempt to see anything beyond their own reflection. I translated the menu for August and then ordered for us while he got us a table in a corner where we could escape the light.

'What was up with Thora last night?' he asked when I sat down.

'I'm not sure. Jens brought up the Stiller business.'

'Ah,' August said. 'Awkward.'

'Yeah. But she seemed mostly angry at me afterwards.'

'Why?'

'I guess I said something wrong. I don't know. In any case she seems to agree with Jens.'

'Jens asked how Eliel and I were even thinking of working in advertising.'

'Really?'

'That's what he's like. He enjoys making other people uncomfortable. He thinks that he's pointing out things you haven't already thought of.'

'Principles are easy, but everyone needs to eat and pay rent,' I said.

'Yes,' August said and took a sip of coffee. 'But it's not as if I *couldn't* work in something else. Advertising salaries tend to cover way more than rent and food. Like expensive sneakers and festival tickets. Though so far I'm not selling my services to any dictators.' He played with the old wine bottle in the middle of our table, which someone had filled with three stems of flowers.

'But you are a cog in the capitalist system,' I said, since I knew the solemn song by now.

August smiled and I felt his gaze on my face like a soft leaf – both tickly and itchy.

'So you and Thora had a fight yesterday?' he said.

I wiggled my little coffee cup, the liquid in it bitter and dark, and the saucer rattled.

'Yes.'

'It will pass,' August said. 'You're not the one she's mad at, either.'

'I don't know what to say,' I said, looking out across the café rather than meeting August's gaze. 'I don't know what to say when she shuts down like that.'

'Yes, the two of you are similar in a lot of ways,' August said.

The softness in his voice made me want to cry.

'Are you really in love with Eliel?' I asked.

'He's not the love of my life. But he can be fun sometimes. After all, you've taken Thora from me.'

I looked at him, stunned.

'Is that how you feel?'

'Or maybe it's her who's taken you from me,' he continued, as if he hadn't heard my question. He smiled. 'What do we want to do today?'

I swallowed. 'We could go to the war museum?'

Eventually we decided to go to the Käthe Kollwitz Museum. I texted Thora with directions from the apartment and she agreed to meet us there. August and I arrived first and paid the entry fee, then started looking around without her. I was more impatient than him and moved faster through the rooms.

When I circled back to August I found him sitting on a bench with Thora, their backs to the doorway. As soon as I saw them I thought, as if the idea had been waiting for me in that room: I am never going to stop feeling lonely. I looked at them, her head on his shoulder, his arm around her back, and then I quietly turned around and took the stairs up to the next floor. After a while I heard their laughter in the stairwell and I slipped into a small room at the end furthest from the entrance, but it only took a minute before I felt Thora's hand on my arm.

'There you are,' she said. 'We were trying to find you.'

I turned to look at her. She'd drawn her hair up into a ponytail. A few strands had come loose and were hooked behind her ears. She smelled like shampoo and sunscreen.

'I went ahead,' I said. 'I didn't know you were here already.'

'It didn't take that long to get here,' she said.

I felt her trying to catch my eye, and though I let her I was still holding back, as if I was collecting up my feelings and strapping them onto my back where she couldn't see them.

'I should have been nicer to you last night,' she said. 'It wasn't fair to you.'

'Okay,' I said, and I could hear how laconic I sounded. 'It's fine,' I added. 'I'm not mad at you.'

She rested a hand on my shoulder and came up on her tiptoes, and I bent down to her. I kissed her lips first, then her forehead. I could taste the sunscreen.

'I do need you,' she mumbled into my neck, and there was that sucking feeling deep inside me again. 'I think that sometimes I say mean things just to see if you care.'

I hugged her and closed my eyes. I wondered how it was possible to feel at once so close to someone and so far away from them.

Thora

A few weeks into the fall semester Hugo told me that he'd started dating a classmate.

'Who?' I asked.

'I don't think you know her,' he said. 'She's not from Stockholm.'

As if I only knew people from here. I cupped my mug with my hands. We were at one of the cafés on campus; sun outside, dusty windows, lawn strewn with yellow leaves.

'I didn't think you would mind,' he said. 'We're not together, right? And you have August.'

I smiled and concentrated on the people in line at the counter, the café staff bustling to put together the lunch orders.

'Am I wrong?' he said when I'd been silent long enough that I thought he should understand that the question was redundant and therefore idiotic.

'No,' I said, surprised by how calm I sounded. 'You're not wrong.'

'You said this summer—'

'I know what I said. And I meant it.'

I pressed my hands around my mug even though it was so hot it made my palms hurt. I knew that Hugo was observing me, and yet I wasn't sure what my face was communicating. My mouth and my eyes were twitching and I felt a crawling sensation over my skin.

'You seem upset,' he said.

'I'm not. You can do whatever you want.' I was afraid I'd start crying if I stopped smiling. 'Does this mean we're no longer sleeping together?'

'No. I don't know, I hadn't thought of that,' he said. 'Olivia and I aren't together either.'

'Did you tell Olivia about me?'

I pronounced the name like a word in a foreign language neither of us had mastered.

'No.' He gave a little laugh. 'I don't know how to explain our relationship to her. Tigran thinks that you and I and August are living in some kind of love triangle.'

I looked at him, thinking that I hated him. Hugo's smile slowly faded. Dust floated in the sunlight behind him, big clouds that swirled whenever someone passed through with a lunch tray.

'You *are* upset,' he said.

I turned my phone on the table to see what time it was. 'I have to go.'

'Thora—' He stood up with me.

I stuffed my belongings into my bag while he watched.

'I didn't think you'd mind,' he said. 'I'm sorry.'

I squeezed the phone in my hand, felt the greasy screen against my fingers.

'My class starts soon,' I said. 'I'll see you later.'

Heading downstairs to the auditorium, I took a seat at the back, so far up that the lecturer resembled a stick figure without a face. The light from the ceiling was hard and dirty and made the white pages in my notebook wax-like. The black lines on the paper rippled like waves. I felt dizzy, like I was sliding back into my own head, the rows of students in front of me appearing as though through a tunnel. When I moved my hand I had the impression that another person had instructed me to grasp the pen. My scrawl looked unfamiliar.

In the break I took my stuff and walked down the corridor, out the exit, past the students smoking outside. The air was cold and smelled of rotting leaves, wet soil, cigarette smoke. The trees were glowing in the sun, lone leaves floating down from the branches. I walked slowly in the direction of the bus stop, jacket in hand. I was wearing a short-sleeved cashmere top and I felt the skin on my arms prickle with goosebumps, but the cold anchored me in my body. I focused on my breath. The tunnel opened up. On the bus I listened to music, rolling the white cord of my earphones around my finger as I watched the autumn colours slide past outside the window. How small I was, just one lonely person on a bus in a city in a country in the Nordic backwoods of the world. Thinking about myself was like lifting the roof off the bus, seeing myself in all my smallness, and it was strangely liberating. A way of giving in, letting myself be swept along by the futility of it all.

In the afternoon I went to the law firm to take care of the reception desk. I watered the orchids and picked up the phone when it rang. Looking at the petals, I wanted to tear them off, one by one, and throw them into the trash. I saw my phone screen light up with messages from Hugo and August; I replied only to August.

After work I went straight to August's apartment and told him what Hugo had said. I was sitting cross-legged on his bed while he went back and forth between me and the kitchenette, stirring the pots on the stove. I tried to sound calm. August came back from the kitchen again, apron on, frying pan in hand.

'Tell him,' he said.

'I can't.'

'Why not?'

'I shouldn't have to tell him,' I said.

'Maybe he's a little slow.'

I folded my hands in my lap. 'He knows exactly what he's doing. I'm not about to humiliate myself in front of him.'

That night I slept over at August's. As we lay next to each other in the darkness he said: 'You know you don't have to pretend to be okay with it, right?'

I closed my eyes. They hurt.

I could tell he was about to say something else, so I told him I was done talking about Hugo. August squeezed my hand. I fell asleep shortly afterwards. In the morning he made us breakfast, frying eggs, putting out bread and cheese and butter. He told me he was thinking about breaking up with Eliel, and asked what I thought.

'I don't know,' I said. 'You'll have to do what feels best for you.'

August's gaze on me was so mild that I thought it must surely break against my hardness. A collision of two incompatible materials.

He flicked on the coffee maker and set two cups on the counter. The machine rumbled in the kitchenette. August got dressed while I poked at the egg on my plate. I felt nauseous. As he poured the coffee and handed me a cup he told me he was planning to quit his job at the ad firm.

'But you're good at it,' I said.

'I don't like it. And I work all the time.'

'Can you make a living from painting?'

'No,' he said. 'I never will. But I don't know if I would want to anyway.'

'That's fair,' I said.

'I've applied for a temp job as an art teacher,' he said. 'If they don't hire me I can find something else. As a personal assistant, maybe. Or take a job at a warehouse.'

I nodded.

He looked warily at me. 'Do you think you can live with that?'

'What do you mean?'

'That I won't have a career. Or make a ton of money.'

The morning sun glittered on the water outside the window. The roofs of the cars on the bridges gleamed. August sat still, looking at me.

'I don't care about your job,' I said. 'As long as you enjoy it.'

'You won't be embarrassed by me?'

'No. Do you really think I would?'

'I know that stuff is important to you.'

'Making money?'

August hesitated. 'Prestige.'

'I'm not like your brother,' I said.

'I know,' he said. 'Sorry.'

I smiled. 'I guess I'll be the breadwinner.'

'I can stay home with the kids,' he said.

I laughed, but my head hurt. While we were putting our jackets on, August pulled me close, rested his hand on my hair and told me everything would be fine, would work itself out. I shook my head, face pressed against his sweater.

'No, it will,' he said.

We walked to the subway. It was a beautiful fall day. I liked walking next to August in the morning rush, feeling his arm against mine. He kissed my forehead before he got on his train.

I replied to Hugo during my morning class: *i'm not mad, i'll see you later this week*. He didn't respond. My short sentence looked flat under his long messages, as if it couldn't quite support their weight.

We saw each other at Aron and Laura's house that Friday night. Hugo had moved into student housing in early September but had a standing invitation to the Friday dinners. On my way to my parents', I almost texted him to invite Olivia. Last-minute I decided not to. A message like that would be tantamount to acknowledging that he had power over me, that what he did affected me, and I didn't want to give him that, in black and white.

I spent the dinner talking to Samir, asking him about his current research project, the students he was advising. I liked hearing him talk about academic life in Uppsala, a world he both romanticized and bemoaned. I told him about the classes I was taking, about my classmates who wrote papers in clunky legalese with long sentences and archaic words. I tried to ignore Hugo, talking loudly and gesticulating a lot. I knew he was looking at me, and I liked feeling like I was keeping something from him by not meeting his gaze. Seated at Aron and Laura's dinner table I knew who I was, what my role was; my presence was a given here, and even when a cynical comment slipped out there was always someone willing to smile at me – I was young. My parents' friends still viewed me as a child older than my years, something I took advantage of, effortlessly making them laugh.

Hugo was unusually quiet and excused himself early, saying he had a paper due after the weekend. I watched him disappear down the hallway. He didn't come back. The power I'd juggled during the dinner no longer seemed desirable, but rather like an intoxicant that had caused a lapse in judgement.

A few days passed. A week. Two weeks. Dusk came early, and all that had been green was now red, yellow, brown. I spent a lot of time on campus, writing to-do lists and then checking them off with a sense of satisfaction that didn't correspond to the indifference I felt towards each accomplishment. Our group chat continued to light up with screenshots, articles, snippets of conversations overheard at cafés, on the subway or in line at the grocery store. It was as if we were crafting a story about ourselves through this collection of impressions and opinions, but the story had no relation to reality outside of the chat. Sometimes I wondered if we were creating this assemblage for an absent, imagined audience who would never see it.

I withstood the temptation to google Olivia's name. Every time I had the urge, I imagined Hugo watching behind my shoulder. It was an efficient deterrent.

One day I ran into them by the lockers at the National Library. I was about to leave; they were on their way into the reading room. I understood who the person standing next to Hugo was before he introduced us. I wondered if he was jolted the way I was, as if a lock had been cracked open. He looked embarrassed, holding his computer against his chest like a shield when he said hi. I looked at Olivia and smiled and shook her hand. She was blonde and wore round glasses. She was pretty. Hugo and Olivia looked good together; they fitted each other. Olivia brought out Hugo's softness, accentuated the amused spark in his eye as his gloominess faded.

When I told August about the meeting he listened without any indication of his thinking.

'They look good together.'

'Yeah, you said that.'

'I mean it. I'm sure Olivia is good for him. Maybe she can help him get in touch with his emotions.'

'You don't have to be this rational.'

'Just because I don't react the way you would doesn't mean I'm doing the wrong thing.'

August's gaze moved casually over my face, orienting itself in familiar terrain.

'Fine,' he said. 'All I'm saying is it's okay not to be so accommodating. You're allowed to feel things.'

We were in the kitchen in the Styrmansgatan apartment, sitting across from each other at the kitchen table, laptops open. Harriet and Iris were out.

'He's not worth it. I don't need him,' I said.

'He doesn't seem very happy to me.'

I didn't say anything for a long while, focusing instead on rubbing a stain on my keyboard.

'It feels like I have to enact violence upon myself to love him in a way he's comfortable with,' I finally said. 'And I can't. I care too much about myself to do that.'

I got up and poured my coffee down the drain. August looked at me over the edge of his screen. When I met his gaze there was nothing that needed to be unbolted – I opened without effort. It made me think of the little animal skeletons at the Museum of Natural History in Paris, their chests pried open, exposed for all to see.

'Do you think it makes me a bad person?' I asked.

'No,' he said. 'Of course not.'

'But am I a severe person? Cold?'

He got up and stood in front of me. Softly, he placed his hands on my face, as if he was handling a fragile object. I closed my eyes.

During exam season you had to get to the library early in the morning to have a chance at a locker or a seat. There was always a group of students waiting on the stairs to the entrance right before the clock struck nine. Afternoons had a faded atmosphere, the café smelling of old coffee. Every single table was occupied and messy with computers and plastic bags and water bottles and takeout containers. Long charger cords slithered from outlets to laptops.

One Friday morning I found Hugo there, waiting to be let in. He smiled at me as if it didn't matter that I hadn't replied to the message he'd sent several days earlier. He asked if I wanted to get lunch with him and a few others. I wondered if he was trying to establish some kind of new normal between us. I said yes, and at noon I left the reading room for the café, where I sat down with Hugo, Tigran, and a guy in a red roll-neck sweater who was a PhD student in the history of ideas and a friend of Tigran's. I'd seen him at the library before; he was always wearing that red roll-neck. We discussed our work. When Hugo told us about his exam in the advanced class in international law, Tigran's friend commented, his face serious: 'Really – there are still people doing causal relations?'

Hugo looked at me as if he wanted my help. I looked away but smiled.

After lunch he asked if I wanted to take a walk in the park.

'Okay,' I said. 'A short walk.'

We said goodbye to the others, got our jackets from the lockers and stepped out into the chilly air, a greyish sky above us.

'It was awkward,' Hugo said. 'The other week.'

'When?' I said, though I knew very well what he was referring to.

'With Olivia.'

'Yeah,' I said. 'It felt weird.'

Hugo seemed relieved that I agreed, as if that agreement gave the conversation a stable foundation to build on.

We rounded the library building. Hugo had his hands in the pockets of his jacket and I could feel him watching me from the side. I imagined Hugo and Olivia having sex, how he'd lie between Olivia's legs, the golden lustre of Olivia's skin, his hands on Olivia's hips, maybe he liked taking her from behind. I bit the inside of my cheek.

'I thought you'd want to know if I met someone,' he said. 'That it would be worse if I didn't say anything.'

'Are you in love with her?'

'I don't know.' He hesitated. 'I like being with her. It feels easy.'

'And it doesn't feel that way with me,' I said, matter-of-fact.

I understood from his expression that I'd said something he didn't want to put into words, even though it was true.

'Do you think we're good for each other?' he asked.

The question made me suddenly angry. It was a new kind of fury, more pure than the hazy rage that rattled in my chest whenever I thought of Olivia.

'What does that even mean? That we're good for each other?' I said. 'That everything is easy? That it never hurts?'

'You and me and August – it feels like I have no control over what's happening between us,' he said, and pulled his shoulders up like he was cold. 'It's difficult. Complicated. And I have friends who think—'

'What does it even *matter* what your friends think?'

He sighed and I watched the muscles move around his jaw. I looked down.

'You care so much about what other people think,' I said.

'I know,' he said joylessly. 'It's one of my less charming traits.'

I looked at him and then away, at the trees. The trunks were dark and slender and the branches reached for each other across the walkway, an uneven network that almost blocked out the sky. Hugo's hand grazed mine, a tentative touch. There was laughter and screaming coming from the playground, the hum of cars on the roads enclosing the park, and gravel crunching beneath our shoes. We returned to the library in silence and went our separate ways at the entrance to the reading room. When I sat down at my seat I felt that something had changed in me. I looked around at the people hunched over computers and books and notepads and thought that it was a dizzying prospect. To belong to nobody but myself. To be my own.

On Sunday I went to the Thiel Gallery with Karla and Laura. I biked to the southern edge of the island. The white building was perched on a hill and shone between the trees like a meringue with light green trimmings. It was cold, and my hands on the handlebars were frozen even though I had gloves on. I parked my bike near the bus stop and waited.

I'd spent the night at Hugo's. I wasn't sure why – to prove something? I could still feel him moving inside me. When he'd asked if it felt good I'd pretended not to hear. Afterwards I wasn't sure who had the upper hand. Had I won it back or given it up by sleeping with him?

The leaves on the ground rustled in the wind. I shivered. Karla and Laura got off the bus and I waved at them. When they spotted me I felt for a moment like they could see straight through me, as if my physical appearance was a public register of all the mistakes I'd ever committed and would ever commit in the future. Then the mass of time came flooding in between us, and I wondered if the generational gap was too big for us ever to understand each other. Would they think me weak?

We paid the entrance fee and hung our coats in the cloakroom. The heels of our shoes clattered against the parquet, softer on the stairs which had been covered with a rug. Karla bumped into two acquaintances and stopped to chat with them in a mellow, penetrating voice, while Laura and I continued on through the gallery.

'How are things between you and Hugo?' Laura asked out of the blue.

I had never discussed Hugo with my mother before, and I looked at her with surprise. I shrugged, aware that I was blushing.

'I'm not sure,' I said. 'Not great.'

'Did something happen?'

'It's hard to explain,' I said. 'I think maybe he's not that good at *feelings*.'

'Hmm,' Laura said. 'Even though he reads so much poetry.'

I gave her an amused look. I wasn't sure if she was joking or not. I leaned my head against her shoulder as we paused in front of a sculpture. She stroked my hair.

'Men in general are bad at talking about feelings,' she said. 'Young men in particular.'

'I'm not sure if I'm very good at it either,' I said.

Laura smiled at me and moved away, walking slowly through the room, hands clasped behind her back. I sat down on a bench and took my phone out of my pocket, resting it in the palm of my hand. The screen was empty of notifications. August called it our 'serious game', when we both held out in the hope that the other would crack and text first. It felt less like a game with Hugo. When Karla entered the room I put my phone away and joined her as she told me about the people she'd talked to downstairs, interspersed with comments on the paintings. She linked her arm with mine.

'They wrote that book,' she said. 'About us.'

I looked at her, surprised. Her hold on my arm tightened. 'You know the authors?' I asked.

'No. But they work for us now.'

I raised my eyebrows. 'For *us*?'

Karla smiled. 'They've got full-time jobs at Philip's magazine. *Full-time jobs*. So they'll be dedicating themselves to other things now. Things of greater importance.'

I laughed softly and exhaled through my nose. I looked at Karla's profile. She was studying a painting but I knew she was aware of me looking at her. I thought of that night in Berlin when Jens had asked me about the Stiller conglomerate. I put my hand on Karla's arm and cleared my throat.

'I've decided to move out of Styrmansgatan,' I said. 'As soon as I can.'

Karla leaned closer to one of the plaques hanging next to a painting by Edvard Munch.

'Oh, are you now? Where to?' she said without looking at me.

'Into student housing. I've been collecting days on the clock.'

'Are you not happy with Iris and Harriet?'

'I am. But I want something of my own,' I said. 'I just wanted you to know. That I'll probably be moving out soon.'

'Sure, sure, I'm sure that will be good for you,' Karla said and let go of my arm.

I looked up at the Munch painting. A group of women were standing in a circle on a bridge, one of them turned away from the circle and facing the viewer. Her arms hung down by her sides, her face inscrutable. I took a deep breath. My body felt strangely light.

Later we had lunch in the gallery café and Karla asked if I was planning to move in with August.

'No,' I said. 'But I might, later. Further down the line.'

'I like his brother,' Laura said.

I didn't know what to say to that.

'Is August still seeing a psychologist?' Karla asked.

I looked at Laura, an accusation in my gaze.

'It's a trap women fall into,' Laura said in a calm voice. 'Getting stuck with someone who is troubled in that way.'

'Everyone goes through rough patches,' I protested.

'You have to think of yourself,' Karla warned.

'I can think about others at the same time,' I said and straightened my back. 'What's wrong with needing another person?'

I saw Karla and Laura exchange a glance across the table. They changed the subject.

It was snowing as I biked back across the Djurgårdsbron bridge. I was cold and sweaty at once, my cheeks smarting from the chill. There was cloud cover over the buildings, but at the horizon the sky was pink and orange. The street lamps threw bands of light on the water.

I met Hugo and August at a bar off Hornsgatan. We were seated on tall stools around a table near the red door. Outside, snowflakes were whirling in the dusk. A multitude of small lights were glowing in the ceiling, a starry sky over the bar counter. I listened in silence as August told Hugo about his plans to leave the ad firm. Hugo nodded supportively, now and then throwing a glance at me. I felt warm, languid, resting my head in the palm of my hand, tracing the dots of light in the black ceiling with my eyes. The murmur of the other bar patrons was like a soft blanket thrown over the space. I returned my gaze to Hugo and August. I'd given each of them parts of myself, but for the first time in my life I didn't feel that giving had hollowed me out: I was still myself. It was like getting back on my feet after a jump from a height – a jump I had voluntarily made – and being astonished to realize that nothing had broken. I could jump again. I thought of recounting my conversation with Karla and Laura to Hugo and August, and then I thought I didn't need to. They already knew and understood, and if they didn't I wasn't sure I'd be able to explain anyway. And the snow fell and fell.

Hugo

Every time I hung out with my classmates they talked about internships, grants, career plans. If drinking was involved, they'd grill each other about different lecturers and the grades they'd received in various classes. It was the first time I'd found myself in a context where there was a genuine interest in knowing what was on someone's CV. Initially I'd liked it – there was a comfort in knowing I wouldn't have to share anything personal to retain people's attention. I listened to my classmates talking about their involvement in various student associations, their board positions and their internships at the UN and the EU and the Department of Foreign Affairs, even as I was embarrassed by my own lack of experience.

I spent a lot of time thinking about what I'd do after the spring semester, how I'd make a living. Everyone said you needed a master's to have a chance at a job relevant to our degree, and I realized that they were all in the process of putting together applications to several master's programmes. I had a vague sense that everyone around me knew how things were done, how to navigate their lives and in what order, whereas I felt shut out from this knowledge. Olivia tried to debate the pros and cons of various programmes with me, wavering between Swedish and foreign universities. When she talked about wanting to do work that made the world a better place, I found myself unable to explain the fatigue I felt without coming up against the idea that I was a bad person who doubted other people's ambitions and intentions.

At the same time, I tried to feel something for Olivia. Something lasting. It was like squeezing a dry dishcloth to see if anything would come out. But spending time with her never left me with the pressure building behind my eyes – that feeling of being too exposed, vulnerable.

I still saw Thora, but she only came to my place when we were alone. Whenever August joined us, we met up at a bar or a café. Thora would text me late at night, asking if I was home and if she could come over. She insisted that she only called because she wanted sex, not because she wanted to see me.

'You know, I'm taking advantage of you too,' she said one evening in my bed. 'I hate dating in the winter.'

I understood that she was joking, at least partly, but I didn't find it funny. I smiled and frowned at once, to please her while still showing my displeasure.

'What do you mean, *too*?' I asked.

'What do *you* mean?'

'Do you think I'm taking advantage of you?'

'Yes.'

'In what way?'

'Come on,' she said. 'Of course you are. All I'm saying is that I'm doing the same. So neither of us needs to feel bad about it.'

It was her old trick, saying things in a flippant voice that belied the seriousness in her eyes. I never knew which one I should take my cue from.

'I don't think of it that way,' I said. 'I care about you. I don't want you to think that I'm taking advantage of you.'

'What am I supposed to think, then?'

I sat up and put my feet on the floor, resting my face in my hands for a few moments. I felt the mattress shifting as she sat up next to me. She placed a hand on my back, a question.

'I just don't think I can be who you want me to be,' I said.

'All I want is for you to be you.'

The flippancy was gone; her voice had a more cautious tone. Somehow that was worse. When I didn't respond, she added: 'Who do you think I want you to be?'

'Someone who is always available to you.'

Her hand slipped off my back. 'And what does that mean? That you'll pull away as soon as something is difficult?'

'I don't feel like a good person,' I said in a low voice.

'What do you mean?'

I turned to face her. The bedroom nook was dim, half hidden from the rest of the room by a curtain. Thora's hair was tousled; her face, without mascara and lipstick, was open – questioning – and I felt a tenderness for her that overwhelmed me, not because it was the first time I'd felt it, but because it seemed logically wrapped up with a desire to distance myself from her.

'I don't think I'm a good person,' I said. 'And I don't think I like myself very much, either.'

'It sounds like you're just trying to find an easy out,' she said.

'I'm trying to do you a favour.'

'Oh yeah? And in what way do you think you're doing me a favour?'

'I don't want you to think that I'm something I'm not.'

'Because of course it would be just *terrible* if someone actually liked you.'

I looked away from her. My face was hot. The words that matched my thoughts stuck in my throat like a physical object, and I tried miserably to think of a way to change the subject which would allow me to put my arm around her without her flinching or pushing me away.

Before I could think of something to say, she stood up and walked into the kitchen, out of sight. I wanted to ask her to come back, but I could tell from the sound of the cabinet doors opening and the tap being turned on that she was angry. I knew she would twist anything I said, that she would toss my words right back at me, newly filled with a sense that hadn't been there when I spoke them.

It was already dark outside. The apartment was quiet aside from the humming of the fridge and the sound of water poured from the kettle. The scent of fresh coffee. I heard the chair scraping against the floor as she sat down at the kitchen table. I thought of the bruise on her knee that she'd shown me last week, of the birthmark on her neck that came into view when her hair fell away as she lay down and faced me in bed, of the mark her sunglasses left on the bridge of her nose, the way she rubbed her fingers over it to make it go away faster though it only made it more red. I wondered if this experience was common or unusual — were there people who lived their lives without feeling particularly close to other people? Did the way I felt indicate some kind of defect in me, an inability — acquired or congenital — to approach life the way others seemed to? I didn't understand how anyone could bear the ever-present risk of being misunderstood and, ultimately, abandoned. I could hardly even bear to think about it.

I got dressed and moved to the couch. Then I reached for my computer on the floor and pulled up a report about drones that I'd begun reading earlier that day. After a while I was so engrossed that I didn't notice Thora coming out of the kitchen.

'I'm leaving now,' she said.

I looked up and put my computer down. She gave the impression of having watched me from the doorway for a while.

'I thought we were going to have dinner together,' I said.

'I don't feel like it.'

'Will you come back here later?'

'I don't know,' she said. 'I think I'm going to sleep at home tonight.'

Fear hit me like an external force, pushing against my back and my chest at once.

'Do you have to go?' I said.

'I *want* to go.'

I put my computer in my lap again and held on to it with my hands the way I would grab the armrests on aeroplane seats during take-off and landing.

'Okay,' I said.

Thora gave me a long look before she turned on her heel. I heard her put her shoes on in the hall and close the door. Then I sat in the silence that lingered in her wake, while winter's darkness pushed up against the windowpanes.

The next day Thora texted me to ask if we could meet up and talk. I read the message several times, trying different emphases, different tones of voice, and wondered what mood she'd been in when she wrote it. I didn't reply. The following day she sent yet another message: *Are you mad at me?* It appeared on my screen during a lecture, and I swiped left so it wasn't there the next time I looked at my phone. She called me that night; I didn't respond and she didn't get in touch again.

Then there was nothing.

A strange stillness materialized, like the pressure building before a storm. I walked through Stockholm with the sense that the city was closing itself to me, expelling me, as if it had finally identified me as someone who didn't belong. I developed a new pain in my shoulder, and searched the internet for stretching exercises that showed figures in various positions with pedagogical arrows pointing at muscles I couldn't identify. One night I woke in agony from my muscles contracting, and my vision went black while I plugged in the heating pad Thora had forgotten at my place. I pressed it against my shoulders until the pain came from the heat on my skin, not the muscles.

Sometimes my pulse ran so fast and so erratically that I thought I was dying; never before had I been so conscious that there was a heart beating in my chest. The only thing that could calm me down was nature documentaries with dry, British voiceovers describing landscapes, animals and weathers which made me feel small and insignificant. I stopped smoking and drinking coffee; I printed the stretching exercises off in the university library, and decided the time had come for me to leave Stockholm. When I finally called Thora, my unspoken decision lay between us like a physical distance.

'Hey,' I said. 'Sorry it's been a minute, I needed time to think.'

'And now you've finished thinking?'

'I needed some time to myself.'

'Okay. Sure. Take the time you need.'

Her voice was careless, a thin layer on top of heavy sarcasm. I closed my eyes.

'I don't know why this is so hard,' I said.

'Talking to me?'

'No,' I said. 'You're not the problem.'

'Oh, please.'

'What?'

'*It's not you, it's me.*'

'That's not what I was going to say.'

'Okay, what were you going to say then?'

'I'm sorry.'

She was silent for a long while. Then she took a deep breath and I felt myself tense up as if waiting to be scalded.

'I don't know if I can do this anymore,' she said. 'I'm always so worried that I'm going to say the wrong thing with you. It feels like you're going to disappear at the drop of a hat, as if you don't care.'

'I do care,' I said.

'It doesn't feel like it.'

I looked around the room, at the ceiling. 'It sounds like you've made up your mind,' I said. 'So I'm not sure what to say. I can't ask you to stay if you don't want to.'

'*Ask me?*'

'If it's hard for you to be with me, then you shouldn't be with me. And it sounds like you do think it's hard,' I said.

I was glad she couldn't see I was crying.

'Just because something is hard doesn't mean it's worthless,' she said.

'You just told me yourself that you can't do this anymore.'

'Hugo.'

'Thora.'

She laughed, sharply.

'Okay, fine,' she said. 'Goodbye.'

Then she hung up.

I called August but he didn't pick up. The ringing tone echoed in me, sounding in an empty room.

I switched up my study routines, from the National Library to the Government Library in the Old Town. I knew I wouldn't run into anyone I knew there. Stepping into the silence was like wrapping myself in a thick duvet. That's where I wrote my dissertation, my applications, my emails. That's where I began to dismantle my Stockholm life without telling anyone. From my seat I looked out the windows at the tourists in the narrow alleys, at Stockholm Cathedral poking out from behind the chimneys, thinking that by next winter I'd be somewhere else, far from here.

I still saw August occasionally but we didn't talk about Thora. The only time we discussed what had happened was shortly after my final phone call with her. August looked me right in the eye and told me I was acting like an idiot.

'Okay,' I said. 'Yes. That's probably true.'

August didn't say anything. He seemed to expect an explanation.

I took a deep breath, held it. 'I'm not like you two,' I said finally.

'What does that mean?'

'It's so *easy* for you both.'

'No, it's not easy at all.'

'It seems easy,' I said.

'Don't you think I feel insecure too?'

The truth was that I didn't think so.

'I just think we're different,' I said, since I didn't believe I'd be able to explain what I was really thinking. 'Too different.'

August looked at me with a defiance I associated more with Thora than with him.

'I'm not like that. It's just how you see me. It's how you *want* to see me.'

I didn't know how to respond. Was it true?

That was the end of the conversation. I wasn't sure if I imagined that August was more distant towards me afterwards.

I paid three thousand kronor to complete a mandatory English proficiency test. I felt both amused and mildly offended by every part of the exam. The oral section included questions like: Do you work with a computer? Did you enjoy your childhood? What is your favourite song? The listening section consisted of audio clips with people speaking British, American and Australian English. One of the scenes featured a man calling a bus company to ask for the timetables of different buses going to British villages with strange names. I was so bored I sometimes zoned out looking at the icicles on the eaves outside, until I remembered I was meant to listen to the people on the tape. A week or so later I learned that my score was high enough for the overseas universities. I scanned the test results at the library and attached it to my applications.

One day I bumped into Eliel on campus. We both stopped and said hi. In the silence that followed I was about to head towards the subway station when Eliel announced that August had broken up with him a few weeks ago.

'I didn't know that,' I said.

'You don't hang out with them as much anymore?'

'No,' I said. 'I guess I don't.'

Eliel then told me he'd started a class in intellectual history and asked if he could buy me a coffee. I hesitated before saying yes. Somehow it felt like switching sides, like taking yet another step away from Thora and August. Then I remembered that I had already chosen my side – wilfully, and perhaps irrevocably. The thought was both painful and absurd.

We went to one of the cafeterias near the station. Eliel started talking about Thora and August the minute we sat down.

'All they care about is themselves,' he said. 'And it always seemed like you were idolizing them.'

I frowned. I thought he was wrong, but I didn't bother trying to correct him.

'I don't think it's healthy,' he said. 'To be that close to someone. At the very least you have to choose. You can't love several people at once. It's not real.'

Once we'd finished our coffees I said: 'I don't know who I'd have been if I hadn't met them.'

The realization came to me suddenly, but the moment I spoke it, I knew it was true. Eliel's eyes widened. We said goodbye shortly thereafter and I understood from the look he gave me that this revelation had rattled the foundation on which he'd built his opinion of Thora and August.

Snow crunched under my shoes as I walked to the subway. The platform was wet, full of students. When the train rolled in I spotted someone who looked like Thora getting into the car closest to the escalators. I paused for a moment, considered following her. She glanced my way, let her gaze linger on me, and then she looked away, impassive as she disappeared into the car. I hurried onto another carriage further off. The doors closed behind me.

I received the first acceptance letter sitting in my regular spot at the Government Library, in the room upstairs with a view of Storkyrkobrinken. Some windows in the buildings across the way still had their Christmas decorations up. One of the facades was dark orange, like clementine ice cream mixed with soot. The people plodded through the snow, sometimes raised their eyes to check the eaves for the icicles whose points gleamed in the sunshine like newly sharpened daggers. I read the email several times before closing my inbox and all my tabs. I shut my computer. Pale sunlight streamed over the wooden floors, like it was stretching out in the warmth of the radiators. I slid my computer into its case, put it in my backpack and slipped on my winter jacket. Then I set off through the city, its alleys and parks, not sure where I was headed until I found myself en route to August's studio.

When I stepped through the door, I considered that I should have texted first. It hadn't been necessary before, I'd always stopped in whenever I felt like it, but I wasn't sure if we had that kind of a relationship anymore. The realization came too late; I was already in the doorway, the late-winter weather behind me. August sat hunched over his desk, dressed in a scarf and a bulky sweater, with wool socks and fingerless gloves. The same old coffee smell lay in the air.

August looked up.

'Hey,' he said. 'I didn't know you were going to come by today.'

'Are you busy? I can leave if you have a lot to do.'

August put down the piece of charcoal he'd been holding, his hands stained with coal and paint.

'No, it's okay,' he said. 'Everything alright?'

I remained in the doorway. My ears burned from the shock of the warmth after the cold outdoors.

'I've been accepted to a university in the US,' I said. 'I just heard.'

The light from the small desk lamp flickered, the light bulb whirring softly like an insect.

'Congrats,' August said. 'I didn't know you'd applied to study abroad.'

'I didn't think I'd be accepted.'

'Do you want to go?'

'Yes.'

'I thought you'd started to take to Stockholm.'

'I have.'

'But you don't want to stay here.' August paused for a few moments and then asked, tentative: 'Is it our fault?'

'What? No,' I said. 'But I don't know if I feel at home here. And the housing situation is hard. Expensive,' I tried.

'Ah,' August said. 'The housing crisis. Another one bites the dust.'

I shifted my weight between my feet. I was hot and sweaty in my winter clothes but I didn't know if August wanted me to stay or leave.

'It's not because of you that I'm moving,' I said.

Saying it like that, with such exaggerated emphasis, I thought that it wasn't a lie.

If I'd been a different type of person I would have stayed. I pictured another life, a Stockholm life with the water and the changing of the seasons as the backdrop, a life where I was a person who didn't recoil before everything that was bigger and stronger than me. When we locked eyes it felt like he'd had the same thought.

'Okay,' August said. 'Does Thora know?'

'No, she doesn't know anything,' I said and looked at my feet. A small puddle of slush leaked out from beneath my shoes. 'We don't really talk anymore.'

'I know,' August said.

My hand was in my pocket, holding on to my phone. August asked if I wanted a cup of coffee, and I said yes. I took my shoes off and hung my backpack and jacket on a hook, then sat down on the couch. August poured two cups of coffee from a thermos and gave me one of them.

'You should tell Thora,' he said. 'That you're moving. I think she'd want to know.'

'I don't know,' I said. 'We don't see each other anymore.'

'Still.'

'I don't think she cares.'

'Maybe not,' August said. 'It's hard to know.'

I sipped the coffee, a burnt taste.

'The United States, huh. So far away,' August said.

'Yeah. I know.'

He smiled weakly. 'Maybe we can come visit.'

'Yeah. Maybe,' I said.

I knew it wouldn't happen and I understood that August knew it too.

We were silent.

Something was throbbing behind my eyes and I found it hard to swallow the coffee. The silence was too loud; I wished for a spring storm to blow through the studio, toss the papers about, disperse the coffee fumes that were giving me a headache. For the first time since I'd got to know August, I couldn't think of anything to talk about. It seemed we had nothing more to say to each other. I regretted having come and threw back my coffee, before excusing myself with a string of courtesies that made me depressed. I'd never felt like I had to talk to August that way before. And I could tell that he was confused by my formalities, too. Suddenly we were strangers to each other.

On an early morning in mid-April I took the bus to the US embassy, which was situated on the edge of the city centre. The embassy resembled a bunker, a foreign object plunked down that had spread out across the greenery. It wasn't even eight o'clock, but the line was long already. Children ran up and down the streets while the adults waited mostly in silence. Any conversation that did take place was quiet, as if everyone was scared of making a sound the implacable building might interpret as noise. I held my passport in a tight grip along with a transparent folder containing a stack of printouts. I had checked the expiration date of my passport several times to confirm that it was indeed far in the future. My fear was that the tiniest of missteps – a missing document, a misinterpreted question – might put an abrupt end to my move to the United States. I'd had so many fantasies about the journey – the body of the aeroplane over the dark depths of the Atlantic; leaving everything behind – that the thought of staying in Stockholm gave me cold sweats.

The line to the embassy grew longer with each bus that stopped. The other embassies in the area were old; some looked like little mansions. The US complex was the only new construction, and the only building surrounded by a tall fence. To get through, everyone had to take off all their outerwear, put their bag on the ground, and extend their arms while slowly revolving until a guard behind bulletproof glass allowed them to step up. I watched as the people ahead of me in line spun with their arms stretched out like they were imitating an aeroplane. The kids laughed and the adults smiled nervously, and when it was my turn I followed suit – I spun, smiling nervously. Once I'd completed my spins the guard waved at me to walk through.

The first building was small, with an airport-style security check. Then I walked through yet another set of doors and continued into a waiting room in the main building. I took a number and sat down with the others on one of the benches facing wall-mounted television screens. Nobody was talking.

When my number was called I wasn't taken to a windowless interrogation room like I'd expected; instead I was directed to a counter where a bored-looking man in uniform stood at a computer terminal, behind bulletproof glass. I slid my plastic folder and passport through the opening and told him my name, explaining in English why I was applying for a visa. The man took my documents out of the folder. His name was Greg, according to the name tag on his shirt.

Greg looked at my passport, then my face. Greg nodded. Greg asked if I'd been to the United States before and I told him no. Greg asked why I was travelling to the United States and I told him I was going there to study. Greg asked how long I was planning to stay in the United States and I told him until I'd graduated. Greg asked how I was planning to finance my stay and I told him about my grant and my student loan. Greg fell silent and looked at his computer. I couldn't see the screen. Greg looked through the documents in my plastic folder, and then, after a few minutes, nodded and said, with a smile: *You'll like New York*.

My visa had been approved.

I left my passport at the embassy, and it came back to me in the mail a few days later with the visa pasted onto one of the pages. It was no more than a piece of paper, with my name and photo superimposed on a US flag and an eagle with its wings stretched out. Yet right then, that piece of paper seemed like the most valuable thing I owned.

It was Aron who told me that Thora had moved into student housing in Marieberg. He sounded surprised as he described the apartment: unusually nice for student housing, he said – tall ceilings, large windows facing a backyard. Aron asked if I'd seen it and I told him I hadn't and then, unable to stop myself, added the treacherous word *yet*. Apparently Thora hadn't told him we no longer talked. Imagining her new home was like cutting a vein to let out a stream of rejected possibilities. I could picture us – Thora, August and me – sitting around a small kitchen table with wooden chairs, and though the scene made me ache, the sensation was strangely pleasant; it negated my other feelings.

I'd bumped into Aron one afternoon when I was strolling around the Old Town, having spent several hours at the Government Library. The city seemed much louder and sharper after the silence of the reading rooms. I saw Aron smoking on the quay near Gustav Adolf's Square, and when he caught sight of me he waved. Cigarette smoke trailed his hand movements, a tail dispersed in the wind.

We went to the Medelhavsmuseet's café, where Aron got us coffee and cannoli. We took a table in the atrium, surrounded by glass cases containing ceramic figures. The museum visitors on the floor below were visible between the marble pillars. Aron asked about my studies, and I told him about the university in the US, about the visa application and my dissertation. I asked about Laura, but I didn't mention Thora.

'Do you know what you want to do?' Aron said. 'When you're done with your studies?'

'No,' I said. 'All I want is a job. With decent pay.'

I didn't tell him I found it difficult to imagine a life after university. Whenever I tried to brainstorm future scenarios, all I could feel was a listlessness I figured I'd somehow need to tame by spending long days at some office. This was of course not an ambition I could highlight in a personal letter. I found it increasingly difficult to shake the suspicion that work was all about pretending to care about pointless stuff, and that success hinged on your ability to trick even yourself.

'You're smart,' Aron said. 'Things will go well for you.'

I wondered what *well* meant in this context, but I didn't ask. Aron's gaze reminded me of Thora's, and I evaded it by looking over the balcony, down to the white sculptures on the floor below. The air was still, and the food smell was underlaid with something old, as if the objects on display emanated a scent that had been bottled up for centuries.

'It's not good to have high ideals,' Aron continued. 'Some students believe they are going to change the world, and then when they enter working life they're disappointed to find that the world doesn't care about their ambitions.'

'I don't think I know anyone who wants to change the world,' I said. 'It seems to me that most people just want a steady job and a successful career.'

Aron smiled. 'Nothing wrong with that.'

I wondered if Aron knew that August had quit his lucrative advertising job and started working as a substitute art teacher at a school in Högdalen. It seemed like the kind of thing Thora wouldn't share with her parents. But perhaps Aron would, in due time, find a way to describe August as a bridge to the cultural world.

As we said goodbye out on the square, we shook hands and Aron wished me luck. He winked at me. I managed to produce a smile. I assumed we would never see each other again.

My dissertation defence took place in a narrow room with yellow overhead lighting that made everyone look slightly bilious. Tension and excitement mingled in the air, like everyone was holding their breath in anticipation of the moment when they could all exhale. I caught myself imagining the way I'd recount the opponent's comments to Thora and August. Olivia smiled at me from across the room. Her discourse analysis of a UN resolution had been met by an approving murmur. The test administrator sat silently at her own table and paged through the documents while observing us with a look of mild tolerance, as if we were amateurs playing a game that could never be more than a pale imitation of real academia.

When the viva was over we went to a café to analyse the sparse comments offered by the administrator. Then we talked about our plans for the future, the cities we were going to move to. I felt my shoulder muscles contract and finally I got up and went to the bathroom, where I threw up. I returned to the table and my coffee cup with white blazes still flashing in my field of vision.

I kept seeing Thora and August everywhere, from afar. I saw them through bus windows, across the street, at cafés, bars, clubs, libraries. Maybe I imagined it. Sometimes I was certain it was them; sometimes I knew it was wishful thinking that had materialized their likeness. I liked seeing them. They looked happy. There was a certain inverted pleasure in imagining that they were happy, as if I'd managed to prove to them and to myself what I'd always known: they were doing just fine without me. Seeing them at a distance was like watching my own life set off by itself, walking away from me.

One evening I ended up at a bar near Mariatorget with Olivia and a few other classmates. I'd just finished my third beer when I saw Thora and August by the counter. The space was lit in a dull red and there was a DJ in a booth near the stairs to the dance floor, playing music so loud that you had to yell to be heard. I couldn't tear my gaze from Thora and August. They didn't see me and I didn't try to catch their attention. They seemed as distant as they had before I knew them.

Towards the end of May I texted Thora to ask if she might be willing to see me someday. I saw that she had read the message but she didn't respond. I added that I had something to tell her. A day later she replied: *okay.* We met at a café across from Vasaparken. I got us coffees and sat down, waiting for several minutes before she showed up. She glanced at the little yellow mugs on the table and said she didn't feel like coffee. She went to the till and returned with a salad and a Coke. I tried to find a comfortable way to sit. I cleared my throat.

'I'm moving to the US,' I said.

'I know,' she said and poured her Coke into a glass with ice. The ice fizzled as the foam shot to the top of the glass and then retreated back down.

'Did August tell you?' I asked.

'Yes. He wasn't sure that you'd tell me.'

I wanted to catch her eye but she kept evading me. 'I didn't know if you'd want to know.'

'Okay. But I do know.'

'And?'

She raised her eyebrows. 'And what?'

'What are you thinking?'

She was silent for a moment before she said: 'It doesn't matter anymore.'

My hands were resting an inch or two from her hands and I looked at them, wondering if I might attempt to touch her, but in that same moment she took her hands from the table and folded them in her lap. She sat up straight, looking past me, her focus on the other diners.

'Tell me what you want me to say,' I said, finally.

'I can't. That's not how it works,' she said.

To my surprise she hugged me when we said goodbye, and I rested my face on her hair. When she pulled away I tried to catch her eye again, but she didn't look at me, just turned on her heel and left without another word. I could still feel the warmth, the mass of her body. I stood motionless and watched her go.

It was a beautiful day. Children played in the park. Cars and buses drove down the road and people were wearing sunglasses and light jackets and drinking coffee outside the cafés. It seemed to me that everything should have stopped, that some of what was happening inside me should have an effect on my surroundings – even just a cold breeze, or a dark cloud passing across the sun. But the world would not be moved.

I took the express train to the airport. The sky was blue and smooth, like a newly ironed shirt hung over the roofs. I had a lot of time and would have to spend several hours in the departures lounge, but I didn't mind. I hadn't wanted to wait at the apartment. It was several days since I'd finished packing. There was no more food in the cupboards. I'd felt light as I dropped the key in the letterbox and stepped out of the door of the building, even though I was pulling a heavy suitcase and the straps of my backpack cut into my shoulders. Looking out the train window, I saw the water glitter in the sun and it was the first time in a long while that I appreciated how beautiful this city was. Then, highways, fields, suburbs, forests. The news reports on the TV screens were in English.

After check-in and security, I ate lunch at one of the restaurants in the terminal. The food was expensive and bland, but I ate every last crumb. I texted my mom to let her know I was at the airport. Since a few months back I'd started talking to her regularly – more regularly than ever before – until she joked that I really seemed to be missing her. Embarrassed, I'd laughed and said something about how I had to take advantage of the lack of time difference now; it would be more difficult to call from the US. But I called her less frequently after that. I didn't want her to worry about me. I thought of texting Thora and August – I even opened our group chat – but I didn't know how to word it. Even a short and simple sentence seemed to require a tone that sounded fake, and finally I swiped out of the chat and put my phone back in my pocket. Maybe I'd text August when I arrived instead.

I'd forgotten to pack anything to read in my carry-on, so after finishing my meal I went to the bookstore across from the duty-free. I picked up a few paperbacks I hadn't read. In line to pay, I spotted the Stiller book. I hesitated for a few moments before picking it up and sliding it across the counter, along with the others. Then I found a café, bought a cup of coffee and watched the people passing by on the walkway between the shops and restaurants. I started reading.

The Stiller book was shorter than I'd expected, designed with wide margins and big line spacing. The sentences were short and the line breaks frequent, as if to emphasize a certain rhythm. It was a quick read, and when I closed the book I felt underwhelmed, wondering if it was because I always had such a hard time summoning the kind of distress over the state of things that I'd often seen my classmates and August's friends express. I took out my phone and searched the names of the family members. I found encyclopedia entries about Laura and all her siblings, but Jacob was the only one with a photo on his page. Then I closed the tabs and cleared my history. What was the point? Their hypocrisy had nothing to do with me and I couldn't change anything.

I finished my coffee and left the book on the table.

The gate was already crowded. I found a seat near the window and charged my phone. Looking around at the other passengers, I thought that I was on my way to somewhere new, where nobody knew me, where I didn't need anyone. The thought made me feel free.

PART THREE

The gallery is a small, narrow space. They walk past it twice before they notice the door. Thora stops at the threshold to take it all in, thinking: did we really cross the Atlantic for the sake of these four walls? But she doesn't say anything; she just adjusts Frances on her hip and follows August. The gallerist, an American who August met in Stockholm, greets them and double-taps Frances's nose with his finger. Frances pushes his hand away with a loud *no* and then presses her face into Thora's collarbone. He laughs. Since she doesn't know if the gallerist understands Swedish, Thora refrains from tartly asking August if he would do the same to an adult.

She puts Frances on the ground and watches the child trundle about August's legs as if trying to trip him. The gallerist serves them iced tea and they talk about the weather, their plane ride and the time difference before the conversation turns to the hanging of the paintings. There is no furniture in the space, so Thora leans against the wall with her phone and catches up on emails. Whenever August asks for her thoughts on the positioning of a particular painting, she looks up from her screen. Frances plays with the bubble wrap the paintings were shipped in, pops spattering like hail through the room.

They eat lunch at a restaurant down the street recommended by the gallerist. Thora's English is better than August's, but he's more charming and has a knack for the American habit of small talk that she does not possess, so she lets him drive when it comes to chit-chatting with servers and sales staff. She refrains from pointing out his grammatical errors.

'You must have been an American in a previous life,' she says.

'Americans are so nice,' he says. 'I could imagine living here.'

Frances sits in his lap. He holds her plate in place while piling food onto a fork.

'I couldn't,' Thora says.

He smiles at her. 'I know.'

The fork scrapes against the china. They have a street-view booth to themselves, and she senses August's gaze climb over her face, as if he is trying to find somewhere to plant a thought. She knows what he's about to say before he's opened his mouth.

'I think we should call him to say we're here.'

'You call if you want,' she says and leans back. 'But I'm not going to.'

'Don't you think he'd want to see us?'

'See you, maybe.'

He's silent for a few seconds, moving the fork in the direction of Frances's mouth. She opens.

'He did get in touch when Frances was born,' August said.

She purses her lips, and in the ridges of her skin she can taste the sunscreen she applies every morning. 'Yeah, sure. He got in touch with you. How nice of him.'

'I'm going to call him.'

She shrugs. 'Just don't drag me into it.'

August tries to catch her eye, and she lets him, meeting his gaze for a short while before she leans in to wipe Frances's mouth. Frances bangs her arm on the table and topples Thora's mug. The swoosh of coffee running over the edge of the table sounds like a faint sigh. Frances laughs and then covers her mouth with both hands, looking like she's trying out a gesture she's picked up from a movie. They toss napkins onto the floor and the waitress comes out from behind the bar with a bunch of paper towels, smiling at August as if the mess is no bother whatsoever. August moves to crouch on the floor to help wipe up the coffee, but the waitress makes a dismissive gesture. Thora resists an impulse to put on her large black sunglasses, which are poking out of her handbag on the seat next to her. A fresh coffee materializes. Once again August tries to find her eyes across the table, like there was no interruption.

'Will you be upset if I call him?' he asks.

Out of the corner of her eye Thora notes that the waitress is watching August from behind the bar. Frances sits immobile, looking at Thora with the same big eyes as August's, as if she were asking the same question.

Thora smiles at them both. 'No. You do what you want.'

She feels a drop of sweat trickle down her back, closely followed by another. She wonders if it's stained the white cotton shirt.

The summer has been one long heat wave, even in Europe. The news is full of reports on forest fires, people fleeing their homes in cars, helicopter water shuttles and cooling centres in the cities on the continent. A scorching state of emergency from which a stillness has been born, a kind of involuntary reverence akin to the silence that spreads on winter days when the air is so cold it hurts to breathe. The heat wave has reached as far north as Stockholm; by the time they left for New York, fans were sold out everywhere and the air quivered over yellow lawns. Beaches and docks were full of people shuttling back and forth between the water and towels spread out on grass and cliffs, dunking themselves in the river as soon as the sun dried them. They drank soda and ate ice cream and spoke about the end of the world.

New York is even hotter. And it's a different kind of heat – more humid, oppressive like a stranger's smelly breath. The subway station in Crown Heights is so warm that Frances begins to cry when they pass through the turnstiles. Thora, dripping with sweat, holds a cold water bottle against her child's forehead, watching as condensation trickles down her face. Eyes shiny, Frances gazes at her – accusingly? The plastic bottle creaks. The air is so thick it feels like swallowing something fleecy and sticky that expands in the mouth, a taste of bodily fluids and dust.

It took two days for August and Frances to adjust to the new time zone. Thora still hasn't adjusted. When one out of the three weeks of their stay has gone by, she decides it's pointless trying to switch her circadian rhythm. So she wakes up early in the morning, gets dressed and takes a walk through the neighbourhood, heading towards Prospect Park. The water towers protrude from the roofs like tumours, but she tries not to linger on that image; the word makes her nervous – *tumour* – sharp edges, doughy middle, she doesn't want it in her thoughts. She stops at a café on Rogers Avenue, where women in long skirts and men with black hats and beards drink coffee on brown leather couches, laptops on their knees. She exchanges a few words with the barista who started to treat her like a regular after just a few days. She buys fresh bagels to bring back to the apartment, where she slices them for the toaster. She makes coffee and sets plates and butter on the table, then turns to answer work emails even though she's on vacation. Frances usually wakes up around this time and enters the kitchen in her pyjamas, rubbing her eyes.

'Mamma,' she says from the doorway. 'Hungry.'

Thora gets up, pours a glass of juice and prepares two halves of a bagel which Frances eats with great focus, the bread crunching between her teeth.

August wakes up soon after. Like Frances, he rubs his eyes as he enters the kitchen. Then he pours himself a cup of coffee, strokes Frances's hair and kisses Thora on the forehead. And there they sit at the kitchen table in an apartment they've borrowed, until they decide it's time to step out into the heat.

*

August is better with Frances. It's been that way since the baby was born. In fact, it's been that way since long before Frances was born – children have always taken to August. And it was August who wanted to have a child. She was more sceptical. None of their friends had kids at the time, and though she liked the idea of a child that was his and hers, she wasn't convinced she'd like that idea made reality. They agreed that August would go on longer parental leave than her. She worried about turning into someone who only cared about baby stuff; so worried that she actively avoided reading any articles or books at all on the subject, and she gave him the responsibility of getting a stroller and baby clothes and a crib.

He usually picks Frances up from preschool in the afternoon and takes her to his studio, where he lets her draw with colourful crayons and markers beneath the big reproductions of paintings by Sigrid Hjertén and Hilma af Klint. It makes Thora happy when she gets there after work and finds August and Frances sitting side by side, facing away from the door – happy, because they're hers, but also downhearted, since it's difficult to know that she's intruding on their peace with her reminders of dinner, cleaning, bedtime.

During pregnancy she couldn't help but feel that she was erasing herself as she was creating new life. Being a mother feels like stumbling around in shoes a size too big – she can't quite find her footing, the ground keeps shifting. Even before Frances's birth she could easily imagine August as a dad, but conjuring a picture of herself as a mom wasn't as immediate. She told Laura this in passing and Laura grabbed hold of the confession like it was something precious blowing past them in the wind. She looked Thora in the eye and said she'd felt the same way, that she'd been depressed in the post-partum period. It was something her mother had never mentioned before, and Thora didn't know how to respond. She wasn't prepared for any confidential admissions from Laura, and suddenly, after the birth of Frances, there was a steady stream of them, as if Laura had kept parts of herself hidden for so many years that they were now all tangled up in each other, and untangling one piece meant unrolling the entire ball of yarn. It was like catching sight of Laura from the outside, a person Thora had never known before, who sometimes stepped into the role of a mother just as Thora herself sometimes feels that she steps into a role that doesn't quite match her true identity. She wonders when Frances will discover that gap.

She marks the subway stations that are equipped with an elevator on her phone, memorizing their names, but sometimes those stations are too far away, and sometimes the elevators, even when they do exist, are out of service. It's easier when August is with them, but when he's at the gallery or meeting with art buyers she faces the choice of staying in the borrowed apartment or heading out into the city with the stroller. Frequently a stranger will ask if she needs help, sometimes multiple strangers at once, so Frances is hauled up and down the stairs of the underworld like a sleeping queen with a pacifier in her mouth. Thora thanks them and wipes the sweat from her forehead with the back of her hand, and the strangers smile and say *no problem* and sometimes, if they have time, they linger for a moment to ask where she's from, how old Frances is, why they're in New York. American English makes her think of someone standing wide-legged in bootcut jeans, or maybe it's like the words are stretched out, the letters separating like toffee, making everything sound sugary, porous.

August comes home late one night and smells like Hugo. She can't explain how she knows it's him, but she recognizes the smell as instantly as she would recognize a face she's kissed, caressed, dried from tears. Perhaps a move across an ocean doesn't change the way a person smells. She rolls onto her side in bed, her face turned away from August, pretending to be asleep. In the morning she doesn't ask about Hugo. August says, simply, while they're eating breakfast:

'I didn't tell him.'

'Okay.'

'It felt unnecessary.'

She nods.

'Yes,' she says a few seconds later, as if to emphasize the nod. 'It would be unnecessary.'

'It's funny, but he reminds me of someone,' August says thoughtfully. 'I just can't think of who.'

She looks up from her phone. 'Who?'

'Hugo.'

'Ah,' she says.

August lifts Frances up. Thora looks at them and feels her throat constrict like there's an invisible belt strapped over it, and she moves her fingers to loosen it but it tightens instead, though she smiles and the sun filters through her eyelashes.

She thinks to herself that every single adjective could be used to describe her, and they'd all be equally true and untrue.

She tries to fetch Hugo's image from the recesses of her memory. Recall his face. It burns. She pulls her hand back.

She walks in and out of the narrow churches that spring from in between the skyscrapers on the avenue, and wonders what it would be like to breastfeed in one of the wooden pews. To unbutton her blouse, take out the breast, let light fall on the dark areola. Frances is eating an apple in her stroller. The sound of her chewing reaches up towards the ceiling, a leap of the quotidian that gasps and vanishes like an insect in a gust of wind. Frances hands her the apple core and she holds it in her palm; there's no trash can anywhere. The air is cool in between the marble pillars, a scent of wood and something vaguely sweet she might have been able to identify were she more conversant in religion. She wanders from cool cathedrals to air-conditioned department stores, where the staff give her blinding smiles and call her *ma'am*. She realizes she's put the apple core in her pocket when she's fishing for her wallet.

August's phone rings early one afternoon, and Thora automatically calculates what time it is in Sweden. He walks into the hall to pick up. Thora sits immobile, her back a few inches from the back of the chair. She listens to Frances playing in the living room, hears her say *mom* and *dad* in that tone of voice that turns the words into toys. When August comes back Thora turns to look at him, arm on the back of her chair.

'What did he say?'

August returns to rinsing the dishes. 'He asked me to come in when we're back in Stockholm.'

Her jaw makes a cracking sound when she opens her mouth. 'Why?'

August puts plates in the drying rack. Iridescent soap bubbles float up from the sink. 'He said something about a referral. He wants to run a few more tests.'

'Why?'

August looks at her over his shoulder and smiles. 'You sound like Frances.'

Thora does not smile.

'Maybe we should go back now? We can change our tickets.'

'No.' August dries his hands on a kitchen towel. 'We're leaving next week. It's fine.'

He rests his hands on her shoulders, squeezing them. She wants to crumple to the floor and cry but instead she asks if he wants coffee, he says yes, and it's only when she takes two cups out of the cupboard and spoons the grounds into the filter that she realizes her hands are trembling. She holds on to the kitchen counter while the coffee maker gurgles up water that slowly drips down through the filter. August and Frances have put on a movie in the living room.

The child slips down into the imprint August makes in the cushion, leaning against him, her mouth half open as her eyes follow the action on the screen. August is more focused on Frances than the screen. He looks at Thora through the doorway to the kitchen and smiles. She smiles back. Her knuckles are mottled red and white. She wonders if her throbbing pulse is visible from the outside, a finger knocking for a soft spot. The coffee maker makes one last gurgling sound, as if to dislodge phlegm from deep down in the throat. And she pours the coffee.

Handing August one of the cups, she decides that nothing bad can happen to him. This resolution feels like grabbing hold of a shaking object in order to make it stop. She can feel it resisting between her palms, feel the reverberations, but she doesn't loosen her hold. Finally it quivers, almost as if despondent, and when it stops it goes cold too, like she's strangled it. She shakes off her discomfort, drinks the coffee quickly, and breathes in the scent of Frances's newly washed clothes and skin, her smooth child's body.

Lydia lives on one of the top floors of a building on Riverside Drive. She left the Paris attic studio with its book piles on the floor and its candles in wine bottles, and married a wealthy American. Julian is still in Paris, where he smokes weed and reads dusty books in the light of the neon signs outside his apartment. Thora knows this because she and August have visited Julian in that apartment, where they sat on stiff, sequined cushions, trying to make out his face through the smoke. Thora doesn't know if Lydia is still in contact with Julian; she doesn't ask. People drift away in the mass of time and get stuck in the undercurrents of artificial oblivion, which eventually does turn into real oblivion; nothing sticks, everything drifts away. At least that's the way she thinks, and so she's surprised whenever she moves her hands over her body and finds a lump, a protrusion, a mark from something she thought had washed off. It's like discovering a tick that hasn't let go even though it's gorged on blood.

These days Lydia dresses exclusively in loose-fitting clothes in a neutral palette, with embroidered shawls she drapes around her shoulders with such painstaking care that Thora wonders if she uses them to communicate her moods. Lydia's wrists are very thin and when she extends her toes her joints crack, but she just keeps walking, unaffected, through the hallways with cream carpeting.

The living room has a piano with several rows of photographs on it, and windows show the river and the tall buildings across the water. Thora carries Frances on her hip as Lydia shows them around. The weight of the child in her arms keeps the heaviness at bay, though she can sense it lurking in the dark corners of the apartment. Thora and Lydia discuss their other cousins, their careers, their plans for the future. Lydia asks about Aron and Laura, and Thora tells her about the residence they moved into when Aron was named ambassador, and about the pool area where the diplomats gather at dusk after a long day at work, with drinks in their hands and bug spray in the inside pockets of their blazers. Thora thinks of her parents' home in Stockholm, shuttered and desolate with white sheets protecting the furniture they left behind. A monument to the certitude felt by the entire family that nothing could ever dislodge them from their position.

Lydia sighs that it's nice to talk about something other than the president, but then she starts talking about him anyway, as if she touched a bug bite she can't help but scratch.

'Everyone asked if we were going to move to Europe when he won the election.'

'Did you consider it?' Thora asks.

'No. Why would we?' Lydia says with a frown. 'But I have several European friends who cancelled their trips here for a while. Some kind of statement. Against what, I'm not sure.'

There are so many cushions on the couch that there's only room to actually sit on the edge, so that's where Thora perches, back straight, legs crossed. Frances wriggles down from her lap.

'She's so cute,' Lydia says and leans down to get on Frances's level. 'You're so cute.'

Frances waves her fist violently, as if to dismiss the compliment, and Lydia laughs.

Thora smiles.

Her brain fog is intense, a haze that makes it difficult to seize any thought that might be fashioned into a coherent observation, question, comment on the state of the world. These days she rarely reads the news; she can't imagine conjuring the energy to care about things that hardly concern her – they're so far away. August reads both Swedish and foreign newspapers, follows the news, debates the current situation, and when he asks for her thoughts on some question she looks at him, wanting to tell him that all she cares about is him, that she'd give the world for him, but she doesn't, because she knows he wouldn't want to hear it. He thinks caring about the world is important; she thinks that the world, singular, is an abstraction that an individual can't relate to – neither with care, nor even with indifference.

She's the one who spots Hugo. They're on opposite sides of the street, a crosswalk at an intersection near Central Park. She stops in her tracks. People jostle her to get past. She clings to the stroller. When he catches sight of her in the crowd their eyes meet, a short moment in which she has time to think that everything in her life has led up to this. Her insides heave, it's a forbidden thought, she pushes it away. She has the sense that an enormous mass of water is rushing up the avenues, surging forth between the skyscrapers, and she hangs on to the stroller for dear life, trying to resist the currents.

Then she wakes up.

She buys a pair of thin black nylon tights for August's private view. She's planned to wear heels; she hopes to avoid blisters in her low black pumps. She looks at herself in the mirror, tugging at the wrap dress, pulling the tights up past her bellybutton by wriggling her hips. Frances watches in delight. As Thora applies lipstick, Frances pouts her lips and says, voice nasal, eyes closed: 'Me too.' Thora pats a bit of red on her daughter's lips and makes a smacking sound that Frances imitates.

Frances opens her eyes and looks expectantly at her own reflection. She frowns. '*More*.'

Thora shakes her head with a smile. 'Your dad wouldn't like that.'

They take a cab to Manhattan to drop Frances at Lydia's with two backpacks: one small knapsack Frances has filled herself, and an overnight bag that August packed with a change of clothing. Frances talks incessantly during the cab ride, about what she and Lydia are going to get up to, about which room she'll sleep in, about what they'll have for dinner. But when they're about to say goodbye she suddenly gets anxious; Thora can tell from the way Frances starts fiddling with the straps of her little yellow knapsack, and she gives August a look. He gets down on his heels in front of Frances.

Frances comes close to him and asks in a whisper what time they'll pick her up.

'Nine thirty tomorrow,' August says.

'Nine thirty,' Frances repeats. 'When is that?'

August draws a circle in the air and explains what the hands on the clock look like when it's nine thirty.

They're standing in the long hallway outside Lydia's apartment. Thora strokes Frances's hair. She imagines Hugo observing them from afar, can almost feel the weight of an outsider's gaze even though the corridor is empty.

Her tights keep slipping down and there's already a run at the left ankle.

She's become used to socializing with artist types; by now she thinks of them as a nice distraction from the lawyer world. The difference between American and European artist types soon becomes evident:

the Americans talk more; they talk so much, in fact, that she doesn't need to ask any questions. It also means that when she does speak, she doesn't need to worry about going on too long, since everybody does. The conversations revolve more around politics than art. Several months have gone by since the election, but the Americans still look pale, jumpy, and they question the usefulness of art in a world like this, only to retract the question, add more nuance to it, and then look around in bewilderment and sigh. She tries to discreetly pull her tights up while she nods consolingly along with the other foreigners, as if they were giving condolences after someone they didn't know had died. One of the artist types floats the idea that art must be complex, perhaps even incomprehensible: 'What kind of art would it be otherwise? It's what life is, right? Complex, incomprehensible.'

Thora goes to the bathroom to touch up her lipstick and take off her tights, which she bundles up and tosses in the trash can. As she steps back into the gallery she sees that August is standing next to Hugo. They're close together, as if they're discussing things they don't want others to hear. August is nodding, his eyes are bright, intense, even when he directs his gaze at the floor as if to pause, rest from the conversation for a moment. And Hugo. Does he look the same? His hair is still thick and dark, curls at his neck and ears. He smiles and frowns at once. He's wearing a button-down shirt and a blazer – a formal look next to August and all the artist types. Did he come straight from work?

August and Hugo look up, as if both of them can sense her watching them. August smiles at her. Hugo's gaze only grazes her face. She has the sense that it's snowing on this summer night, that the sky is glowing blue, as if the northern light has heaved itself over the Atlantic to get to them. She walks over as shadow figures around them laugh and talk and drink. August pulls her close for a kiss, which tastes of wine and cigarettes. He's tipsy.

'There you are,' he says.

'Hey,' Thora says.

'Hey,' Hugo says.

She spreads her toes in her shoes, feeling the blisters throb like angry little hearts. Out of the corner of her eye she thinks she sees the snow whirling in the light of the street lamps. She looks up and briefly locks eyes with Hugo. There's an entire life there, a life she knows nothing about.

'How are you?' he asks.

'Fine,' she says.

One of the artist types puts a hand on August's arm, asks him something in English, and August excuses himself. He smiles at them over his shoulder.

Thora is mute.

She knows what questions she's supposed to ask, she knows the whole repertoire of topics by heart; she has frequent reason to trot them out when she runs into old acquaintances in Stockholm. But she has no desire to ask Hugo things like that. The idea of small talk with him is depressing. She would rather stand in silence. Hugo, however, doesn't seem to feel the same. He starts rattling off questions like live ammo, asking what she thinks of New York, what she does for work these days, where she and August live in Stockholm, how Aron and Laura are doing, if Frances likes her preschool. She jolts when he says the child's name; she's not sure why, of course she knows that August has told him about Frances. Hugo apologizes without seeming to know what for. Suddenly she's aware of how tightly she's clutching her wine glass. She tries to relax her grip.

'I've thought a lot about you both,' Hugo says. 'About you.'

Thora doesn't know what to say so she says nothing.

Hugo slouches his neck. She glances at his head, looking for a hint of a receding hairline. Then she looks out across the room and finally asks: 'How are you?'

Hugo smiles. 'I walk around in a long monologue.'

Thora raises her eyebrows but he keeps smiling. When she meets his gaze she sees that the smile doesn't reach his eyes. It's just there to hold the curtain up, to maintain the distance between stage and backdrop. She thinks: how could something so vast get compressed into nothingness, be split into two strangers? She doesn't get it. Maybe she'll never get it.

'It's weird,' he continues. 'Do you remember when we were studying literature?'

'Yes,' she says, apprehensive.

Hugo doesn't seem to notice, or care about her tone. He looks thoughtfully at the other gallery patrons. 'When I moved to New York I was surprised by how lonely it felt to know that people who read books here have never read or even heard about authors like Cora Sandel or Tove Ditlevsen or Hjalmar Söderberg.'

'There are lots of people in Scandinavia and the rest of Europe who have no idea who they are.'

'I mean people who read.'

Thora shrugs. She finds herself unwilling to agree with him on anything. 'It's not that weird. I guess they don't translate very much from small European languages into English.'

'I know,' he says with a hint of irritation in his voice. 'I just didn't think it would feel so strange. So lonely.'

'I didn't think you cared about loneliness.'

Hugo looks at her and she understands, when she sees the disappointment on his face, that the topic – the reference to their university years, their common history – was a clumsy attempt at closeness, at re-establishing an intimacy. She grows stiff and looks away. They stand together in silence.

Late that night they go to a 24-hour diner. They're a big group, and they take up several booths. The waitress is unfazed. August shows Hugo photos of Frances. Thora looks at their reflection in the window. Yellow, red and green lights from street lamps, store signs and traffic lights flicker in the glass.

'She's so cute,' Hugo says and returns the phone to August. 'When are you going back home?'

'She mainly takes after Thora,' August says. 'Thankfully.'

'We go back the day after tomorrow,' Thora says.

The table between them is the size of an ocean. She smiles an impersonal smile and Hugo smiles back, just as impersonally. It stings. She thinks of the person she was when he knew her, when she, Hugo and August were a trio. She conjures an image of the three of them in winter jackets, boots, scarves and hats, with library books in tote bags and laptops weighing down messenger bags and back-packs, and she can picture their silhouettes so clearly it's as if they're shuffling past outside the window, somewhere in between the fluttering lights. Then they disappear, engulfed by the lights, the people they once were, dissolved. She blinks. Yawns.

They order milkshakes and French fries. August says his teeth are hurting and she tells him to book a dentist appointment when they're back in Stockholm.

'Perchance the great artist has cavities,' she says.

'Can't be,' he says and stirs his drink with his straw.

Later, in the cab heading back to Crown Heights, they roll down the windows in the back seat, and the summer air, ripe with city smells, tousles their clothes and hair.

'It's strange,' August says. 'But I realized just now who Hugo reminds me of.'

'Who?'

'Samuel,' he says, and frowns as if he's surprised by his own words. 'He reminds me of my brother.'

Thora is silent for a short moment and looks out over the sky-scrapers, the bridges, the river.

'It's the suit,' she says, finally.

They take the subway to the airport. The stations replace one another. It's late in the afternoon, the car is warm and smells of sweat and urine. August holds Frances in his lap. Thora is clutching the suitcases to stop them from rolling away whenever the train lists. Frances is unusually still, watching the people getting on and off. Some of them smile at her when they look up from their phone or book. The stations replace one another. A long darkness. At last the train exits the tunnel, comes up above the roofs, a long way from the skyscrapers. The sun thrusts through the clouds and comes flowing through the scratched windows. There's a halo around Frances's hair. Thora looks at August. His eyes are closed. So she does the same, closes her eyes and listens to the beating of the wheels on the rails, the sighs from the doors as they open. The contours of shapeless figures are visible through her eyelids. Black on red. She can feel the sun on her face. August takes her hand in his, pressing it, and she smiles and presses back without opening her eyes. Everything is beautiful for a short moment. When she lets go she can still feel the warmth of his hand.